She was

Lily pressed a hand against her stomach, remembering all the times she had prayed for a child before adopting Annmarie. She didn't dare hope for the impossible, especially under these circumstances. Not after learning how Quinn felt about family—and being abandoned.

She was at once terrified and exhilarated. Quinn's baby. The contract Franklin Lawrence had put out on her life. The need to leave before someone—maybe her daughter—got hurt or killed.

Her already impossible choice had just become even worse. If she was pregnant, what did she do about Quinn?

For a moment she allowed herself to believe the baby was a foundation on which they could build a life together. For the moment she wanted to pretend that she didn't have to run again....

Dear Reader,

Welcome to another month of the most exciting romantic reading around, courtesy of Silhouette Intimate Moments. Starting things off with a bang, we have *To Love a Thief* by ultrapopular Merline Lovelace. This newest CODE NAME: DANGER title takes you back into the supersecret world of the Omega Agency for a dangerous liaison you won't soon forget.

For military romance, Catherine Mann's WINGMEN WARRIORS are the ones to turn to. These uniformed heroes and heroines are irresistible, and once you join Darcy Renshaw and Max Keagan for a few *Private Maneuvers,* you won't even be trying to resist, anyway. Wendy Rosnau continues her unflashed miniseries THE BROTHERHOOD in *Last Man Standing,* while Sharon Mignerey's couple find themselves *In Too Deep.* Finally, welcome two authors who are new to the line but not to readers. Kristen Robinette makes an unforgettable entrance with *In the Arms of a Stranger,* and Ana Leigh offers a matchup between *The Law and Lady Justice.*

I hope you enjoy all six of these terrific novels, and that you'll come back next month for more of the most electrifying romantic reading around.

Enjoy!

Leslie J. Wainger
Executive Editor

Please address questions and book requests to:
Silhouette Reader Service
U.S.: 3010 Walden Ave., P.O. Box 1325, Buffalo, NY 14269
Canadian: P.O. Box 609, Fort Erie, Ont. L2A 5X3

In Too Deep
SHARON MIGNEREY

INTIMATE MOMENTS™

Published by Silhouette Books

America's Publisher of Contemporary Romance

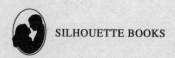 SILHOUETTE BOOKS

ISBN 0-373-27298-7

IN TOO DEEP

Copyright © 2003 by Sharon Mignerey

Visit us at www.eHarlequin.com

Printed in U.S.A.

SHARON MIGNEREY

lives in Colorado with her husband, a couple of dogs and a cat. From the time she figured out that spelling words could be turned into stories, she knew being a writer was what she wanted. Her first novel garnered several awards, first as an unpublished manuscript when she won RWA's Golden Heart Award in 1995, and later as a published work in 1997 when she won the National Reader's Choice Award and the Heart of Romance Readers' Choice Award. With each new book out, she's as thrilled as she was with that first one.

When she's not writing, she loves enjoying the Colorado sunshine, whether along the South Platte River near her home or at the family cabin in the Four Corners region. Even more, she loves spending time with her daughters and granddaughter.

She loves hearing from readers, and you can write to her in care of Silhouette Books, 233 Broadway, New York, NY 10279.

Acknowledgments:

I would never have been able to imagine
microbes that live in high pressure and high temperatures
around deep sea hydrothermic vents, nor would I have
had any idea about how to create a disaster in a lab,
without input from my brother, Paul Noble Black, Ph.D.
Thanks, Paul, for answering endless questions about life
in a lab and microbiology, and for providing invaluable
suggestions that made the science come alive.
The good stuff is yours, and the mistakes are mine.

Thanks to Jo Mrozewski,
whose knowledge of village life on the Inside Passage
gave me wonderful tidbits, including basketball
and hot strong tea laced with sugar and cream.

Dedication:

To Barbara, Amy, Patty, Daniele and Karen...
I love our Wednesday-night laughter and your friendship
more than you know.

Chapter 1

"Mommy, look at what we found." Five-year-old Annmarie's call was filled with enthusiasm from where she was bent over a tide pool with her new best friend, Thad.

Lily Jensen Reditch grinned at her daughter's excitement as she clambered around several large boulders to reach the rocky beach. *Act the act until you feel the feeling.* Normal was the feeling she wanted, and today felt…normal. Her daughter's carefree joy as she skipped through life was something that Lily would give a lot to have back in her own. She'd done all the right things to be better—gone through grief counseling and completed the regime recommended by victim's advocacy—and she was determined to be her old self. The optimistic one. The naive one. That thought made her smile. Optimistic—oh, she hoped so. Naive—never again.

Movement farther down the shoreline caught Lily's attention. She breathed a sigh of relief when she realized it was just Thad's uncle Josh, hiking around the Hollywood Bowl.

It was a collapsed mineshaft that had eroded into a clamshell shaped cave at the water's edge.

Lily deliberately reminded herself that the whole reason she had moved here was so she didn't have to assess every person she met as a threat. No threats here, despite the sleepless nights that continued to plague her and despite the nightmares that made sleep something to avoid. Dismissing Josh from her thoughts and reminding herself to smile, Lily returned her attention to the children and the beach, which was dotted with tide pools that reflected the misty noon sky of late August.

By Alaska standards the day was warm. Cold, though, compared to the balmy weather of California where they had lived until two months ago. Despite the gray sky that promised rain, Annmarie's blond hair gleamed, and Lily touched her daughter's head when she reached the kids. Wrapping her thick red cardigan more firmly around herself, Lily bent over the pool where the children crouched.

A small scallop and an equally small crab rested at the bottom of the pool. A second later the crab bumped the scallop, and it shot through the water with surprising speed.

Annmarie laughed. "Wow, did you see that?"

Lily grinned at her daughter's unabashed delight. "I did."

"How do you suppose he did that?" Thad asked.

"He clamped both halves of his shell together, which squirts the water out and makes him leap forward," she responded, demonstrating with her hands. The mechanics of how a bivalve moved was elementary compared to the mountains of research data she had been absorbing during the last few weeks.

A hydrothermic vent discovered last year was the major project under way at the Kantrovitch Research Center. Lily had uncovered several interesting areas where she could put her background to work…if she chose to get back into the research fast track. She was tantalized, a surprise since all she had wanted was to come home so she could be closer to family, especially her sister Rosie.

During the past month, the center had been practically deserted, evidently a planned break until additional funding arrived in September. Max, a jack-of-all-trades and handyman, had been the only other person around, caring for the specimens in the various aquariums, setting up the pressure tanks needed for deep-water specimens, and providing her with the extra muscle she had needed to drag new file cabinets out of the middle of the floor.

The project leader, Quinn Morrison, had interviewed her by phone, hired her sight unseen, and had encouraged her to settle in. He'd left her a set of keys and told her to take any desk in the main room except the one closest to the windows.

"How do you know it's a he?" Annmarie wanted to know, drawing Lily's attention back to the discovery at hand—the small scallop. "It might be a girl."

"Could be."

"How do clams make babies?" Annmarie asked, pulling at Lily's sleeve. Whether talking about her aunt Rosie's pregnancy or other animals, babies—or, more accurately, the making of them—recently held endless fascination for Annmarie.

"I bet they do it like snails. I've seen 'em in my brother's aquarium," Thad said before Lily could answer.

"But this is a clam," Annmarie said.

"Not it's not. It's a scallop," Thad said with the superiority that came with being two years older. "I bet they open their shell real wide so they can touch like snails do."

"Actually, the male and female never touch," came a voice from behind Lily, deep, as gravelly as the surf over rock, and pure Texan in the accent. "The male's sperm is drawn through the water to the female when he senses eggs are present."

Lily whirled around to look at the man, alarmed they were no longer alone and that he'd managed to arrive without her seeing or hearing him. His statement could have been salacious, but it was, instead, the matter-of-fact explanation of a scientist.

She sized him up through the haze of warnings that she hated...that she wasn't safe, that strangers were potential threats. The man's deep voice matched his appearance. Tall, broad-shouldered. Bigger than life, in fact, from where she knelt on the rocks next to the children. His sandy hair curled at his nape and over his ears, mussed as though he had repeatedly run his fingers through it. His eyes were dark, the color of a fjord when the shadows stretched over the water.

He smiled as he knelt next to them and said to Lily, "Hi, I'm Quinn Morrison." Before she could respond he smoothly turned his attention back to the kids with, "This scallop will be lucky to even find a mate." He pointed at the sea star that also occupied the tide pool. "See this guy here? He's *Pacific Henricia* and his favorite food is the scallop. And if he gets close enough—"

"The scallop will be lunch," Thad finished.

Lily's galloping heartbeat settled. This was her new boss—and, of course, he knew the scientific names of the local sea life.

"That's right," the man agreed.

"Maybe we should take her out of this pool and put her into another one," suggested Annmarie.

"What if the sea star is hungry?" he asked. His glance skipped over Lily before focusing on her daughter.

Each time he looked at her, Lily could feel a charge in the energy around her. She hadn't felt a spark of awareness like this in nearly forever. She shivered and openly watched him. The tanned lines of his face and the deep smile lines around his eyes reminded her of the men in her family—men who wrestled a living from the sea by fishing the waters of the inside passageway.

He smiled easily as he talked to the children, the expression encompassing his entire face. It wasn't so much handsome as interesting. Prominent cheekbones sculpted a deep hollow at his cheeks and a cleft emphasized his chin and square jawline. Clearly in his element, he wore a long-sleeved denim shirt, a micro-fleece vest and worn, button-fly jeans.

Annmarie asked, "Why does he have to eat this scallop?"

"Because Mother Nature intended that some animals be food for others. Sure, we could move it, but it could end up being somebody else's lunch." He winked at Annmarie. "Yours or mine."

"That's right," Thad agreed with an emphatic nod. "I've eaten scallops. Lots of times."

"So, how does the boy scallop know when the girl scallop has eggs?" Annmarie asked, returning with single-minded purpose to her earlier topic. The child had babies on the brain.

"Well," the man answered, "we don't actually know for sure. We think the female's scent changes. That's the trigger for mating behavior in most animals."

"You mean, they smell? Like perfume or something?" She wrinkled her nose.

He laughed. "Yeah. Like perfume or something."

Once more his gaze slid from Annmarie to Lily, who felt her color rise. She became aware of his scent—not cologne or sweat. Something far more subtle and altogether… pleasant. A nudge of awareness became something more, a primal recognition that welled out of the depth of her heart. *He's the one.*

She shoved the thought away. John had been *the one*. Her beloved John who had died so suddenly more than two years ago. Whatever spark she felt was loneliness, she reasoned. Maybe even envy at seeing her sister and her brother-in-law so deeply in love. Maybe missing someone to hold her through the night when her thoughts were consumed with a past she couldn't change.

He smiled and extended his hand. "You must be Dr. Jensen."

"You're back." She automatically shook his hand. A common, ordinary act. Still, she was aware of his touch, his hand large and warm and inviting around hers.

"Just last night."

"I'm Annmarie," her daughter interjected. "This is Thad."

"Your children?"

"Just me," Annmarie said with one of her infectious grins. "Thad, his mommy is Hilda. She's my mom's friend from when they were kids. Did you know that?"

"Ah, no."

"Do you have kids? We could play with them," Annmarie said.

He laughed. "No. No kids." His gaze skipped back to Lily. "No wife. Not even a dog."

"Aunt Rosie has a dog," Annmarie informed him. "And I have a cat named Sweetie Pie." When he looked back at her, she added. "You could play with them or I could help you get one of your own. Which do you like better? Dogs or cats?"

Quinn stood up, and his "Oh, no!" expression at the thought of being fixed up with a pet made Lily grin.

"You'd better say no quick," she said. "Once my daughter gets hold of an idea—"

"I get the picture." He smiled down at Annmarie. "Thanks for the offer. But—"

"You'll think about it." She gave an exaggerated sigh. "I don't know why grown-ups have to think about all the fun stuff. Come on, Thad, maybe we can find an octopus."

Quinn laughed and offered Lily his hand. "Now that would be an unusual find."

He pulled Lily up when she placed her hand within his. The detached-scientist part of her wanted to know how it was possible to feel each separate pull of his fingers against hers.

The man was not quite as tall as her brothers-in-law, both of whom were well over six feet. Unlike them, Quinn had the breadth of a linebacker. Broad shoulders had never before been alluring. Next to this man's bulk, she didn't feel so much small as sheltered. She reminded herself that she really did prefer men who didn't make her feel quite so small.

She watched Annmarie and Thad scamper down the deserted beach, pausing here and there to lean over and peer into the tide pools.

"I was expecting someone older," Quinn added, releasing her hands, ignoring that it wasn't politically correct for employers to bring up the subject of age. "Someone with your publishing record ought to be at least fifty."

"A scientist without a publishing record is also one without grants…and a job." Lily met his gaze and told him the truth. "I was expecting you to be older, too."

One of his eyebrows rose and another engaging grin lit his face. "I'm only nineteen."

"It's not the years, then, but the miles." The man had an impressive record based on what she'd been able to glean from the university Web site. With his investigation of this hydrothermic vent he had the chance to establish himself as one of the top marine biologists in the Pacific.

"They do pile on." He laughed again, a deep, rumbling purr that encouraged her to laugh with him. And she did, feeling a rapport with this man she had experienced with only three other men in her life. Her father. Her husband. Her brother-in-law, Ian. Fleetingly, she wondered, if like Ian, this was a man she could entrust with her life. Her laughter faded. She turned away that thought as her gaze fastened on her daughter. Act the act, she reminded herself. This wasn't California. She and Annmarie were safe.

"Are you responsible for that major cleanup project in the front office?" Quinn asked, pulling her attention back to him.

The question sounded to Lily like an accusation. When she had first set foot in the facility two weeks ago, she had found the office in complete chaos. Quinn Morrison might be a brilliant marine biologist, but organized he was not. Papers and files had been piled on every available surface of the office area, and two huge file cabinets that still bore their shipping tags were empty. Ignoring the mess on that one desk he'd told her to leave alone, she had gradually read, labeled and filed everything.

"Responsible?" She shook her head. "No. I've settled in like you told me to and acquainted myself with the research."

"Getting acquainted with the research is one thing. Cleaning is another."

"I was trying to find a place to sit. And since you had those empty file cabinets—"

"If I'd wanted a janitor, I would have hired one." The instant the words left his mouth, Quinn heard the annoyance in them and reluctantly admitted he was irritated. When he'd left a month ago, the place had looked a shambles, but at least it was *his* shambles. When he'd walked in a half hour ago, he'd barely recognized the office. The homey touches on one desk—pictures and a plant—were an invasion to his space.

"I've moved something you need—that's why you're upset." Her gaze openly searched his face. "What are you looking for?"

Quinn stared at her, surprised she hadn't taken offense. Her willingness to take responsibility for his being annoyed took away any fun that he might have had in continuing to bait her.

"There were a bunch of files on clams we collected from the vent site. I'd like to find the ones on the hemoglobin levels found in the dissected clams," he said. He'd need those reports sooner or later, he decided, but now was as good a time as any to figure out if he'd ever lay hands on any of his data again.

"I know exactly where that is. And since I couldn't find the electronic file, I scanned them, so they're also in the computer." Lily's glance went to the children who were bent over a tide pool. "Come on, Annmarie," she called. "Time to go."

Quinn looked at the shoreline, noting the tide was still going out. "They can stay here if they want."

"Says the man with no kids." Lily grinned. "I might let them walk from the research center to Thad's house, but leaving them alone on the beach..." She shook her head.

"Asking for trouble, huh?" Time to be agreeable, though he thought she was being a little overprotective. Then again, maybe this was the way caring mothers acted. Like he would know.

"Big-time."

As soon as Lily saw that the kids were right behind them, she headed toward the path that led up the steep slope to the research center. The bounce in her step matched the enthusiasm in her voice. "Do you have the data for the clams harvested from the Juan de Fuca site? Since this vent isn't as deep, any variances should be interesting."

Quinn followed her, wondering if she'd managed to really bring enough order to the files that she really did know *exactly*. He would have spent a couple of hours looking for the files, much as he'd never admit that to her. "Given your previous research, I would have thought the microscopic life around the vent would be more interesting to you."

She glanced over her shoulder. "Like the barophiles? Or the autotrophs? They're magical."

That wasn't the word he would have applied, but he liked the thought.

"Have you isolated any organisms yet?" she asked.

He shook his head. "We're still in the survey stage. We've scheduled a week to gather samples when the summer break ends."

"Figuring out how a living thing creates food from inorganic material," she continued, "could keep a scientist happy for years."

"You?"

Her smile faded. "I...left that behind."

He still couldn't believe that he'd managed to snag someone with her credentials for the research assistant's salary that he could offer within the budget of his current grant. Now that he'd met Lily Jensen, Ph.D., he was even more confused. Especially after she'd made it clear during their phone interview that she was now using her married name. Since all of her publishing had been done under her maiden name, why in the world was she distancing herself from it?

"What made you give up the publish-or-perish career track to come here? There's not much challenge for someone who's had her own lab and grants big enough to support a staff." He didn't elaborate that the grants he'd secured so far were much too small to do the research needed. If she had come across those documents, she would have already figured that out. He gave her one of his practiced smiles. "Kick me if I'm being nosy."

She didn't respond for several seconds, then carefully said, "I needed a career change. No. More than that. A life change. My sister Rosie lives here, so we came here."

"Ah."

"Ah?" She turned face him.

"Everyone sometimes does," he said with a nod. "Needs a change that is. After a divorce—"

"I'm not divorced."

"After being fired." His smile stayed firmly in place. He knew he was prying, and he wondered how long it would be before she told him to back off.

"I wasn't fired. The university even offered me a bigger lab as an inducement to stay."

That didn't surprise him. She had a slew of papers that made his own publishing record look meager. "After rescuing your kid from drugs."

"Annmarie is only five-years old, for pity's sake," she responded. The corners of her eyes crinkled as though she couldn't decide whether to laugh at him or to be mad at him. "Okay, yes, wanting a good place for her to grow up was part of it. But I'm not so idealistic as to think children in small towns don't have their problems. I grew up in a small town—"

"Where?"

"Petersburg."

"Alaska? You're not a California girl?" From her blond hair, casually secured in some kind of big clip at the back of her head, to the honey tan of her skin, she conjured images of the old Beach Boys' song about California girls.

Lily shook her head with a chuckle. "Not me, though I lived there for the last ten years."

"Which explains why you're cold." The long red sweater belted around her waist hadn't kept her from shivering, even while they walked up the slope.

She shivered again, glancing back toward the beach where the children were tagging along behind them. "It's a nice day."

Without hesitation, he took off his vest and draped it over her shoulders. She stopped walking and turned around to face him. Since she was higher on the slope, they were eye to eye, and he realized she was petite, her bone structure fine.

A question formed in her eyes. "Are you always this—"

"Inquisitive? Pushy? Nosy?" he finished.

She shook her head, her gaze deeply searching his eyes as though she saw a hero. For an instant he wished he were.

She simply watched him with those dark brown eyes that were unusual in a complexion as fair as hers. He'd been around enough women to recognize the spark of interest in her expression, which was totally at odds with her body language.

Thinking she was way too likable for his peace of mind, he said, "You moved here to escape the scandal of being involved with a student."

"Outrageous." She laughed.

"That bad, huh?"

"Your behavior," she said. "Pushy, maybe. Nosy, absolutely. And definitely outrageous."

"That's my stock in trade." He grinned at her. She hadn't taken his barbs seriously, and she'd responded with humor. An assistant with a sense of humor was a plus. Double if she was easy on the eye, and she was.

They reached the crest of the slope and she stopped walking so suddenly he nearly ran into her. She glanced at him, then away. "My husband died two years ago—"

"I'm sorry." Something in her voice made him believe that she wasn't beyond that. That put her in the do-not-touch category, which was too bad since he'd been thinking she was a woman he'd like to touch. All over.

"—and," she rushed on, "I had a grant that ran out. So the timing to make a change was good. And I really did want to be closer to family again."

He figured she was telling him the truth—just not the whole truth. He'd read her curriculum vitae and her papers. Her work was original, brilliant, and represented years of commitment.

"So you're giving up research?"

"For now," she said.

A shadow chased through her eyes, and he again wondered what she wasn't telling him. Beneath her easy laugh and open smile, he sensed a flicker of sadness that he suspected she worked hard to hide. Deliberately teasing, he said, "Now that I know you can file…"

As hoped, she grinned. "I knew there was a down side to this job."

"I have a theory about how the office got to be such a mess." He waited a beat before adding, "In the dead of night, the files and papers get together, mate, reproduce and create new piles."

"A topic for your next paper, hmm?" she returned. "Something you could publish in the *Journal of Organizational Science,* maybe?"

He laughed. "Maybe."

Lily watched the kids coming up the trail behind them. She gazed at her daughter as though the child was more precious than life. Nobody had ever looked at Quinn like that, but until now he hadn't thought it mattered.

The kids came over the crest.

"We made it!" Annmarie exclaimed, throwing her arms wide. "I'm king of the mountain."

"You can't be king," Thad said. "'Cause you're a girl."

"I can be anything I want," she informed him. "My mom said."

"Okay if we go inside and look at the aquariums?" Thad asked Quinn.

"Sure."

"Last one there has to eat raw fish eggs," Annmarie taunted. They took off toward the building at a run.

Quinn grinned. "Now that's one I'm going to remember."

By the time the two children reached the door, they were neck and neck. Something had caught Annmarie's attention, and she pointed.

"Mom!" she shouted, her voice full of fright. "Look out!"

Quinn's gaze followed the line of her pointing finger. A dark-green vehicle was rolling down the slope, picking up speed...and headed directly toward him and Lily.

Chapter 2

Lily glanced over her shoulder, her first thought for her daughter. To her relief Annmarie stood on the stoop in front of the door.

"Move!" Quinn pushed Lily out of the vehicle's path. Then he sprinted after the car.

"You stay there," Lily shouted. When her daughter nodded that she understood, Lily started after Quinn. Dear heaven, he was a crazy man. Didn't he realize he could get hurt?

The vehicle—her car, good God, *her car*—rolled across the shallow slope like some monstrous, lumbering beast, tipping when one of the wheels rolled over a small boulder. The vehicle veered in a new direction. Quinn caught up with it and pulled on the door handle. He stumbled back, swore, and made a second grab, this time at the back door. The vehicle picked up speed and jerked him along like a rag doll.

"Let go!" Lily's heart rose to her throat. Any second he was sure to lose his balance and end up under the wheels. The car was headed directly toward the cliff between a huge pine and a flatbed trailer parked in the lower lot—a trailer she didn't remember seeing earlier.

A tire rolled over another large rock and knocked Quinn to the ground. He disappeared from view and she screamed. A second later the car hit the trailer with a grinding crunch.

Lily came to a skidding halt by Quinn, who was already sitting up. She dropped to her knees next to him. He had a gash on his head that pumped blood. It ran down the side of his head and neck. His attention was focused completely on the car. She spared it only a fleeting glance while raw fear for him pulsed through her.

"Oh, God," she panted. "You're hurt." She grabbed a packet of tissues from her pocket and pressed a wad against the gash. Instantly the blood soaked through.

"Damn it all to hell." Rolling to his feet, he ignored her and the blood streaming from his head. He stalked toward the crash.

Shaking, Lily stood and trailed after him. Head wounds, even minor ones, bled like the devil. How hurt could the man be when he was swearing? Her attention shifted to the accident. One wheel of her car was in the air, still spinning. Her car, that she had just paid off, looked as though it was permanently attached to the trailer. She hadn't taken fifteen steps when he turned around to glare at her.

"That's not my car." He waved up the hillside toward the parking lot. "That is."

"It's mine," she said, following the line of his finger. His vehicle was nearly identical to her dark green SUV. Except hers was perched precariously against the open trailer. She finally gave the trailer a closer look. Sitting on its flatbed was a small robotic submarine—a huge white and silver ball with headlights—one of them broken—and mechanical arms—also one broken—that looked alive.

"And that—" he was beginning to sway as he gestured toward the trailer "—is a submersible that has been here for exactly—" He squinted at his watch as though he couldn't read it. "Forty-three minutes. I parked it down here so no-

body had a chance in hell of running into it. Do you have
any idea what I went through to get it? Only sell my soul.''

Her legs rubbery, Lily's gaze followed his accusing finger.
The whole passenger side of her car was caved in, and the
trailer was dented where the car had hit it. She wrapped her
arms around herself, which did nothing to lessen her shaking
or the fear that made her throat tighten.

Once again, Quinn tried to open one of the doors on her
car, then leaned down to peer inside. Straightening, he swore
again.

"You left the keys in the ignition," he accused. Blood
continued to pour down the side of his face, and he was
looking more pale by the minute.

"We've got to get you to the clinic." She laid a hand on
his arm to steady him. "You're bleeding."

"I'll get a Band-Aid later." He shrugged off her support
and looked back up the hillside. "How the hell did this happen?"

"I don't know." What she did know was that Quinn
looked worse.

His knees buckled. Before Lily could reach him, he fell.
She cried out and knelt beside him. Pounding footsteps made
her look up. Max and the children were running toward them.

"Well, damn," Quinn said, struggling to stand up.

"You stay put." She pushed him back down.

"Damned if I will." Somehow, though, Quinn found himself without the energy to stand. Which was ridiculous. The
woman couldn't weigh more than a hundred and ten pounds
sopping wet. He bench-pressed triple that. Of course she
couldn't hold him down.

Except that resting for a minute seemed like a better idea.

Through a haze of red he watched Max and the two children come to a halt next to him. Lily's child threw her arms
around her mother. Lily automatically hugged Annmarie with
words of reassurance and a gentle admonishment to stay out
of the way.

That didn't keep the child from kneeling next to him and

peering into his eyes. "You're going to be okay," she crooned, patting his hand, then said, "I don't think he's in there, Mom."

Where else would he be? Especially since his head was beginning to feel like it would crack open if he so much as moved it.

"Got your car keys in your pocket?" Max asked, appearing in Quinn's line of vision.

"Vest," Quinn responded, his voice sounding thick to his own ears. Everything was growing more blurry by the second.

The next time he looked up, his car was parked right next to him and Max was getting out of it. Didn't make sense since they'd just been talking.

Lily's face appeared in front of him and Quinn tried to smile. Her hair framed her face in a golden halo. God, but she was pretty. Why had he been mad at her?

"Can you stand up?" she asked.

He nodded.

To his complete irritation, he felt as weak as a wet noodle, and it took both Lily and Max to hoist him up. Just moving…made him sure that any second his head would simply explode.

After an eternity of awkward moves to get in the car, he collapsed in the back seat with Lily. Max and the two kids were in the front seat. The ride down the hill to Lynx Point had never seemed longer, and Max didn't miss a single pothole on the way down, Quinn was sure of it. He wanted to know where they were going, but didn't have the energy to ask.

He slumped over, somehow found his head resting on Lily's lap. He opened his eyes and looked at her. Her mouth was moving, but it took too much effort to figure out what she was saying, so he watched her. He didn't think anyone had ever smelled better, and he turned his head toward her belly and inhaled. She smelled like comfort. Through the soft texture of her sweater against his cheek, her body was warm.

He decided being right here like this would be about perfect if his head weren't pounding.

"I'll go get a gurney," Max said sometime later.

Quinn managed to open an eye. Through the window he could see a weathered sign. Medical Clinic. A scant two months had passed since he was last here. No way was he being wheeled in.

"I can walk." Straightening and opening the car door required a Herculean effort that made him break into a sweat.

This time he managed to stand with only Lily supporting him, her shoulder fitting under his arm like it was meant to be there. She wrapped an arm firmly around his waist. Somehow he managed to walk the eight or ten steps to the door of the clinic.

Thad opened the door, and Quinn made every effort to walk through in a straight line. He'd had to do that once for a cop after he'd celebrated getting a scholarship for college. It had been easier then.

At the jingling sound of the bell, Hilda Raven-in-Moonlight came out of one of the back rooms of the clinic. Remembering something about Thad being her son and being Lily's childhood friend, Quinn studied her. As usual, she was dressed in jeans, a unisex sweater, and jangly earrings he'd never seen her without.

"You never told me you had a kid, Doc." Quinn flashed her a smile, straightening to his full height, and hoping for her usual tart reply to being called "Doc." The very first time he'd been to see her, she had informed him she was a physician's assistant, not a doctor. In his book, she was better than an M.D. any day of the week. Hopefully she hadn't noticed that he'd fall over if Lily wasn't holding him up.

"I have four of them, and that gash on your head will get bigger if it involves any of them." For all the gruffness in her tone, she was gentle when she put an arm around his other side and steered them toward an examining room. She settled him on the examining table, hoisting his feet up.

"How did he manage to get you involved in one of his hare-brained schemes, girl?"

"No scheme." Lily caught his bloody head as though she somehow knew it was killing him and gently eased it back until he was lying down. "A stupid accident. This happened when he tried to keep my car from running into a trailer."

Quinn heard tears clog her voice. Realizing she was more affected than her casual words suggested, he reached for her hand and found it was trembling.

"You should have seen it," Annmarie said, close enough that she could peer into his eyes. "Mommy's car bumped along and then it crashed right into the other one with a big kaboom."

"Everybody else okay?" Hilda asked.

"Fine," Max said. He came through the doorway and dropped the keys to Quinn's car in Lily's hand. "I'm going to go and see what needs to be done to take care of things at the lab."

"Do you need a ride?" Lily asked.

"Nah. It's not that far." With one of his quick smiles that always looked vaguely foreign on his face, he turned around without waiting for a goodbye.

"Me and Annmarie are gonna play video games," Thad said.

"I want to watch Hilda sew Mr. Quinn up," Annmarie said. "Okay, Mom?"

Lily shook her head. "Not okay. Go play with Thad and I'll be along in a bit."

"Mom."

"Go."

Quinn liked the way Lily was firm with her daughter—as though what she did really mattered. Mrs. Perkins had been like Lily in that way. He closed his eyes and allowed himself to remember, just for a moment.

He had been one of five foster children in her house. She had made sure they studied and did the chores and remembered to say "Yes, sir" and "Yes, ma'am" when talking to grown-ups. Quinn had been pretty sure she was a mean old biddy until she died less than a year after he had gone to live with her. Kenny Jones had been in the car with her, and he died, too. Not the drunk who hit them, though.

As foster parents went, she hadn't been so bad. She'd never taken a strap to him. She'd never treated him like she figured he'd steal whatever wasn't tied down. She insisted that "sir" and "ma'am" be used when addressing adults and that he do his homework in the kitchen under her watchful eye. After she died, those two habits were key to his staying out of trouble.

His hand tightened around Lily's and her fingers pressed reassuringly back. He sighed and opened his eyes, staring at the ceiling until the crack he remembered from his last visit came into focus.

"A mundane car accident?" Hilda said from the vicinity of the sink. "That's a first. Last time it was pulling seaweed out of a propeller."

When Lily glanced back down at him, he nodded toward his arm closest to her and tried to waggle his eyebrows. That hurt to much, but he smiled anyway. "Wanna see my scar?"

"Stop bragging. Not every woman is impressed with scars," Hilda scolded, appearing in his line of vision. "Let's see how big this hole in your head is."

She pulled off a huge gauze bandage he had no recollection of anyone putting on him. When had that happened?

"Close encounters of the accidental kind—happens to this guy all the time."

Lily cleared her throat. "This one is my fault."

"No, it's not." Quinn's gaze snapped to her. To his shock her eyes shimmered as though she was a breath away from tears.

Hilda patted his arm. "I get to sew you up again, big guy."

"Okay." His attention didn't leave Lily, though. She had taken off the enveloping red sweater. The blouse underneath was cream-colored...and smeared with his blood. She still gripped his hand, but didn't look at him.

"He's going to be okay?" She glanced at Hilda.

"Fine," Quinn said for himself. "This wasn't your fault."

"It was my car." Finally she looked at him. "And like you said, the keys were in the ignition."

"Little sting while I deaden this," Hilda said, adding, "He's got a concussion. Somebody needs to keep an eye on him, wake him up every couple of hours."

Lily's expression became even more guilt-ridden. "Do you have anyone who can do that?"

He searched her gaze. A man could drown in those dark, beautiful eyes. "Do what?"

"Be with you tonight?"

He managed a grin despite the needle pricks against his forehead. "Are you volunteering, darlin'?"

A blush swept up from her cheeks, then turned her fiery-red to her hairline. He couldn't remember if a woman had ever blushed when he teased her.

"Last I knew, he lived alone." Hilda wasn't as gentle as Lily as she washed the blood away from his forehead, and he closed his eyes to keep his focus on something besides the pain.

"I still do," he muttered.

Time blurred after that, and Quinn drifted in and out, absorbing bits of conversation between Hilda and Lily, who bantered like old friends. There was something about a house being built for Lily with somebody named Ian overseeing the project. And Rosie, who still had morning sickness.

Each time Quinn opened his eyes, he found Lily watching him. Each time, she squeezed his hand and gave him a soft smile as though his being hurt really mattered to her. Wasn't that a hell of an idea.

When they began discussing him again, he forced himself to pay attention.

"He really does need to be checked on for the next twenty-four hours," Hilda was saying. "Maybe the handyman..."

"Max?" Lily finally inserted.

"Yeah. Maybe he can look after Quinn tonight."

"No," Quinn said. "I don't need a nursemaid."

Lily looked at him as though she knew differently. "Ready?"

He nodded and sat up. Surprisingly, he didn't feel nearly as bad as he had a few minutes earlier. "Take me home and let me down a couple of aspirin. By morning, I'll be good as new."

"And ready to kayak over to Foster Island," Hilda said, her voice dry. She took off a pair of latex gloves and dropped them into a trash can. "Stay away from the aspirin. Do you have any Tylenol?" When he didn't answer right away, she added, "I'll give you some. And I want to see you back here in the morning."

"Yes, ma'am."

"Agreeable, now." Hilda smiled. "Keep that up and you could tarnish your swashbuckling reputation."

He stood and took step toward the door. "Like I said, tomorrow I'll be back to normal."

"I'll get Annmarie and be ready in a minute." Lily picked up the red sweater she had been wearing earlier and disappeared through the doorway.

He watched her walk down the hallway toward the door to Hilda's apartment. Lily might be small, but the curve of her bottom was all woman, round and sexy despite the full cut of her slacks. The lady looked damn near as good walking away as she did coming toward him.

Hilda cleared her throat and he turned around. She handed him a small bottle. He glanced at the label and put the bottle in his pocket. When he looked up, he found her watching him.

"So that's the way the wind blows," she said.

"What?"

She folded her arms over her chest. "Don't you 'what' me. I see how you look at her."

"Last I heard, looking wasn't a crime." He didn't add that

Lily had been looking back. In fact she was the one who'd started it.

"She's still getting over the death of her husband."

"She told me."

"She's not the type to have a fling."

Quinn pressed a hand against the bandage at his hairline. "Do you always fight her battles?"

Hilda grinned suddenly and the heat disappeared from her voice. "Since we were seven years old. She'd take in a stray and never check to see if he had rabies."

"Talking about me behind my back again?" Lily asked, coming down the hallway from Hilda's apartment, Annmarie holding her hand. "I haven't picked up a stray since Sly Devious Beast." She grinned at Quinn. "He turned out to be a great dog and quite without rabies."

"I'm worried," Annmarie said. "We've been gone a long time and Sweetie Pie is probably missing me."

"Most likely." Lily urged her daughter toward the outside door and gave Hilda a quick hug. "I promised Thad that I'd bring caramel corn when we come down for videos tomorrow night."

"You're spoiling my son rotten."

"I know."

Lily opened the exterior door and waited for Quinn. Annmarie ducked under her arm. He followed her outside where she said, "I'm driving."

"Okay."

She held open the car door for him, which made him feel like an old man, then waited until he was settled into the passenger seat before going around the vehicle to the driver's side.

"I live up the hill from the dock. Second house from the end," he said after she got in the car and was scooting the driver's seat forward to accommodate her shorter frame. "You live with your sister, right?"

"That's right." Lily started the car.

"Then you should take the car after dropping me at home."

She smiled at him. "Does your head still hurt?"

He nodded. "Like hell."

"He said a bad word, Mommy," Annmarie said.

"Sorry." Now that they were moving again, his brief surge of feeling better had all but disappeared.

Lily drove right past the turnoff to his street.

"You missed the turn."

"I know," she said. "I'm not taking you home. Like Hilda said, you need someone to check on you tonight, and you yourself said there's no one to do that."

"I'll be fine."

"I'm sure you will," she agreed.

"But you're not taking me home." He really ought to be more upset about that, he decided. Instead the idea of being babied somehow appealed more than being one of the strays she took in bothered him.

Again she smiled. "I'm not."

"Who would have thought you're stubborn?"

As they headed south from Lynx Point, he figured his brain cells were still mostly intact. He didn't have to be a genius to figure out they were on their way to Lily's sister's house. There were only a couple of places out this direction, and the nursery was at the end of the road.

On the drive to her aunt's house, Annmarie maintained a running monologue, informing Quinn how impressed she was with his car, which was green like hers only much nicer and with lots of dials and stuff, pointing out the turnoff to the house where she and her mom were going to live only couldn't right now because the house had no walls yet, and relating how her kitten tormented the dog.

He'd seen the house the last time he had been kayaking, the straight lines of new lumber standing out from the surrounding forest.

They came around a final bend and the road ended at a gate with a hand-painted sign above it that read Comin' Up

Rosie. Quinn had ridden his mountain bike out here a couple of times, but he'd never been through the gate, which framed a traditional Tlingit totem in the middle of the yard. Beyond the house was a gorgeous yacht anchored next to a pristine dock.

As Lily parked the car, a woman clad in jeans and a dark green apron came out of the greenhouse. She was followed by the ugliest dog he had ever seen.

"Do you have a totem pole in your yard?" Annmarie asked him.

"Nope."

"In California, we didn't have one, either." Annmarie sat up straighter and waved. "That's my aunt Rosie," she informed him. "She's going to have a baby real soon. Did you know that?"

"No." Or maybe he did—something about her having morning sickness. She showed no sign of an advanced pregnancy despite her niece's assertion.

The instant that Lily shut off the ignition, Annmarie scrambled over her and bounced out of the car. She skipped across the yard and threw herself into her aunt's arms.

"Guess what happened? Mommy's car was in a crash and Mr. Quinn, he got stitches from Hilda, and Thad and me, we found lots of stuff in the tide pools."

Quinn's impression was that anyone could tell Rosie, Lily and Annmarie were related. Rosie was taller than Lily, but not by much. All three had blond hair and dark eyes. Even without the similarities in their coloring, the family resemblance would have stood out.

"What's all this?" Rosie removed her work gloves and stuffed them into the pocket of the canvas apron.

When Quinn walked toward them, the dog sniffed his hand, then ambled toward the wide porch that wrapped around the house.

Lily briefly related what had happened with the accident. At the end, she glanced toward Quinn and introduced him.

"I think we met once last spring when you moved your

lab to the new place.'' Rosie shook his hand. ''You probably want to go sit down somewhere.''

''Yeah.'' He remembered how surprised he had been when about forty people showed up to help him move. A job that he had anticipated would take a week had taken, instead, hours. It was his first experience with the neighbor-helping-neighbor support commonplace in Lynx Point. Given the independent nature of the people who lived here, their generosity and support had been a surprise and had proven to be an integral part of the character of these people.

''You might as well stay for supper,'' Rosie said.

''Actually, he's staying a bit longer than that,'' Lily said, taking him by the arm and steering him toward the house. ''He has a concussion and needs somebody to keep an eye on him tonight.''

''He's spending the night?'' Rosie's eyebrows rose and she gave Quinn an even more thorough look.

Hilda's comment about strays struck home. He was done with being the odd man out, the stray, the one nobody really wanted. God, but he was tired.

''Lily was driving—''

''Which put me in the driver's seat.'' She led him up the steps to the porch. ''So, yes. He's staying.''

''I never agreed to that.'' He stepped around the dog, who was sprawled in front of the door.

Somehow he found himself led into the house. Lily came to a halt, then gave him a long, considering glance. ''You're not as tall as my brother-in-law, but I bet he has something you can wear. The blood on your shirt—''

''Isn't that bad. I'm fine.'' Quinn didn't tell her that he'd made a point of never wearing anyone's else's clothes since he'd gone off to college when he was eighteen. By then he'd had more than enough of hand-me-downs.

Annmarie came from somewhere in the house, carrying an apparently boneless calico cat in her arms that she held up for his inspection. ''This is Sweetie Pie. Would you like to hold her? She purrs and everything.''

"Maybe later."

"This way," Lily said, urging him toward a doorway. Through a short hallway, he found himself in a comfortable-looking living room. As with the kitchen, the walls were a cheery yellow. The sofa and chairs were large enough to accommodate a man of his size. Lily pointed toward one of the blue-upholstered chairs in front of a large television. "That one is a recliner."

"You're going to let me sleep?" When she looked up to meet his gaze, he grinned. "I still haven't agreed to stay."

To his surprise, she handed him his car keys. "If you feel well enough to drive, go."

No one had ever called his bluff as neatly. He gave her back the keys. "Maybe after a nap."

"I'll get you a glass of water so you can take the Tylenol that Hilda gave you." She went back to the kitchen, and a second later he heard the sound of running water.

A poster-size photograph over the mantel caught his gaze—a family gathering. He wanted to look away, hating the feeling that always wound through his chest with the whole family thing. Other people took pictures like that for granted. Easy if you had a family…and he didn't.

This photograph chronicled a wedding, he realized a second later. Right away he recognized Lily and Annmarie wearing traditional Norwegian dress. Rosie stood next to a tall man in a tux and another woman looking much like Rosie and Lily stood next to another tall man, this one in a full dress uniform. Annmarie hadn't changed much, so he figured the photograph had to be a recent one.

The other picture that snagged his attention was one of Lily with a man and a baby—clearly one of those portraits that had been taken to commemorate the beginning of a family. The man and Lily cradled the baby, but their eyes were on one another. Their expressions made Quinn feel as though he was peeping through a window at something too private to be shared. Lily's husband…. No matter what kind of signals she had given Quinn this afternoon, no man could com-pete with this dead husband she obviously adored. Him least of all.

He fished the bottle of pills out of his pocket and sat down. The chair was as comfortable as it looked. He had just lifted the footrest when Lily returned. She waited for him to take the pills, then covered him with a knitted blanket. The novelty of it all had him searching her gaze and snagging her hand when she would have stepped away.

"Hilda was right, you know." When she raised an eyebrow, he added, "About checking for rabies."

"If you were some stray, she might be right, but you're not." She pulled her fingers from within his and brushed his hair away from his forehead, lightly skirting the bandage that covered his stitches. "You belong here more than you realize." Patting his shoulder, she walked away. "Rest."

Rest? Not likely. He fingered the handmade blanket, his thoughts following the woman. Of all the words he'd wanted to hear his whole life and never had, hers were the ones. *You belong here.*

Chapter 3

A loud rhythmic rumble made Quinn open his eyes. A pair of brown eyes within a pixie face peered into his. Annmarie. He turned his head slightly and found her cat resting on his chest, her paws kneading. The source of the rumble, her purr, was loud, satisfied and inviting.

"I'm s'posed to wake you up when the timer rings," Annmarie said, lifting a handheld timer for him to see. According to the dial, he had less than five minutes.

"Looks like I woke up just in time." He pushed the recliner into a sitting position, and the cat slid to his lap. He glanced at his watch, surprised that nearly two hours had passed. He'd slept, and he hadn't intended to.

"Sweetie Pie likes you."

"I can see that." He petted the cat, discovering that she was far smaller than he had imagined, her long calico coat disguising her size. He'd forgotten how soft cat fur was. She opened her green eyes, her expression one of complete contentment.

Quinn glanced around the room, which was bathed in the

light of early evening. Everything about the room suggested this was where Lily and her family spent a lot of time—books stacked on one of the end tables, a basket filled with skeins of yarn, and a coloring book and crayons on one end of the coffee table. Again, his gaze lingered on the family photos on the mantel.

This place was a home, in all that word conjured. And, as always, he was the outsider.

If asked, he'd deny he had ever wanted this, but for a moment he allowed himself to imagine being right here enjoying one of the Alaska's long winter nights with a family—a woman like Lily and a little girl like Annmarie.

The timer pinged and Quinn gave himself a mental shake. e had tried the family thing right after college and it hadn't lasted a year. No way was he repeating that experience. Bad as it was for him, he wouldn't subject anyone else to his Dr. Jekyll and Mr. Hyde behavior ever again. The honeymoon period, doing everything he could to please. The rebel-without-a-cause period, being a royal pain and sabotaging the very relationships he wanted. He'd finally grown up and admitted the obvious. Wanting a family and having the goods to make it work…those didn't come in the same package—at least, not with him. End of story.

He lowered the footrest and handed the cat to Annmarie. She grinned at him, then skipped toward the kitchen, the cat draped over her shoulder.

"He's awake, Mom. Guess what? He snores. I heard 'em."

Quinn grinned at that. Annmarie really was a pistol. He stood, deciding he really did feel better, not good enough to whip anyone, but at least his still-aching head didn't feel as though it would fall off when he moved it.

"And snoring sounds like?" Lily asked from the kitchen.

"Like Sweetie Pie when she purrs, only louder."

Nothing had ever been more inviting than Lily's soft, answering laugh. Or maybe it was the mouthwatering aroma coming from the kitchen.

At a slower pace, Quinn followed Annmarie. Lily stood at the stove, her back to him. She had changed out of the tailored slacks into a print skirt that skimmed her ankles. An oversize towel was wrapped into an apron around her slim waist. Her feet were bare and tapping to the rhythm of a Country tune on the radio. The scientist had been replaced by an earth mother cooking in a cheery yellow kitchen.

"Are you making cobbler yet?" Annmarie pulled a chair across the floor toward the counter. "I want to help."

"Fine, but put the cat down and wash your hands first."

"Hi," Quinn said.

Lily turned around, her smile welcoming, her gaze frankly searching his face. There it was again…an invitation in her dark eyes that he found all too tempting.

"Hi. How are you feeling?" She came toward him and pulled one of the chairs away from the table in the center of the room, motioning for him to sit down. "What can I get for you—a soda, milk, coffee?"

"Nothing, thanks."

She wiped her hands on the makeshift apron and returned to the stove where something sizzled in a large cast-iron skillet.

"Whatever you're cooking smells great." What he had intended was to make his excuses, thank her for her hospitality, and leave. Instead he moved closer, drawn by both the woman and the tantalizing aroma of her cooking.

She flashed him another smile over her shoulder, then expertly turned over the pieces, cooked to a crisp golden brown. "Comfort food—fried chicken. I thought you might enjoy that."

"Sounds great." The same thing as agreeing that he'd stay for dinner. Then he'd go home.

"And smashed potatoes," Annmarie said from the sink where she was washing her hands. "Uncle Ian says they're his favorite, did you know that?" Without waiting for an answer she added, "And he likes cold pizza, too, but Mommy thinks that's yucky."

Quinn caught Lily's gaze. "What about cold fried chicken?"

"On a picnic…"

"With potato salad…"

Lily shook her head. "Cole slaw and chocolate cake."

"Sign me up." *The way to a man's heart,* he nearly said, which was the same as admitting he wanted more from this surprising woman. He merely offered, "Your picnics sound better than mine."

"Aunt Rosie and me, we planned lots of picnics, and then it always rained," Annmarie said, once again pulling her chair toward the counter. "Can we make cobbler now, Mom?"

"Yes." Lily set a mixing bowl in front of Annmarie.

The little girl looked at Quinn. "You could help, too, Mr. Quinn. Mommy measures and I get to put everything in the bowl. But I can share."

"Thanks, but I think I'll just watch."

Annmarie grinned. "And you get to put your finger in to see if it tastes good."

He laughed. "Would I have to wash my hands?"

"Certainly," Lily said, giving him a mock frown that he didn't believe for a minute.

Within seconds he figured out that he was in the way by simply standing around, so he retreated to the kitchen table and sat in the chair that Lily had pulled out. He had never imagined that he'd find watching a woman and a little girl so fascinating, but it was. The flour that ended up on the floor instead of in the bowl didn't seem to bother Lily a bit. She was patient and funny with her daughter, both of them clearly enjoying the process.

Throughout the interplay, Lily somehow managed to maintain a running dialogue with Quinn, eliciting from him that his head still pounded and bringing him a Dr Pepper after he mentioned that was what he liked.

"Where's your sister?" he asked as Lily slid the raspberry cobbler into the oven.

"I have two. Rosie is on a walk with Ian. And Dahlia is in Colorado."

"With Uncle Jack," Annmarie piped in. "He was Mr. Jack and Uncle Ian was Mr. Ian and then there was the wedding and I got two uncles on the same day."

"I see," Quinn said.

Lily smiled. "Can you believe we planned a double wedding in less than two months?"

It was the sort of question that required a "No, I don't believe it," so he shook his head.

"We had a great time. Lots of family, lots of food. And perfect for Rosie and Dahlia."

Family. That again.

"Mommy says just because Aunt Rosie is having a baby doesn't mean Aunt Dahlia is," Annmarie offered. "I really, really want a baby sister or a baby brother, but Mommy says she won't be having any because that takes a mommy *and* a daddy."

"Aha." Quinn had the feeling this was part of an ongoing conversation between the two when he noticed the chastising look Lily gave Annmarie.

She tousled her daughter's hair. "Time to help me set the table, sweetie."

Quinn stood. "That's something I can help with."

"Okay." Lily pointed to where the plates and flatware were kept, then returned her attention to the stove and the dozen things that suddenly all needed to be done at once.

In the middle of setting the table and smiling at Annmarie's direction where the forks and knives should be placed, the outside door opened. Rosie and the dog Quinn had seen earlier came in, followed by a tall, rugged-looking man whose gaze lasered in on him.

"I'm Quinn Morrison." He offered his hand. "You must be Rosie's husband."

"Ian Stearne," the man said, shaking Quinn's hand. "Rosie tells me you've been playing chicken with Lily's car."

"Chicken-brained is more like it," Quinn said. "I had the dumb-ass idea that I could catch it."

"And he would have, too, if it hadn't been locked," Lily offered. She carried a steaming platter of crispy fried chicken to the table.

Ian gave her a sharp look. "Your car rolled down the hillside, and it was locked?"

"And the keys were in the ignition." Lily returned to the stove where she poured steaming green beans into a serving bowl. "I would have sworn I put them in the drawer of my desk, but I must have left them in the car." As had happened before, Lily's casual words belied the pain in her eyes, which gave Quinn the impression she didn't want anyone to know how frightened she had been.

"That makes no sense," Ian said.

Rosie motioned for them to all sit.

Quinn pulled out a chair, wondering what was behind Ian's protective attitude toward Lily.

"The handyman—Max—called," Ian said. "Frank Talbot picked up your car and towed it down to the garage."

"That was good of him." Lily took the seat next to Quinn and promptly passed him a napkin-covered basket that he discovered was filled the warm corn bread. "I bet I have to send it off to Juneau to get it fixed."

"Not as convenient as San Jose," Ian said.

"Speaking of California," Rosie said, glancing at Lily. "Cal called today asking for you. Said he was just checking in."

If Quinn hadn't been watching Lily, he would have missed the shadow that chased across her face before she smiled. Old boyfriend, maybe? The twinge of jealousy over that thought surprised Quinn.

"He's been calling a lot," Ian said. "Everything okay?"

"As far as I know," Lily said. She gave Ian the sort of smile that suggested the subject was closed, then asked, "Did the windows for my house arrive today?"

"They did," he said. "We're right on schedule to have the exterior weather-tight by the first of October."

The next few moments were taken up with the discussion of Lily's house, which was under construction, while food was passed around the table. The routine was clearly ordinary to Lily and her family, but for Quinn... He figured the last home-cooked meal he'd had like this was last Thanksgiving. Lily hadn't been whistling "Dixie" when she promised comfort food. Fried chicken and corn bread. One of his favorite meals...one he'd enjoy a whole lot more if his head wasn't once again pounding.

"Any strangers hanging around the center?" Ian asked.

Lily uttered a soft chuckle, her gaze amused when she looked at Ian. "You have the most suspicious mind. No, it was nothing like that. Just a stupid accident."

Ian's expression suggested that he didn't agree.

Quinn realized that he didn't think it was an accident, either.

With a sudden rush of clarity, Quinn remembered a conversation he'd had with Dwight Jones on the ferry yesterday. As chief geologist for Anorak Exploration, Jones's views on the natural resources surrounding Kantrovitch Island were diametrically opposed to Quinn's. Jones had been more than a little hot that Quinn had filed a request for an injunction to stop the exploratory drilling within a twenty-mile radius around the hydrothermic vent.

"If you want to play hardball," Jones had said, "you'll be getting yourself in way deeper than you can imagine. We will be drilling. Get used to it."

Until now, Quinn hadn't thought that anything about their conversation could be construed as a threat. Was it? He wished he didn't feel so woozy and out of it, which left him with the feeling that he had overlooked something important.

Though their professional differences kept them from being close friends, Quinn liked Dwight well enough. They had gone kayaking a couple of times, which had been fine. As had their occasional Friday afternoon basketball games on the dock.

"That's some mighty deep thinking you appear to be doing there," Ian said.

Quinn nodded, meeting the other man's narrowed gaze. "Just remembering a conversation I had on the ferry yesterday. I'll check it out."

The narrowed gaze became a frown. "You bring trouble to Lily's door—"

"Stop it." Lily flashed Quinn an apologetic smile. "You'll have to forgive Ian. He sees a boogeyman behind every bush."

"That's 'cause there were bad mens. Lots of them," Annmarie piped in.

"As for those bad men—" Lily said "—that's behind us, and they're in prison." At Quinn's questioning glance, she added, "I testified in a murder case last spring, the man was convicted and he's in prison. Since then, Ian has been a little edgy."

Quinn caught the other man's gaze, certain there was a wealth of information that Lily had left out of her light explanation. Ian Stearne didn't strike him as a man who imagined things. He did strike Quinn has the kind of man who took care of his own, though. Quinn admired that.

"Lily's car is almost identical to mine." He cleared his throat. "If today wasn't an accident, it has to do with me…not her."

"Something involving Anorak?" Rosie asked. "They've made it real plain to the fishermen they expect to begin drilling soon."

Quinn knew better than to throw even the most casual of stones before checking his facts. "I don't know, but like I said, I'll check on it."

"Eat," Lily urged. "Our dinner is getting cold, and I've had about enough of this. Today was an accident. That's all."

Quinn hoped she was right. He flat-out hated the idea that somebody else's argument with him could have put Lily or

Annmarie in danger. The quicker he figured out if Anorak or Dwight Jones had anything to do with today, the better.

His name being whispered brought Quinn wide awake.

After a second of disorientation he remembered where he was. Spending the night with Lily and her family. He really had intended to go home, but instead found himself in Lily's queen-size bed, while she slept with her daughter.

He'd watched Lily and Rosie put clean sheets on the bed, but they still smelled like Lily, a scent he liked better by the hour. Long after he'd gone to bed and turned out the light, he had imagined having her in bed with him, naked, hot and willing. She wouldn't be so worried about waking him at the two-hour intervals that Hilda had prescribed if she knew how unruly his thoughts were.

He turned his head toward the open doorway. The hall light behind Lily backlit her slim figure. To his disappointment, she was wrapped in some kind of thick bathrobe that prevented the light from revealing a bit of her body.

"What time is it?" he asked.

"A little before one." She came into the room, knotting the sash of the robe more firmly around her waist.

That meant he'd been asleep not even two hours.

"How are you feeling?" she asked.

"Like hell." He wished her face wasn't hidden in the shadows. "Which probably means I'm going to live."

"Is there anything I can get you?"

That was too good to pass up. "What are you offering, darlin'?"

She chuckled as though she understood exactly what he meant. "Company—" she held out a glass of water as he sat up "—Tylenol."

"I guess that will have to do, then." He took the pills from the palm of her hand, washed them down, then set the glass on the nightstand.

"Are you hungry?" she asked. "There's milk and chocolate cake. Or maybe you'd rather have hot chocolate."

"I'm fine. You shouldn't have to give up any sleep on my account."

"I'm not."

He snorted. "Sure you're not. You're up in the middle of the night all the time."

"More than you might think." Her expression was hidden in the shadows, but it was impossible to miss the sadness in her voice. "Go back to sleep, Quinn."

"Sure. Just so you can come wake me up again." Truth was, he was looking forward to it. He slid back down until his throbbing head rested on the pillow.

She turned off the light in the hallway and he heard the soft click of the other bedroom door as she closed it.

He fell asleep in the middle of wondering about her confessed insomnia. True to her word, she came back at three. The only other time in his life that he remembered anyone checking on him during the middle of the night was when he'd been in the hospital with appendicitis. At the time he'd been sure the nurse had woken him simply to give her something to do. Thinking about the kind of caring a man might attribute to Lily's actions was dangerous thinking in the middle of the night.

"Are you doing okay?" she asked. Perching on the edge of the bed, she touched his shoulder. That simple touch shot straight to his groin.

He took her hand and kissed the back of it. "Fine." Gruffly he asked, "What about you? Did you sleep?"

"I was hoping you would have forgotten about that."

"So you didn't."

She didn't say anything, but didn't deny it, either.

"What are you thinking about?" he asked, taking one of her hands within his, rubbing his thumb against her palm.

She sighed. "If there weren't nights, this would all be a lot easier."

"What?"

"Getting on with my life." A long moment of silence stretched before she added, "I felt like I was just getting back on my feet after John died when I saw this guy murdered one night. I'd just gotten into my car and was leaving the parking lot, and there they were—these three men. One of them was on his knees and one of the others shot him in the back of the head.'' Her voice had a soft, overcontrolled quality to it that showed just how close to the surface her emotions lay.

When she paused, Quinn didn't say a word, just continued to hold her hand. What could he say that wasn't totally meaningless? But he ached with the fear that he knew she would have felt.

"God, I don't even know why I'm telling you all this."

"Maybe because I'm interested. Maybe because there's something about the dark that feels safe."

"Sometimes I just wish there was someone to hold me during the night—" She broke off suddenly. Then, in a strangled whisper, added, "I'm not asking… I didn't mean—"

"It's okay," he said. "I didn't think you were inviting yourself into my—your—bed."

"God, I'm embarrassed."

"Don't be."

"During the day, I'm busy and I do okay. But at night…"

"You have too much time to think."

"Yes," she breathed. A smile was back in her voice when she said, "So, you're doing me a favor. Giving me something to do during the long hours of the night, something other than my puny fears to think about."

"They aren't puny, so stop right there," he said, cataloging all she had been through the last couple of years—at least the obvious things. Her husband dying, witnessing a murder, walking away from a career, moving, and all the while keeping things normal for her daughter.

Though his head was throbbing, he liked having her with him, liked knowing that in some strange way his being here was somehow helping her, too. She didn't say anything more, just sat there with him, her hip warm against his side. And despite wanting to stay awake, to keep her company, he felt himself drift back toward sleep.

When she came back at five, though it was still dark outside, sleep was the last thing on his mind. He'd been awake for maybe half an hour, anticipating the moment when she'd slip inside the room. Knowing she fought demons during the night somehow made her even more likable. Like? Who was he kidding? There was like and then there was *like*. What he was feeling at the moment had nothing to do with friendship and everything to do sex. Morning arousal didn't usually have the direct focus of a warm, fragrant woman.

She sat close to him on the bed, apparently oblivious to the danger, and brushed his hair away from his forehead. "Are you doing okay?"

"Lie down with me," he whispered, wondering where the hell those words had come from the instant he said them. Sure, he'd been thinking about it, but that was no excuse.

Her breath caught, and he wished for more light than came from the hallway so he could see her expression. She looked away from him, then stood.

Ah, damn. The apology he owed her remained stuck in his throat. She'd been nothing but kind, and she was bound to take his invitation as an insult rather than... Than what? he wondered.

He closed his eyes and a second later heard the click of the door. He looked over at it and, to his astonishment, saw that she was moving toward him as if in a shadowy dream. He heard the soft swish of her robe, then sensed more than he saw as she let it drop from her shoulders to the floor. She pulled back the covers and slipped in beneath them.

She scooted closer as he shifted onto his side, then she was in his arms, pressed against him full body to body. Hardly daring to breathe, he wrapped his arms around her. He had to be dreaming.

No way had she just climbed into bed with him.

Chapter 4

"Oh, Quinn," she whispered, her arms coming around him, gently for an instant, then fiercely, as though she expected him to be wrenched away. "You feel so good."

"So do you, darlin'." Against Quinn's feet, hers were like ice. As soon as he touched them, she tried to pull away. "Shh," he murmured, cradling her cold feet between his much larger ones.

Breathing in the fragrance of her hair, he decided that if he was dreaming he didn't want to wake up. If he wasn't dreaming...he sure as hell didn't want to do the honorable thing and send her away.

He wanted to kiss her. He wanted to roll her onto her back and to plunge into her soft body. He wanted to know the sounds she made while making love. Instead he held her, feeling her feet warm.

Beneath his hand, the silky fabric of her nightgown slid against his fingers. Soft, but not as soft as her skin at the nape of her neck. He couldn't have kept his hands from wandering to the swell of her bottom or the sweet curve of her breasts if his life had depended on it. As he did, she somehow snuggled even closer, her breath hot against his cheek.

He buried his face in her hair. Silky. Fragrant as sunshine. In his arms, she was so damn small. Smaller by far than any other woman he had ever held. He shifted against her, absorbing the slide of her body against his, the friction undoing him a bit at a time. Oh, she fit him perfectly.

He pressed his lips against that fragrant hair, then on her cheek. Soft. Then at her jaw. Smooth. Then the other cheek. Silky.

Her small hands were warm through the fabric of his T-shirt; he would have given just about anything to feel them against his bare skin. Through the pounding of his head, he couldn't decide what the mixed signals meant. She was in his arms, being held so intimately that with a couple of shifts of their clothes, he could be where he wanted—buried in her. Though she held him tightly, offering the comfort of her body, he wondered if she meant to be offering sex, too.

God, he wished his head didn't hurt so much. He needed to really think this through.

Her fingers eased into his scalp, finding the pressure points and gently massaging them, the movement easing the throb in his head. Instantly, he relaxed, and his head dropped into the hollow between her neck and shoulder.

''Keep that up, darlin', and I'm yours for life.''

Her soft chuckle vibrated against his cheek. ''Promises, promises.''

Though he was too relaxed to move, the realization that he had said, *Yours for life?* stabbed at him. Where the hell had that thought come from? Who was he kidding? He was a here-and-now kind of man. And she was…definitely a forever kind of woman.

That knowledge didn't keep him from wanting to kiss her, from wanting this innocent embrace to morph into torrid sex.

''Better?'' she whispered, her magic fingers easing the knots out of the tendons in his neck.

"Mmm." He kissed her neck, then had to test that silky skin with his teeth.

She shuddered then arched beneath him in that timeless gesture of surrender that his own body recognized. He released her skin, then laved the tiny hurt, kissing her neck. He inhaled deeply, loving the floral, musky scent of her.

His arms came around her and he ignored the throbbing in his head to kiss her the way he had been wanting to practically from the moment he had met her.

Her lips were soft beneath his, trembling, and so sweet.

"Darlin', let me in."

She sighed, and then he was in, finding her shy tongue with his own. She moaned, or maybe he did, and the sound drove the last coherent thought from his mind. All that was left behind was a need to be connected to her, a need that he'd die for.

The kiss went on and on. Dark. Carnal. More vital than breathing. He pulled her close, sliding his hands across the satiny fabric of her nightgown, pushing the fabric up...until he reached the inside of her thigh. Soft. So...damn...soft.

Barely daring to breath, he lay there, his head pounding and his arousal throbbing...more scared about making that next move than he had ever been. Time stopped except for brush of his thumb against her leg.

From somewhere he found the honor to ask, "Is this what you want?"

"Lying with you?" The beat of a second passed. "Or sex?"

"Either. Both."

"What I want." She cupped his cheek with her hand, the tension seeping out of her body. "You'd have to be a decent man and ask me, wouldn't you?"

"There's not a single decent thing about what I'm thinking."

Still, he had his answer. He dredged a little deeper, found his conscience and removed his hand from the inside of her thigh. Wishing that he'd touched her more intimately, he

smoothed her nightgown into place. She'd have to be dead
not to notice his erection pressing into her belly, but to his
relief she didn't ease away from him. Her body softened even
more, though the thrum of arousal continued its hum through
him, urging him to ignore his self-control and the headache
that had resumed its incessant pounding. He allowed himself
a sweep of his hand over the curve of her bottom and imagined how she'd feel naked.

They lay together like that for a long time, her hands continuing to knead the knots of muscle in his back and neck.
Her touch became more languid, then ceased altogether. Her
breathing became even as her body relaxed against his, and
he realized that she had fallen asleep. He didn't dare let his
mind embrace the implications of that. Sleeping together, in
his mind, was a thousand times more intimate than sex, required way more trust than sex. And yet she had fallen asleep
in his arms as though he could keep her worries at bay. Sighing, he pressed his lips against the smooth skin at her temple
and wished he was the kind of man who could do that for
her. But he wasn't.

He must have slept because sometime later he opened his
eyes and the room was light, sunshine streaming through the
window. He rolled onto his back and stretched, noticing feminine things, frilly things, about the room that he hadn't noticed last night. A stack of paperback novels on the nightstand caught his attention, along with a small lamp. He had
images of her in here inside that tiny pool of light reading
and keeping her worries hidden from her family.

Rubbing a hand over his face, he felt the bandage at his
hairline and realized his headache was mostly gone. He
hoped it stayed that way when he was vertical.

An erotic dream lingered, its focus Lily. He brought one
of the pillows to his nose and inhaled deeply, the scent of
her making him instantly hard. For a moment he wondered
if she had really been in his bed or if he had simply been
wishing so hard that it seemed real. His remembered words
tore through his brain. *I'm yours for life.* What kind of idiot

was he to ever say such a thing? No one else had wanted him for life, and he was about to delude himself into thinking that she would. Thank God they hadn't had sex. He didn't need that kind of grief in his life.

Instead he'd been even more stupid—letting her under his skin with her hidden worries and vulnerabilities that made him wish he was a different kind of man. He needed to re-establish the relationship on a professional level, and fast. Before he hurt her. Because it would come to that. It always did.

He had just met her, didn't really know her. She worked for him, for Pete's sake. Making love with her…what in the hell would he call it, if not that? So they hadn't had sex. Not quite. What they had shared, though, had been a hell of a lot more intimate. He might have sex with the occasional woman, but he didn't sleep with them. *She worked for him.* He had to remember that because he didn't have a damn thing that he could offer her.

Why even think about that, moron? he told himself, yanking on his clothes. Sex without commitment, he was used to. Somehow those words in relation to Lily sounded dirty. What he had felt with her wasn't. Not even close.

He had nothing to offer her. Not a woman who had been as happily married as she clearly had been. Not a woman with a cute little girl like Annmarie. He'd done that once before—acquired the ready-made family he had been so sure he wanted. One word described that experience. Disaster.

He raked a hand through his hair and went to the window. Thanks to the sunshine, the water in the cove beyond the house sparkled and the islands in the distance rose from the water like mountains. The scene was so idyllic he was tempted to hope for the possibilities that skipped through his mind.

The daydream lasted for about a second. Until the old accusation, so true it hurt, ripped through his head. *You're too damn scared to let anyone love you. However much you're hurting me…you're killing yourself. You just don't know it.*

Oh, he knew. His ex-wife had been right on all counts. No way could he risk going there again.

His emotions in turmoil, he glanced around the room to make sure he had all of his things. Shoes in hand, he pulled open the door and stepped into the hallway. To his relief, the door to Annmarie's room was closed—with any luck, Lily was still asleep. Coward that he was, he didn't want to face her.

He crept down the stairs. Uncertainty crawled through his gut, reminding him of being a child in a strange house with people he didn't know, sure that soon he'd be sent somewhere else because he always was. He hated the feeling and reminded himself he was a man, no longer powerless like the scared boy he had once been.

Downstairs, he went through the hallway to the kitchen. As soon as he put on his shoes, escape was within reach. Seconds away.

"Hi, Mr. Quinn," Annmarie said from the kitchen chair where she was sitting, a coloring book in front of her. "I'm having hot chocolate. Do you want some, too?"

"I..." His gaze darted around the room. "Where's your mom?"

"Sleeping." She sighed and took another sip of her hot chocolate, carefully lifting the mug to her lips with both hands. "Everybody is sleeping, 'cept you, me and Sweetie Pie." Annmarie set the mug down and pointed toward the cat who was on the windowsill, her attention riveted on the bird feeder visible through the window.

"I see."

"Is your head still hurted, Mr. Quinn?"

"Only a little." He sat across the table from her and began to put on his shoes. Out of the corner of his eye, he watched Annmarie put one of the crayons in the box, then select another one.

"I can make hot chocolate all by myself. Uncle Ian showed me. Blowing up the marshmallows is the best part."

"What?" When he looked up from tying his shoe, she grinned.

"You put 'em in the microwave, and they get real, real big. Uncle Ian says that I can do it by myself, but I have to follow the rules." She leaned closer to him. "So, Mr. Quinn, you want hot chocolate and marshmallows, don't you?"

"I do." Clearly he had lost his mind. What he wanted to do—needed to do—was to leave before anyone else was up. Still, this little girl with her impish smile made him want to linger—to pretend for a few minutes longer that he really could do the family thing.

He followed Annmarie across the kitchen, where she scooted a chair to the counter, filled a cup with water, heated it in the microwave, added chocolate mix and stirred carefully. Then she added a marshmallow and put the cup back in the microwave for ten more seconds, all the while telling him each step and finishing with, "See? Simple, huh?" and handing him the cup with a huge, puffy-white topping, the likes of which he'd never had.

"That's very grown up," Quinn told her as they sat back down at the kitchen table.

"I know," she agreed solemnly. "And, if I don't get a baby brother or sister soon, it will be too late."

"Too late for what?" Quinn asked, focusing on the one part of the sentence that kept him from thinking about the very activity that could lead to Annmarie having that sister or brother.

"Well," Annmarie said, swinging her legs back and forth, her fuzzy pink slippers making her feet look bigger than they were. "If Mommy waits too long, then I'll be sixteen like Angela."

"I see." In fact, he didn't see anything at all. "Who's Angela?"

"Thad's sister," Annmarie said before returning with laser precision to the topic at hand. "And I asked Mommy why she couldn't do it like last time, only she said things are different now. We can't adopt Aunt Rosie's baby like

Mommy did with me because Uncle Ian wouldn't like it. But he could still be the daddy and Aunt Rosie could still be the auntie.''

Quinn failed to follow the child's logic even as he was sure things made perfect sense to her.

''So I've been thinking. Since Uncle Ian says you have to have a mommy *and* daddy, all I have to do is find a daddy. Mine died, you know.''

Quinn nodded at her matter-of-fact announcement.

''When you were a little boy, did you have a daddy?''

''No.'' The question was as unexpected as everything else about the conversation.

''Oh.'' A tiny pucker appeared between her eyebrows. ''Did you want one?''

Had anyone else asked the question he would have lied. Instead he found himself telling this child a truth that he would have denied anyone else. ''With all my heart.''

She smiled. ''Me, too. But mostly I want a baby. This time maybe the baby can grow in my mommy instead of in Aunt Rosie. That should work, don't you think?''

He didn't know what to think, but he was sure of one thing. Agreeing with Annmarie in any way at all would likely land him in deep trouble.

''I think—'' he glanced at his watch ''—it's getting late.''

''Yep,'' Annmarie agreed.

''And I should probably go.''

''Before breakfast?''

He nodded, standing up, and she expelled a big sigh.

When he looked down at her, she said, ''Are you sure you don't want breakfast?'' She pointed at the cupboard. ''The cereal is way up there. The bowls are over there and, besides, the milk is very heavy.''

''Ah.'' Things were beyond her reach, if he understood the problem. How could he leave without helping her out, especially since she had made hot chocolate for him? ''Okay. I guess I can have cereal before I go.'' He opened the cupboard and found a single box of cereal on the top shelf.

Cocoa Puffs. He had been hoping for cornflakes or something similar.

She beamed as he poured cereal into two bowls and got out the milk. Within no time they were munching on cereal as Annmarie continued talking about babies. This time, thankfully, the subject was the cat that lived in Rosie's greenhouse.

"Where's my punkin'?" Lily called from the hallway.

Annmarie giggled as dread settled into the pit of Quinn's stomach. He should have left. He shouldn't be sitting here waiting for Lily, wanting to see her, wanting, just wanting, all the things he could never have.

Smiling, she came through the doorway an instant later, wrapped in that same thick robe she'd had on when she'd visited during the night. Until now, he hadn't known it was lavender. The smile remained, but something changed in her eyes when her gaze lit on him. Was she glad to see him or wishing he'd left already?

"I'm having breakfast," Annmarie returned.

"Cocoa Puffs," Lily murmured, taking in the contents of the bowl. "Your Saturday treat on—"

"It's not Saturday?" the child asked.

Lily tousled her hair. "You know it's not." She dipped a finger in her daughter's hot chocolate, then licked off the gooey mess of the marshmallow before turning to Quinn. "I never would have figured you for a hot-chocolate kind of guy."

He shrugged, images of licking her fingers destroying any hope he had of ignoring the flare of attraction between them. "When in Rome...you know."

Lily moved away from him, wanting to put her arms around him and discovering that she had used up all her courage a couple of hours ago. Having him watch her with that troubled expression made her opt for pouring a cup of coffee. After adding cream and sugar to it, she sat next to him. "How's your head?"

"Better." He touched the bandage at his hairline. Without meeting her eyes he added, "Thanks for taking care of me."

"I'm done," Annmarie announced. "Can I give Sweetie Pie my milk now?"

Lily looked at her daughter, then the bowl of cereal-flavored milk she was holding up. "You may. Time to go get dressed, sweetie."

Annmarie climbed down from her chair, set the bowl of milk on the floor near the window, then lifted the cat from the windowsill and set her in front of the bowl. When Annmarie skipped away, Lily glanced back at Quinn, giving in to her need and resting her hand over the top of his.

"Thanks to you," she said, "I had the best sleep I've had in weeks."

He grasped her fingers for an instant before letting them go, his gaze far too somber when he met hers.

She didn't need the Ph.D. after her name to recognize the man was uncomfortable in the extreme. Her sisters had both lamented about awkward morning-afters. Personally, she had never experienced one. Though she had fallen asleep in the man's arms, this morning didn't count as a morning after, either.

"Are you okay?" she asked.

He nodded. "You?"

She caught his gaze. "Wishing—" She took a deep breath and plunged ahead. "Wishing I'd told you I wanted to make love. Wishing I were braver."

Something in his eyes fractured and his jaw clenched. "I think you're plenty brave. But the truth is, you don't know anything about me, and I didn't expect…didn't have any way to protect you."

"From what?"

"Are you crazy? From me. From a possible pregnancy." He jumped to his feet and glared at her. "Or… For all you know, I could have HIV or—"

"Do you?"

"No."

"Or anything else?"

"No. But that's not the point, damn it."

She rose to her feet and took a step toward him. "Then what is?" When he glanced blankly at her, she added, "The point."

"I'm not one of those strays you're known for picking up."

That baffling hurt was back in his eyes. "It never occurred to me that you were." She took another step toward him.

He retreated a step. "Why in hell—"

"Did I climb into bed with you?" She shrugged, then told him the truth. "I've lived my whole life being the good girl, doing what was expected of me." She took another step toward him and he backed up one. "That was the old me." She closed the space between them until she could feel the heat from his body though they weren't touching. "An aneurism in my husband's brain burst while he was having lunch. Two days later he died."

"I'm sorry," Quinn murmured.

She met his gaze. "So am I. But you know what that taught me? Finally? That nothing is sure. That today is all there is. That you'd better grab what you want when you have the chance because tomorrow it could be all gone." She touched one of the buttons of his shirt with her finger, not quite sure enough of herself to put her arms around him, but aching for him to give her some clue that she'd be welcome if she took that final tiny…huge…step into his arms.

Pretending to be far more courageous than she really was, she looked up and found him watching her with the eyes of a man being tortured. "So, that's my regret. That I once again took time to think, instead of taking what I wanted. I'm so sick of being a coward."

"That's not true," he said quietly. He held her gaze for a long moment, his eyes deeply searching hers. They held the colors of the earth and ocean and stormy sky, framed with lashes any woman would envy. "Not making love was for

the best,'' he finally said, glancing up when something behind Lily caught his attention.

She turned around and found Rosie at the doorway and
headed for the cupboard where the crackers were kept.

''Good morning,'' Lily said.

''Morning,'' Rosie returned, reaching into the cupboard.
She pulled down a package of soda crackers, then took a bite
of one, giving them an apologetic smile. ''Don't mind me.''

''No problem.'' He glanced down at Lily and managed to
slip from between her and the counter. ''I've got to go.''

''Cocoa Puffs isn't much of a breakfast,'' Lily said. ''Let
me make you something.''

''I really do need to…'' His gaze caught hers once again.

''Go?'' Rosie supplied, looking from him to Lily.

He nodded, pulling keys out of the pocket of his jeans.

''If you can give me about fifteen minutes, I can get
dressed and go with you,'' Lily said.

''I, uh, need to check with Hilda before going to work.''

''Fine. I thought you might.''

A flush crawled up his cheeks, and Lily realized he was
trying to find a tactful way to leave without her. ''I think I'd
like to go home before going to work.''

''I can take you to work, Lily,'' Rosie said, waving one
of the crackers. ''Another half dozen of these and I'll be
fine.''

A look of pure relief passed over Quinn's face. ''There. A
solution. You have a ride to work.'' He headed for the door.
''See you later.''

''Okay.'' Lily watched him leave, one more regret heaping
on all the others. She had ignored the possibility that he
might not want her the way she wanted him.

''You slept with him, didn't you?'' Rosie accused.

The call came into the payphone near the marina exactly
when the man was expecting it—dreading it.

''Is it done?'' asked the raspy voice.

''Accidents are dicey things,'' he said, watching a float

plane land beyond the line of boats. "Not predictable like more traditional methods. This will be a helluva lot easier with the direct approach." Stealing the keys out of a desk— that had been easy. Pushing a car down a slope at exactly the right time to kill somebody—that was a gamble in anybody's book.

"No," was the immediate answer. "So you're telling me that the status quo hasn't changed."

"She's not dead, if that's what you mean," he answered, tired of the stupid game of refusing to name what he'd been hired to do. The chances of anyone listening to a conversation made to a pay phone from a pay phone were slim and none. "You want an accident, that's going to take time."

"And expenses on our clock. Mr. Lawrence expects results from you. I expect to read in the paper that a terrible accident has had tragic results. The sooner, the better."

"And like I said, accidents aren't that easy."

"Let me put this another way, so you'll understand perfectly. Mr. Lawrence is an engineer, did you know that?"

"Get to the point." So he was an engineer. So what?

"He always ensures there are backup systems and fail safes."

Which explains why he's in prison, he nearly retorted.

"If a fail safe is required for this situation," the voice continued, "you won't be needing a single dime of the payment that was agreed to. Now, then. Since you seem to be unable or unwilling to think on your own, you will find a way to get close to her, and you will see to it that she's involved in a very tragic, life-ending accident."

The line went dead.

He stared across the water. A fail safe? A chill slithered down his spine. He got it. Somebody would kill him if he didn't kill Lily Jensen Reditch. So far, he hadn't been able to get close enough, which was only one of the problems with "accidents."

As for thinking on his own, he already had an employment application in to go to work at the research center. He had enough of a chemistry background to create fire out of water, to even blow up a building. Plus, he knew for a fact he had the party-hearty merchandise a couple of the students wanted—they'd already made a buy from him. Trade drugs for a favor or two—a plan that was already in the works. Think on his own. What the hell did the old guy on the other end of the phone even know?

As the opening movement of Tchaikovsky's Seventh Symphony swelled from the small CD player on the counter, Max Jamison, aka Jones, sat at the kitchen table waiting for a collect call. Depending on the length of the lineup to use the phone at the prison, the call could come in the next second or the next three to four hours. His gaze swept over the austere apartment he'd rented after arriving here a week after the double wedding of Dahlia Jensen to Jack Trahern, and Rosie Jensen to Ian Stearne. That's a ceremony he would have liked to have seen, though he wouldn't have been welcome.

The last time he had seen Dahlia, she'd believed he would kill her. She had shot him instead. Luckily for him, hospital prison wards were easier to escape from than prison cells. And now, unlikely as it seemed, here he was—seeking his revenge. Franklin Lawrence was going to pay for blackmailing him into kidnapping Lily's sister.

Oh, he had done it, but he'd hated everything about it. After learning that Franklin Lawrence had since issued a contract on Lily, he had headed here.

A pro bono job—and his last. God willing, his sister would never learn that he had spent the last twenty-plus years as a paid assassin. He liked thinking how retirement would be, being with her without the lies about what he did or where he had gone. Enjoying his favorite music on his state-of-the-art system over coffee that had been ground seconds before brewing. Spending time with his niece and nephew.

The few dishes from breakfast had been washed and put away. The double bed that should have been hauled off to the dump ten years ago was made. The floor was swept, the battered furniture dusted. So, waiting was all he could do, just as he had done for much of his adult life.

He suspected that Lily believed Franklin Lawrence wouldn't still be interested in her now that the trial was over. Max knew better. Men like that—men like him—didn't let go. Since Lawrence was looking at a life sentence of hard time if his appeal failed, Lily still wasn't safe. She might be with her family using her married name instead of her maiden name—but she wasn't safe. Not yet.

Max's cell phone rang thirty-seven minutes later.

"Yeah," he said.

"Interesting proposition," came a gravelly voice on the other end of the line, "assuming you're J.M."

"I am."

"So how does this work?" the man asked.

Max wished for the more secure telephone line he had at his home. "If you agree to the job, I'll deposit fifty Gs wherever you want. After it's done, I'll deposit another fifty."

"One condition," the man said. "Can you make it look legit so my wife and my kid—"

"Consider it done," Max said. He breathed a silent sigh of relief. He'd carefully looked for the right man. A lifer who could be motivated to do a job that could only be accomplished by an inmate on the inside. Someone with nothing to lose.

"You've got a deal."

"Okay," Max said. He ended the call. Franklin Lawrence didn't know it yet, but he would never blackmail anyone again. His life sentence had been changed to a death sentence.

Chapter 5

"**Y**ou did, didn't you?" Rosie repeated.

Lily met her sister's gaze, the last of her euphoria crashing like a meteor. First Quinn, now her sister. As teenagers she and Rosie had shared everything, especially those exciting firsts—first dates, first kisses, first loves. Disapproval... Lily hadn't expected that. Disappointment washed through her. If she couldn't share her confusing attraction to Quinn Morrison with her sister, she was even more alone than she had imagined.

She looked away, feeling guilty that she didn't feel guilty, hating that she had nothing to feel guilty about. Despite Quinn's reaction this morning, she didn't regret the impulse that had made her crawl into bed with him.

"You're too damn trusting, Lily," Rosie said, breaking the silence. "Good grief, he's your boss. You don't even know the guy. And you have a hickey. Explain that."

Lily felt her face heat and for an instant she was swamped with the memory of him dragging kisses across her neck. She raised her collar higher and tightened the belt of her robe. "There's nothing to explain."

"So you didn't sleep with him?"

"Technically, all I did was sleep." She'd been so mortified when her fragile courage had deserted her the instant Quinn had asked if she was sure. Leave it to the man to be a gentleman who wouldn't press to continue what she had started. And then he'd held her, just held her, as she had so badly needed. She hadn't intended to fall asleep, but his warm arms around her had been a healing balm. This morning she felt more like herself than she had in a long while.

"Oh, Lily. You expect me to believe that? C'mon." Rosie's mouth fell open and she laughed. "This is so not you. You're the cautious one who takes forever to make a decision, even if you do always wander around with those rose-tinted glasses of yours."

Lily had given those up a long time ago, something that her family and friends had yet to realize. And how could they? She was content to let them believe she was still an optimist because that meant things were normal. At least on the surface.

This morning, though, she couldn't stand that her sister—her best friend—didn't believe her. "You haven't been with me enough over the last several years to know what I'm like."

"You've done it again. Taken in another stray."

"Quinn is no stray." Lily straightened and glared at her sister, hating that he had characterized himself the same way.

"What were you thinking?" Rosie's question was an echo of their father when one of them had done something stupid.

Now, as then, Lily's first reaction was that she didn't know. Thinking? She hadn't been, not even close. She met her sister's gaze. "Did you know that since John died, nobody touches me?" Lily looked away, raking a hand through her hair. "Oh, there's the occasional hug, but not held...when you're scared or lonely or hurting or, most of all, for the simple pleasure of it. God, Rosie, can't you un-

derstand that?'' Lily sat at the table and reached for her coffee mug. ''Just being in his arms—do you have any idea how
wonderful that was?''

''You're lonely.''

''I'm not.'' Lily had the awful feeling her sister was right,
but darn if she was going to admit it to her. Another sliver
of regret crept through her.

''Like you said, you wanted to be held. And with guys,
sex is usually the price that comes with that.'' Rosie sat next
to her. ''I understand what it's like to be lonely. But, let's
face it, you're not exactly a fountain of experience with men.
There wasn't anybody before John, and since you're new to
all this, you don't have a clue about how uncaring men can
be.''

''Quinn wasn't—isn't like that.''

Rosie shook her head. ''Says you. It's worth repeating.
You just met him.''

''He's a good man.''

''That's what you always say.'' Rosie took another bite of
her cracker. ''Remember Pete Stone? And how mad Dad was
when he got arrested?''

''We were kids then,'' Lily said. ''That was a long time
ago.''

''You've always been too trusting.''

''It sure beats assuming the worst,'' she responded, filled
with an unaccustomed need to defend herself even as she
kept wondering why Rosie was on such a tangent.

''I can't believe you *did it*—''

''Nothing happened.''

''—with Annmarie in the next room. What if she had come
in?''

''Ah, finally. This is really about Annmarie. Like I don't
have good sense enough to lock the door.'' Surprisingly hurt,
Lily looked at her sister. Maybe hormones were to blame,
Lily decided, for her sister being more wired than usual.

Rosie shook her head. ''No, it's about—''

''I would never do anything to hurt Annmarie.''

"You need to be more careful. You heard him last night at dinner. He practically admitted that he's involved in something that caused yesterday's little 'accident.'"

"And your point is?"

"What do you really know about the guy? For all you know he could be a total lowlife."

Lily surged to her feet. "I don't want to listen to this."

"Sure. Go ahead," Rosie said. "Run away. Just like you've been doing for a while."

"Just because I decided to move doesn't mean I'm running away."

Rosie shrugged. "I would have after witnessing a cold-blooded execution. Lily, you witnessed a crime," Rosie said. "A murder. And not just any murder, but a cold-blooded execution."

"That was a random event completely out of my control. It's time to move on." This was the same old pep talk she gave herself daily. Sooner or later it would sink in.

"Sure. That's why you moved home so soon after—"

"I'd been thinking about that for a while. Since John died, in fact."

"So you could feel safe again," Rosie continued, ignoring her. "I do know what that feels like, remember?"

"You make it nearly impossible to forget. I may be cautious, but I can't live my life looking for the boogeyman behind every tree. I won't. I don't want my daughter thinking that way, either."

"If you think I'm such a bad influence on *your* daughter, maybe you should move out."

The words hung there between them, and Lily felt the blood drain out of her face.

Her throat clogged and her eyes burned. She stared at Rosie for a long moment before fleeing toward the hallway before she said something she was sure to regret.

Pregnancy-induced hormones or not, Rosie had gone too far. In her secret heart of hearts Lily had always worried that

Rosie would one day regret giving up Annmarie. Annmarie…Lily's daughter by adoption, Rosie's by birth.

Lily checked on Annmarie, who was singing as she dressed and played with dolls that sat on the bed next to Sweetie Pie. Then Lily moved on to her own room, leaning against the door after she closed it behind her.

Lily had tried to get pregnant for years, and it had become apparent she would never have a child of her own. Rosie, with a pregnancy that was the result of a rape, had been confronted with the awful choice of whether to carry the baby to term. At the time, the perfect answer had seemed so apparent. Lily and John would adopt Rosie's baby and everything would be perfect.

Every day of her life, Lily was thankful for the gift and did her best to live up to her sister's trust. Still…she worried that one day Rosie would regret the choice they had made all those years ago and would want back the daughter she had given up.

Lily was all too tempted to fling herself across the bed and cry her eyes out. Instead she did the sensible thing—stripped the bed, her father's voice echoing through her. *All crying will get you is wet.* Still, the tears came. She buried her head in the sheets held against her chest, smelling Quinn and wanting back that sense of certainty she'd had when she'd slipped into his arms.

No regrets. Who had she been kidding? She had too many to count. Briskly, she made up the bed. Before climbing into the shower, she called Hilda's mother, Mama Sarah, and made arrangements for her to watch Annmarie for the day.

A half hour later Lily and Annmarie were ready to go. Rosie had disappeared into her bedroom. Lily suspected she was still fighting her daily bout with morning sickness. Ian had was nowhere to be found.

"Kiddo, we're going to walk to the village," Lily told Annmarie.

"Okay," Annmarie said. "But it will probably rain."

Lily chuckled. Her daughter had been making that pronouncement more than daily, though she supposed that, compared to California, there *was* a lot of rain. "Which is why we have rain jackets and umbrellas."

They went off the porch and around the totem pole whose stylized figures faced the water, then headed across the yard for the graveled road that led to the village. Thankfully, Annmarie didn't question why they were walking instead of driving, and she had a dozen observations about everything around them by the time they were a hundred yards beyond the gate.

They had passed the turnoff for Rosie's closest neighbor, the Ericksens, when Lily heard the rumble of a motor. A second later Mike Ericksen came into view riding an ATV. It looked brand-new, shiny chrome and blue paint gleaming in the sunlight. When he pulled even with them, he came to a stop.

"And how are you lovely ladies this morning?" he asked, lifting off his hat and brushing a hand through his white hair. "Looks like you could use a ride."

"We could," Lily said, eyeing the oversize seat. The vehicle had more than enough room to carry them both.

Lily lifted her daughter onto the seat behind Mike. "Is this a new toy?"

He laughed and patted the bright blue body. "Yep. Gotta get her broken in before Katrina carts us off to Seattle again. She's set on leaving before the end of the month."

"That doesn't leave you much time since that's only a few days away." Lily settled onto the broad seat behind her daughter, and Mike put the vehicle into gear.

"Never figured that we'd be making so many trips back and forth," he said over the roar of the engine, "but my wife seems to think the grandbabies can't arrive without her. So I'm on a quest for a house-sitter. Don't like leaving it empty with winter coming on."

Talking became impossible as they zoomed along the narrow road that led to the village, which gave Lily time to think. She needed a place to stay until the construction on her house was completed. Mike had the perfect answer. After he inquired where they wanted to be dropped off, he came to a stop in front of the clinic.

"How long do you and Katrina plan to be gone?" Lily asked as she climbed off the ATV and lifted Annmarie down.

"Probably a good part of the winter—if I can find someone to stay that long. Know of anyone?"

She swallowed, her sister's voice once again echoing through her head. "Me. And Annmarie." She smiled, offering part of her reason to be somewhere other than under Rosie's roof. "Ian and Rosie are still newlyweds. They've been great, but if I had the chance to provide them with a little privacy…you know."

"I can imagine." Mike laughed. "Well, that would be great. I'll tell the wife. I didn't want to leave until we had someone lined up, so you've made this real easy." He extended his hand.

Lily nodded, both relieved and feeling as though she was betraying her sister. "Great."

She settled Annmarie in with Mama Sarah, who lived with Hilda behind the clinic, then walked up the hill to the research station. Quinn's SUV was parked in front of the building and she gave it a long second glance—it really did look a lot like her car. She took a deep breath and went through the door.

"Good morning, Dr. Lily," Max said as she came into the office. "You're in bright and early."

"It's not that early." She set her tote bag on the floor next to her desk and picked up her coffee mug. "Anything exciting going on this morning?"

Max nodded toward the double doors leading to the lab. "He's interviewing a guy who had breakfast with us at the Tin Cup—says he's desperate for a job. One of the grad students arrived last night, and he's back there with Quinn, too."

The double doors swung open and Quinn came through, accompanied by two young men who couldn't have been more different. One looked as if he'd walked off the streets of a big city, complete with pierced ears and gelled hair. The other had the Alaskan outdoor look, including scrawny beard and ponytail.

When Quinn's gaze lit on Lily, he said, "Great, you're here." He nodded toward his companions. "Meet Dr. Lily Reditch. She's the senior staff in charge of research. Any requests she makes of you carry the same weight as any I make of you."

Senior staff in charge of research, Lily silently echoed. Yesterday she had been a research assistant.

"Patrick Riggs," Quinn added, nodding toward the bearded young man. "He's one of the grad students who'll be with us this fall." After Lily shook hands, Quinn introduced the other. "And this is Will Baker. He's going to be a lab helper."

What in the world was going on? she wondered as she made the perfunctory greeting. In the communication she'd had with Quinn prior to yesterday, sparse as it was, he had never said a word about hiring anyone else. The graduate students were expected, but not other help. Lily had hired lab helpers before, but only after the research got so busy that the students couldn't maintain the housekeeping activities.

"I have some things to discuss with you," she said to Quinn, "when you have some time."

He was staring at her neck. A muscle tightened in his jaw and his eyes were filled with regret when he met hers. Feeling unbearably exposed, she straightened her collar to hide the mark he had left on her.

He colored, cleared his throat, then muttered, "Sure. This afternoon. Catch me then."

"Okay." She recognized a brush-off when she heard one and was surprisingly hurt by it.

"And show Will around," he added, already heading for the door. "Patrick is going to come with me to see what needs to be done with the submersible. Max, I could use your help, too.''

She watched him go and, after the door closed behind him, Max and Patrick, she met Will's gaze. He was older than she had first thought—closer to thirty than twenty. ''Did Quinn have anything specific he wanted you to do?''

''Not yet. He said I'd just be helping out wherever you needed.'' Will's glance fell to the cup of coffee in Lily's hands. ''I wouldn't mind one of those.''

''Help yourself.'' She pointed toward the alcove. The phone rang and she went to her desk to answer it. Katrina Ericksen was on the other end of the line, thrilled that Lily had agreed to stay in their house. Lily's gaze tracked Will as he crossed the room, then sat next to her desk, openly listening to her conversation.

''I'm sure glad to have this job,'' Will said after she ended the call. ''Starving to death in the Alaskan north wasn't my idea of fun.''

''The Alaskan north is a long way from here.'' Despite his assertion, he didn't have the look of someone down on their luck, from his trendy hairstyle to his designer jeans. Nor did he seem to realize this part of Alaska was a temperate rainforest where subzero temperatures and polar bears were rare. ''What brought you here?'' she asked.

''I came for the summer, and decided to see if I could make a go of it instead of going back home.''

The story was common enough, but he didn't look much like the guys who came to Alaska for adventure even though some of those guys also had pierced ears and wore too much cologne.

''Where's home?'' she asked.

''Anaheim,'' he said. ''You're not from around here, either. The chicks here are all into jeans.''

She glanced down at her slacks, formal for Lynx Point though her choice in clothes would have been too casual for her old job. ''I am, actually. I've just moved back.''

Deciding to ignore his comment about chicks, at least for

the moment, she went through the areas of study currently underway with the vent site. Will picked up on things quick enough, but as they worked through the morning, she was never quite sure if he really knew what she was talking about or if he was simply clever enough to piece things together. He asked a lot of Chemistry 101 questions, which quickly wore thin.

"You're not going to be doing experiments," she said to him.

"I know." He gave her a smile that fell short of being reassuring. "I'm just curious about all this stuff, you know?"

Shortly before lunch she left Will alone in the lab to do some basic slide preparation for spore samples. A simple enough task that would give her some indication about how well he thought things through on his own and whether he really had worked in a lab before.

Despite Quinn's promise to talk later, he wasn't available. When she caught up with him midafternoon, he and Max were busy with the submersible, which had been hauled into the workshop. She found herself watching Quinn like a teenage girl with a hormone overload. The workshop was warm enough that he had taken off his vest and long-sleeved shirt. The physique revealed by that white T-shirt was undeniably masculine, and the ripple of muscle as he moved made her mouth go dry and her palms go wet. When he looked up and caught her staring at him, she felt her cheeks burn.

He glanced at his watch, then back at her. "The time got away from me. I'm going to be a while yet."

"It's okay," she said. "I'll talk to you later."

She fled back to the lab and the mundane task of supervising Will, who was more interested in the Friday night plans he'd made with Patrick than in his work.

Lily kept thinking how wonderful being held against Quinn's impressive chest had felt, how gentle he had been. No matter what task she did for the rest of the afternoon, her thoughts were consumed with Quinn. As a scientist, she admired his intelligence and dedication. She liked his gentleness and his humor. And as a woman…she was totally smitten by his physique. Until today she hadn't known that she loved muscles.

At the end of the day, Lily came out the front door of the research station as Quinn was getting into his car. He looked preoccupied and worried. His SUV headed down the road as Lily zipped up her jacket, wondering if she would ever get reacclimated to the chill and the humidity. Quinn stopped before his vehicle reached the first turn down the hill. She knew that he was watching her approach through the rear-view mirror.

Awareness zinged through her, bringing to life all those fluttery feelings of anticipation that made her feel young and feminine and more alive than she'd been in a long time.

"Busy day," he said when she stopped next to the passenger door, its window rolled down. Her glanced at her, then focused on the misty sky. "How's Will working out?"

"He acts like he's in beginning chemistry," she said, "but he takes direction well enough."

"Good. That's good." Quinn tapped his fingers against the steering wheel, then looked at her. "Need a ride?"

"As a matter of fact…" she returned, climbing into the car before he could change his mind. "How are you feeling? Does your head still hurt?"

He brushed a hand against the bandage at his hairline—a smaller one than he'd had when he'd left her house this morning. "It's fine."

"And Patrick and the submersible. How did things go there?" she asked the way an adult was supposed to. All the while, her heart pounded, which was stupid.

"Fine."

Fine. The one-word response that didn't say anything and effectively put a stop to any further conversation. *Fine.* "Why do you say 'fine' like that?"

Quinn glanced at her, the question echoing in his head. No accusation, just curiosity. He'd spent the day avoiding her avoiding what she made him feel and… "Because I don't want to talk, okay?"

"Fine," she returned, mimicking his tone of voice. "You can take me to Hilda's. Annmarie is there today."

"Okay." He drove down the hill, the tall pines casting shadows across the road. As happened every time he was with her, he was conscious of everything about her. The scent of her perfume—something soft and clean. The way she fingered the strap on her bag. The faint spray of freckles across the bridge of her nose. The mark he'd left on her neck, branding her. That thought made him instantly erect. Insistent as lust was, he reminded himself the right thing to do here was to not get involved. That didn't keep him from imagining her naked, his aching flesh buried in her.

He realized he'd lost track of the conversation when she said, "She told me that she had talked to you about babies. She can be a little overwhelming when she gets an idea in her head."

Her daughter—Lily was talking about her daughter. He cleared his throat. "Annmarie is great." The little girl's conversations left him confused, but he liked her.

"About this morning…"

Oh, man. He didn't want to talk about that.

She looked away, toyed with a lock of hair at her nape, then said, "I've never had a morning after before today, though technically I know that requires sex."

This morning had been better by far than any sex he'd had in a long time. And that scared him to death. Too easily he imagined a life with her—not just sex, but everything. He felt her glance at him, though he didn't dare look at her.

"We have to work together," she added. "So…"

He parked the car in front of the clinic and stared through the windshield. This was where he got to choose, he realized, between having this woman that he liked as a friend or having this woman he desired as a lover. She deserved more than the casual sex he could offer her, and much as he'd like that—it would make being friends impossible.

Finally he looked at her. The hope and invitation in her eyes made him wish he deserved them. "Things will work out a hell of a lot better, Lily, if we forget this morning ever happened. That's a position I should have never put you in, and I can't tell you how sorry I am."

"I'm not," she whispered.

"You should be," he said. "You should expect better for yourself."

"What are you talking about?"

"You're a nice woman, Lily, who has a lot to offer a man. Just so we're clear. I'm not that guy. I'll never be that guy."

"I haven't asked you for anything," she said stiffly. "Especially not a commitment."

"You deserve one, damn it." That came out more harsh than he intended.

Her eyes shimmered and she turned her head away. "Why aren't you that guy?" The question was filled with such anguish he felt like a heel all over again.

"Jeez, Lily—"

"Why?" she repeated, looking at him.

He felt stripped naked, but she deserved the truth. "I've done the marriage thing, complete with kids, and I'm rotten at it."

"You have kids?"

He shook his head. "They were hers."

"How old were—"

"This isn't the time to exchange touching life stories," he said, pushing away those memories. "I'm trying to make a point here."

She lifted her chin. "Don't let me stop you."

"The point is, I know what works for me, and it's not long-term relationships." He stared through the windshield, knowing this conversation hurt her. Better now than later after they got involved in something they were both bound to regret. "I like you, Lily, and I don't want you to be hoping for things that just won't happen." Finally he looked at her.

"So you're warning me off."

He nodded. "I'm doing my best."

She held his gaze a long, long time. To keep from touching her, to keep from cupping her cheek and catching that single tear that slid down her face and sliced him open, he wrapped his hands tightly around the steering wheel. This was better, he reminded himself, though it felt like hell. Not once in his entire life had he been this attracted this quick. Attracted...an utterly tame word for what he felt.

She looked away, her eyes wide as though she was surprised to see they were parked in front of the clinic.

As she opened the car door he touched her arm. "We work together, Lily. On that level I want things to be okay."

She nodded and said, "They're fine."

He recognized that for the same lie he'd told her.

Chapter 6

"**Y**ou look like you lost your last friend." Mama Sarah's eyes were bright behind the thick lenses of her glasses as she let Lily into the apartment that she shared with Hilda.

As usual, it was noisy—the television, the chatter of kids, and from one of the bedrooms the loud music from some rock band. Chaos that Lily found oddly comforting though it would drive her crazy if she had to live in it.

She put her arms around the older woman, who hugged her hard in return. As they had been since she was seven or eight years old, Mama Sarah's hugs were nearly as comforting as her own mother's. Unlike her mother, Mama Sarah wouldn't push to know what was wrong. Lily gave her a last squeeze, then stepped away.

"Hi, Mom," Annmarie called from one corner of the living room where she and Thad were bent over a project. "Guess what? Mama Sarah is helping Thad and me make a crystal garden." She grinned. "I got to pour on the food coloring—I made purple."

"Cool." Already, the crystals were growing in a brilliant

rainbow of color on the charcoal briquettes that rested in the bottom of a cut-down plastic milk bottle.

"We got to bake cookies, too," said Annmarie.

"Chocolate chip," Mama Sarah said when Lily glanced her direction. "Your sister showed up about an hour ago and she looked nearly as bad as you do."

"Guess I'd better go see what's going on." Lily took off her jacket and brushed a hand over her daughter's head as she passed by. As much as she had been dreading her talk with Rosie, she also wanted to get it over with. She found her best friend and her sister in the back room where they often hung out.

The back room was Hilda's sanctuary from her responsibilities as the town marshal, the island's only health care provider, and mother of four. The scent of tea and chocolate-chip cookies wafted from the room.

"Hey, you," Hilda said from where she sat cross-legged on the floor.

Rosie stood at the window. The Friday afternoon basketball game played on the dock next to the warehouse was visible in the distance. Lily recognized her brother-in-law's tall form.

"I saw Katrina Ericksen when I was on my way in." Rosie turned away from the window, her arms folded across her chest.

"Oh, Rosie—"

"It would have been nice to hear from you that you were planning on moving out."

"Not moving out," Lily hedged. "House-sitting."

"Moving out," Rosie stated, shrugging beyond Lily's reach. "Katrina says they'll be in Seattle most of the winter—at least until after Christmas if she can convince Mike to stay."

"Maybe I should go get another cup for the tea," Hilda said, standing in a fluid move.

"Stay," Rosie commanded that same moment Lily implored. "Don't go."

Hilda raised her hands in surrender. "Fine. But I'm not playing referee."

Wishing she had Dahlia's knack for making peace, Lily joined Rosie at the window. As children, they'd experienced very little of the sibling rivalry that they'd seen in others or that Rosie had experienced with Dahlia. Maybe that's why their rare arguments always felt so awful, Lily thought. She felt as out of her depth with this as she had with Quinn.

As though she had somehow conjured him, she watched him get out of his SUV and saunter toward the other basketball players, shedding his jacket on the way, and joining the game.

Fighting the urge to weep as she had most of the day, Lily looked over at her sister who was watching the game. Rosie fidgeted, twisting her wedding ring. Lily found herself equally antsy. She searched for the right words to make up. None came, which made her steal another glance at Rosie, who looked at her at the same moment. They both burst into tears, then wrapped their arms around each other.

"I'm sorry," Lily said through a sob. "I *do* think you're good for Annmarie."

At the same time Rosie was saying, "I was being stupid and spiteful and I didn't mean it. You deserve to be happy. I don't know why I was such a witch this morning." Rosie met Lily's glance, and they both grinned.

"Hormones," they both said at the same time, then laughed.

"Oh, what a pair we are," Rosie said, wiping her eyes. "Mom would have made us sit down right then—remember?" She put a hand on her hip and leaned forward slightly in imitation of their mother's "You've got to settle this, girls" posture, and said, "'Make up, ladies, or I'll do it for you.'"

"I think you got that more than I did." Lily pulled a tissue out of her pocket and wiped her nose.

"Yeah, thanks to Dahlia." Rosie sat on the floor and picked up her cup of tea. "She called this morning and says hi, by the way. She wants to know why you haven't sent any videos.''

''I've been working on one for her.'' Lily didn't realize Hilda had left until she appeared in the doorway with another cup in hand.

''Oh, good, you've made up,'' she said. ''Thank God. I thought I might have to go find two other new best friends.''

Rosie threw a pillow at her. ''Like anyone else would put up with you.''

Lily sat on the floor, and gratefully took the cup of tea that Hilda had poured for her. Sweet and heavy with milk, the way she liked it. She closed her eyes, feeling the weight of the day slide away. This was the way it always had been among the three of them. The best of friends no matter what the world threw their way.

She felt something land in her lap and, when she opened her eyes, discovered a wrapped piece of chocolate.

''Was he good?'' Hilda asked, watching her and unwrapping her own chocolate, then settling more comfortably on one of the oversize pillows scattered across the floor. ''Since you've got a hickey to show for it—''

''A little privacy, please.'' Lily clapped her hand against the telltale mark on her neck.

Hilda grinned. ''This is big news, girl. No secrets here.''

Lily felt her cheeks flame, but didn't even try to pretend she didn't know what her friend was talking about.

''I know you won't believe me—but nothing happened.''

Hilda smiled. ''Nothing? I don't care what you call it, you don't get that morning-after glow by sleeping alone.''

''The man slithered out of the house this morning, guilt painted all over him,'' Rosie said.

Frustrated, Lily waved her hands toward the ceiling. ''I give up. We had sex, okay? Wild, loud, passionate sex that you could have heard clear over to Foster Island.''

Hilda's eyes gleamed. ''He was that good, huh.''

''Ask Rosie if you want salacious details. She's married *and* pregnant, so she's got more to talk about than I do.''

Most vivid in Lily's mind at the moment were the things Quinn had said as he'd dropped her off, not what happened before dawn this morning—not that either Hilda or Rosie would believe her.

"He's an okay-looking guy, I guess, but I never quite imagined him that way," Hilda said.

"That's because you've always been too busy patching him up from one injury or another," Rosie said. "Plus, he's too much the burly linebacker type."

"He's not that big." The memory of being in his arms too visceral to bear made Lily close her eyes for a moment.

"So what do you see in this guy?" Hilda asked.

Lily unwrapped the chocolate and put it into her mouth, letting the flavor coat her tongue while she thought about the question. As a scientist she had done her homework and had read his published papers. In the process of organizing the office, she had read his research notes and looked forward to meeting him. She had been predisposed to like him since she admired his work. That didn't explain her instant attraction to him. "Yesterday when I met him," she finally said, "I just knew. When he held me…" Her throat clogged and she paused a second before continuing. "Oh, man, I'd forgotten how good it can be."

When her voice trailed away, Hilda said, "Nothing happened, huh?"

Since they weren't going to believe her no matter what she said, Lily responded, "Not like you're thinking." Her smile faded as she met Rosie's gaze. "He called himself a stray, even before you did."

"I could do a background check," Hilda offered. "You might be surprised at what turns up."

Lily shook her head. "You say that like you're serious. No. I've read his work and his bio posted on the university Web site. I know what I need to know."

"He lives alone," Hilda said, ticking off a list on her fingers. "Has breakfast at the Tin Cup most mornings. He doesn't hang out at the Lodge, and he hasn't been dating anybody local. At least twice a week I see him paddle over to Foster Island. It's no wonder the man has shoulders the size of a house.''

"It's a good thing you're not a gossip," Lily said.

"Heard you're moving," Hilda said with a grin.

"About that," Rosie said. "You call Katrina back and tell her to find someone else."

Lily met her sister's gaze, more certain now than she had been this morning that helping the Ericksens was the right thing to do. She shook her head. "I can't do that, Rosie. First, you and Ian are still newlyweds. Granted, it's been a long time, but I remember what that's like. If the two of you want to wander around stark naked and make love on the kitchen table, you should." Lily's cheeks burned. She clamped a hand over her mouth. "I don't believe I said that."

Hilda laughed. "Was that a confession? God, I hope so." She looked Lily up and down, her smile remaining in place. "That's a side of you I never imagined."

"And you can stop anytime." Lily wasn't about to admit that the wildest she and John had ever been was the living room couch. "You're bad."

"To the bone, not to mention deprived." Hilda reached for another piece of chocolate.

Lily took a sip of her tea and tried to refocus. "Plus, Ann-marie and I will be only next door, less than a quarter of a mile away from your house, Rosie. Annmarie can come over as much as you both want."

In answer, Rosie squeezed her hand. "Promise?"

"Promise."

Playing basketball when your head hurt was stupid, Quinn decided as he snagged a couple of beers from the six-packs he had brought along to share. He headed for the edge of the court next to the warehouse where Dwight Jones was toweling off his hair. Dwight had a rangy build that was well suited for basketball, and he was as competitive about winning as he was about everything else. That competitive streak had made Dwight a regular at the Friday afternoon game. This particular day, Quinn has happy the man had shown up, true to form.

All day Quinn kept thinking about the conversation they'd had on the ferry the day before yesterday. He still couldn't decide if there had been a threat in anything Dwight had said. Threats, Quinn could handle. Overt action that could hurt somebody else…he wasn't going to stand for that. Not for a minute had he ever figured that Dwight would take the injunction filed against his employer personally. The stakes were simple, Quinn wanted the site around the deep sea vent kept as pristine as possible. If there was oil, Dwight Jones's employer wanted to drill. The injunction would at least buy some time.

"Good game," Quinn said, handing Dwight one of the beers.

"Thanks." He straightened and took the beer, pointing his bottle toward Quinn's in a salute before taking a long pull. "Your play stunk today."

Quinn grinned. "Don't sugarcoat it. Tell me what you really think."

"Playing basketball when you've got a concussion will rattle loose a few more of those brain cells of yours."

"Probably." Quinn took a long pull on his beer. Like playing basketball, the beer probably wasn't on the regimen of healthy things he should be doing.

"Depending on which version I want to believe, you were either nearly killed yesterday or you totaled somebody else's car with a body slam," Dwight said. "You sure you didn't piss somebody off?"

Quinn met his gaze. "You mean, other than you?"

"Wrecking your car sounds a little more personal than filing an injunction."

"Too bad it wasn't my car." Quinn tipped the bottle against his lips and took a long swallow before adding, "So, you didn't take that personally? The injunction?"

"Hell, no." Dwight's gaze narrowed. "You're not implying that I had anything to do with—"

"No, I'm not implying or accusing or anything else." Quinn wrapped his hands around the beer bottle. "You're the second person I've talked to today who seems to think it might not have been an accident."

"I don't know whether it was or not. I thought we were having the good ol' boy talk over a beer." Dwight shrugged into a jacket. "And maybe you did shake loose a few brain cells if you think I had anything to do with it."

"I never figured you for the defensive sort."

"You've lost it. You need to go climb up some other tree, Morrison. Stay the hell out of mine," Dwight said over his shoulder as he walked away.

"Well, hell," Quinn muttered under his breath. That had been a total waste, especially as he had used about as much finesse as a Kodiak bear fishing for salmon.

"Still making friends and influencing people, I see." Ian came around the corner of the warehouse, making no secret that he had been eavesdropping. "So, do you think he did it?"

Quinn shook his head. "No." He spared Lily's brother-in-law a glance, deciding his being here for the game was no more coincidental than Quinn's own presence. "Despite what you just heard, we're friends, after a fashion."

Ian buried his hands in the pocket of his jacket. "So, were you blowing smoke, or do you really think what happened with Lily's car was intentional?"

Quinn set down his beer and picked up his jacket. "You know Lily better than I do. Is she the type of person to lock her keys in the car?" He shrugged into his jacket, then leaned next to Ian against the wall of the warehouse.

"Not usually."

"How come I'm hearing a 'but' in that?"

The corner of Ian's mouth kicked up. "Because there is one. Lately she's been preoccupied."

"The murder trial?"

"For starters. Giving up a great position at her old university, handing her lab over to someone else, selling her house, moving two thousand miles away. It all adds up. So, maybe she did leave the keys in her car."

"Any chance there's some fallout from the trial that has followed her?" Quinn asked.

After a moment Ian shook his head. "I think she would have talked to me if there had been." He stared out at the water a moment, then added, "Lily is one of the best people I know."

In a scant day Quinn had come to the same conclusion.

Ian folded his arms over his chest. "I don't want to see her hurt."

Quinn kept his gaze focused on the water in front of them and counted himself a fool. There was no point in telling the man that nothing had happened. For all practical purposes, he'd made love to the man's sister-in-law under his own roof.

"You might as well spit out whatever's on your mind and get it over with," Quinn finally said.

Like himself, Ian continued to stare across the expanse of the dock to the water and the distant islands beyond. "Lily has this way of accepting people without asking enough questions or being suspicious."

"She's an innocent." The truth in Quinn's mind, but he sure hadn't intended to say so out loud. From the corner of his eye, he saw Ian nod.

"Stay the hell away from her," Ian said. "She doesn't need any of the heartbreak your kind would give her."

The echo of his own thoughts didn't keep Quinn immune from a flash of anger. "What would you know about *my* kind?"

Ian took his time before pushing himself away from the warehouse wall and turning to look at him, starting with his feet and moving up until their gazes locked.

"You take what you want and you don't care about how you get it or what the cost is to other people. You're a love-

'em-and-leave-'em kind of guy. Relationships—they take more work than you'd be willing to give.''

Until that instant Quinn hadn't realized how much he hated the man he had become, even in the name of self-preservation.

He focused on the expanse of water beyond the dock. ''Maybe Lily should be making up her own mind about who she wants to see.''

Ian took a single threatening step closer.

''Like you said, Morrison, she's an innocent.'' His chin jutted. ''You don't want the kind of trouble I can cause you.''

''Trouble?'' Quinn shrugged and gave the man a devil-may-care grin, playing this out the way he always had—by acting like he didn't give a damn. He had no intention of pursuing things with Lily, but no way would he give her brother-in-law the satisfaction of knowing that. ''Stay away from me, and there won't be any.''

Chapter 7

"Winch on," Lily called from the stern of the boat.

She stretched, the move vividly reminding Quinn of the morning he had held her supple body with only their night-clothes between them. Dangerous ground, thinking about that. Deliberately, he reminded himself of the reasons why Lily was off limits. White picket fences, her sainted dead husband, and she worked for him—not necessarily in that order.

"Clear," Quinn returned from his post under the awning next to the bridge.

His gaze strayed from Lily to Patrick Riggs, who was sitting on a box packing away the monitors they had used to sample water temperatures. As was usual for him, the kid was only half paying attention, which was beginning to irritate Quinn more with each passing day. At the stern, Lily waited for the kid to sound off that he was away from the winch.

"Let her know you're clear, Patrick," Quinn called to him.

Patrick looked up with that dazed look he often had, then back at Lily. "Oh, sure. Lily. Clear."

She turned on the winch, and cable began to wind around the big drum behind the A-frame at the back of the craft, dripping sea water that looked nearly black in the fading light.

Patrick's inattention was no doubt due to the nearly nightly partying that had Will Baker at its center. Quinn's gaze moved on to Will who stood inside the bridge, flirting with the boat skipper, Rona Petrokov. Everything in her body language suggested she couldn't be less interested in him, which seemed to make Will even more persistent.

Quinn went to the back of the boat. "Are you doing okay?" he asked Lily.

She gave him her usual bright smile and her usual answer. "Fine."

He grinned at her. "Fine, huh." It was the one piece of conversation from that afternoon they acknowledged, sometimes teasing each other. "How are you really?"

"Tired, but I'm doing okay."

There was nothing remotely sexy about the orange life-jacket or the shapeless, bright yellow wet gear that covered her from head to foot. In his mind's eye Quinn imagined her naked. He hadn't seen her, only touched through the slippery fabric of her gown, but even that now haunted him nightly. Maybe that was why he kept thinking about it—maybe that was all he really needed. To see her naked. Just once.

Yeah, right. Like once would be enough.

Over the last three weeks he had constantly reminded himself that he preferred the course they were on, the one of colleagues and friends. Except, every time he was with her, he had a tingling awareness of her. She had put together an outstanding draft for a grant application needed for the program to move forward. As the project leader, he was thankful for her knowledge and professionalism. As a man who hadn't known he was hungry for her approval, he had read and reread her handwritten note attached to the draft. "Brilliant idea, Quinn. Once your theory is proven, it will become the touchstone for the research that follows.''

Despite the guarded invitation he sometimes caught in her eyes, she hadn't once tried to take their friendship beyond the boundaries he had set. Just like he wanted.

Liar.

He realized she was watching him. ''And how are you?''

''Fine,'' he promptly said with a grin.

She laughed, just as he had hoped she would.

''I'm going to see if I can't get Patrick moving a little faster and Will interested in helping.'' Quinn touched Lily's arm. ''Holler if you need anything.''

She nodded, her attention going back to the cable climbing out of the water. Quinn knew that she was tired. They all were. It was the end of the day, the end of a busy three weeks. They had been on the boat eight times, mapping, collecting water samples, monitoring water temperature and collecting data—work that would keep the team busy through the winter months when the water was too rough and the days too short to do this kind of fieldwork.

''Are you seasick?'' he asked Patrick, who was looking queasier by the second. He hadn't made much progress on putting the equipment away.

Patrick nodded. ''I was doing okay until the wind came up.''

Clouds had been building up all day as had the ever-increasing swells that kept pace with their trek home. A sure sign a storm was coming in from the west.

Quinn urged him to stand. ''You'll feel better if you can see the horizon.'' He went to the bridge and called Will to come give a hand putting things away. ''And put on your wet gear,'' Quinn said.

Will, always interested in looking good, hadn't yet donned the bright yellow Gortex waterproof pants and coat, that obviously didn't fit his definition of cool. Grumbling, Will pulled on his coat and came outside to finish the task that Patrick had started.

Quinn went to the computer tucked in one corner of the bridge where he checked the data that methodically came up row after row on the computer monitor.

"We're going to get rained on before we make it home tonight," Rona said from the wheel.

Quinn noted the bank of clouds that seemed even lower over the water than they had earlier.

"Good thing we came today, though," she said. "I think the sea will be too rough tomorrow."

That was Quinn's hunch, too. "Think we'll make it back before it's dark?" For some reason the question always made her laugh, so he always asked.

As expected, she chuckled, her easy humor as much a part of her as her quiet efficiency in handling the boat. "Hate to tell you, boss, but it's dark now."

She was right. Dark, and getting darker by the minute. Quinn looked at the horizon behind them. Ahead of the boat's bow, Kantrovich Island was shrouded in another heavy bank of clouds.

He made his way toward the stern, past Patrick, who looked even more seasick than he had a few minutes ago, and Will, who seemed more interested in the cable coming out of the water than in the task he'd been assigned.

"Hey," Quinn said, joining Lily. She had an ease of being on the boat that she said came from growing up in a fishing family.

"Hey, yourself," she returned with a quick smile.

"Those two are a pair." He nodded toward Patrick and Will. "I can't imagine how Patrick survived on the N.O.A.A. expedition last summer since he's constantly seasick." Quinn had great memories of his own summer research on an expedition sponsored by the National Oceanic and Atmospheric Administration. The research that summer had been the most exciting of his career until he had come here.

"Hate to tell you this, but they have a bigger boat. That makes a difference."

"I suppose it's held together with a little more than chewing gum and spit," he said.

She chuckled. "Try pulling the other leg, Dr. Morrison. Your adaptations to Rona's fishing boat are pretty ingenious."

Necessity borne of a tight budget had made thinking outside the box a requirement. Ingenious, though? He'd never thought of it like that.

"I've heard there's a state-of-the art lab right on board," Lily said.

He glanced around the boat, his attention coming back to the cable, dripping water across the deck. "I'm not sure where we'd put one."

"You've made progress," she said. "You got Will out of the bridge."

Quinn glanced back at him. "For the moment. If he just had a little initiative."

"I've seen worse." Lily's attention remained focused on the cable. "And he might even manage to learn without taking a dunk in the water."

A gust of wind swept over them and with it a spray of water that felt like shards of ice.

"Spoken like someone who knows."

She nodded, pulling her knit cap more firmly over her ears and the collar of her vinyl coat higher on her neck. "It takes only once."

"Were you ever—"

"Thrown overboard?" She shivered, then finally looked at him. "Yes. Like I said, once was enough." She nodded toward Patrick. "I feel bad for him. I'd hate to be that miserable."

"He's no sailor, that's for sure."

"If you had ever told me that you'd get me back on a fishing boat," she added, "and liking it—"

"That bad, huh?" he teased.

"Not bad," she replied. "Just hard work. Long days."

He chuckled. "Nothing much has changed, then."

The days they sailed to the vent site were fourteen hours long if they were lucky. Not once had she complained about the early mornings or the grueling work or the late evenings back that would have gotten her home after her daughter had gone to bed.

When she met his gaze, he added, "And you like it."

"I do." She was silent a moment, then casually added, "My sister Dahlia always told me she loved fieldwork. Now I understand why." She shivered when another mist-laden gust of wind hit them.

Quinn glanced back at Patrick who had retreated to the awning next to the bridge. Will had finished his project and returned to the bridge to resume flirting with Rona.

"I like days like today," Lily continued. "The whales…" She closed her eyes for a second and a soft smile curved her lips. "Truly amazing."

Quinn agreed with her. For a time today they had been surrounded by a group of gray whales swimming south. For a while, the work had stopped and they had all watched. Some of the whales were half as long as the forty-foot craft. A thirty-foot baby had stayed close to his mother, but he'd watched them, his dinner-plate-size eye reflecting an eerie intelligence. Lily's captivation with the animals had intensified Quinn's own pleasure in the moment.

"No weights yet," Quinn said, mostly because he wanted to stand here and talk to her. Knowing the depth at which samples were collected, coupled with their locations from the global positioning system, should provide clear picture of any variations among their subject locations.

"It shouldn't be much longer," she said.

The one part of the job Quinn disliked was getting the equipment out of the water. They were always later than he wanted to be, and the numbers of things that could go wrong in the dark grew exponentially.

"Think we hit the jackpot with today's samples?" she asked him.

In addition to collecting survey data, today's quest had

been to collect organisms that metabolized sulphur rather than oxygen for their energy production. He was determined to unlock that particular secret, research that could take years.

"It's going to be a long, boring winter in the lab if we didn't."

He glanced down at her and their gazes locked as had been happening more over the past few days. The sound of equipment around them faded. Instead of feeling the icy spray of water that blew across them with each gust, he remembered her breath hot against his cheek, her soft body relaxing against his as she inched toward sleep. She swallowed, and he expected her to look away. But, she didn't.

What kind of stupid fool had he been to think he could ignore the chemistry between them? Standing here with her now, he was more nervous than if he'd been standing at the edge of one of Denali's crevices, hoping the ice wouldn't crumble beneath his feet.

He forced himself to look away and to breathe evenly, though he felt as though he had run to the top of a steep hill. What had they been talking about? With effort he remembered. Water samples.

"As for the samples, they're not *my* collection. There are enough to share," he added. "If it were your lab, what would you want to work on?"

"Barophiles," she immediately answered, her gloved hands gripping the gunwale.

Barophiles were a type of bacteria that thrived in high pressure and high temperatures. Based on what he'd read of her research in California, they would be a natural compliment to work that she had spent years doing.

"Think you could get a grant?" he asked.

She glanced sharply at him. "Probably. The real question is whether I want to. I gave up my lab, passed on my grants, remember?"

"I remember."

Her attention returned to the cable and the sound of the

winch and the rhythmic grind as the line came through the pulleys.

"My own research—that isn't why I came here," she finally said. "I wanted to be closer to Rosie and my parents."

"I know." Her connection to family was clearly the most important thing to her. "Do you see your parents much?"

She grinned. "Not nearly enough to suit my mother. She's trying to talk my dad into buying a float plane so the trip from here to Petersburg would only be a couple of hours instead of all day on a boat." She glanced at him. "What about your parents—where do they live? Texas?"

"Why Texas?"

"Why, the accent, cowboy," she drawled, doing her best to copy his Texan. In her own voice, she said, "So, your parents don't live in Texas?"

He wished he'd kept his mouth shut.

"Quinn?"

"My mother is dead," he said. Why did it always come down to exchanging the old stories? "If my dad was ever around, I don't remember it." Quinn gave Lily his practiced devil-may-care smile. "I'm lucky that the name he left me on a birth certificate was Morrison instead of Frankenstein."

"Oh, I don't know," she said. "Quinn Frankenstein, Ph.D. That doesn't have such a bad ring to it. Better than Quinn Jeckyl, Ph.D."

He gave her points for her casual response. "About that research—"

"It's a nice thought, Quinn, but—"

"Don't answer now," he interrupted. "Just think about it."

When she had first approached him about a job, he had been focused only on how lucky he was to have someone with her skills. Then he'd read her papers, had seen the breadth of her research, had come to realize how bright she was. If she wanted her own research project again, he wanted that for her. It was the one thing he could do for her.

"You wouldn't have the same pressure here that you had

before. Don't tell me that you can be satisfied doing work for me that any first-year grad student could handle.''

"I—"

"Don't say anything." He didn't want to hear her refusal. "We'll talk about it in a few days, okay?"

"Okay."

The sound of the winch motor changed slightly as the weights tied to the cable came into view. Lily slowed the speed of the winch motor and Quinn grabbed the hook at the end of a line secured by the J-frame on the starboard side.

"Engine off," he called to Rona at the wheel.

"Engine off," she repeated, and the boat slowed.

Quinn leaned out over the water, hooked the weights and unsnapped them from the cable. Double checking to make sure everything was secure, he turned on another motor that lifted the weights out of the water through a series of pulleys attached to the J-frame. "Clear."

"Engine ahead," Rona returned.

They repeated the move twice more as additional weights came out of the ocean water. Each time, Lily was right there, giving him the extra hands and extra leverage to make the job easier. They stowed away the weights and prepared the J-frame for the water sampling equipment that would soon reach the surface. Minutes later, the rosette rose out of the water. Four feet in diameter and nearly as long, the rosette held a dozen tubular Niksen bottles that held the water samples. The whole apparatus was heavy and awkward to handle.

"I could use some help here," Quinn called to Patrick and Will.

Will came out of the bridge, zipping up his coat, while Patrick headed toward them.

"You know the rules. Put on a life jacket and your wet gear," Quinn reminded Will.

"For five minutes of work?" he complained.

"Go." Quinn attached the cable from the J-frame to the rosette.

"I've got it," Will said, shrugging into a life jacket. He turned on the motor attached to the J-arm.

The rosette, though, was still attached to the cable and winch used to bring it out of the water. The tiny amount of slack in the line vanished. The heavy rosette quivered between the taut cables.

"Stop!" Lily and Quinn shouted at the same instant.

The line broke. The cable attached to the winch suddenly had too much slack, and the rosette dropped back into the water.

The loose line that had been run through the J-frame tore free and whipped across the boat. The end of the cable struck the deck, then arced in the other direction. Lily dove to the deck, the line snapping where she'd stood an instant before. Quinn took cover to keep from being hit by the whipping line.

On her hands and knees, Lily inched across the deck toward the winch attached to the J-frame.

"Stay down!" Quinn called. "I'll get it."

She ignored him, and the cable snapped again, barely missing her. Quinn felt five years come off his life. The cable could take out an eye or worse. Patrick and Will retreated to the bridge, where they crouched in relative safety.

The cable cracked against the roof of the bridge, then hit the port side. With each turn around the winch drum the line whipped in a new direction.

Rona throttled down the boat. It rocked heavily in the swells driven higher by the storm following them home.

Picking her moment, Lily slid on her belly across the slick deck and hit the brake for the winch. It came to a grinding stop. She sat up and leaned against the side of the boat.

The cable whipped toward her.

"Lily, duck!"

She jerked out of the way, her arms covering her face. But it was too late. The cable caught her square across the back, knocking her the rest of the way to the deck.

Swearing, Quinn rushed toward her, sliding across the wet deck and falling before he reached her. She was so still.

He touched her back. "Lily, talk to me."

"Damn, that hurt." She lifted her head.

Quinn reached for her, thankful for the layers of clothes that had protected her. Her wet gear looked as though someone had taken a knife to it, but the jacket underneath was intact.

"You okay?" he asked, holding her down by the shoulders when she would have stood.

"Never better."

He suspected the words were to keep him from knowing that she was scared.

"Stay there a minute." He touched her face. "Rest."

He stood, his attention first on the cable, which slithered across the wet deck, then on Will.

Quinn stalked toward the bridge. "You damn fool. You could have gotten somebody killed."

"I didn't think the line would snap." Will backed up a step.

"You don't think, period." He glared at the younger man. "Safety comes first, damn it. Go put on your wet gear."

"I don't need it."

"Get on your gear and get out here. Like it or not, I need your help."

With quick efficient movements, his temper barely in check, Quinn tied off the cable. He went to the stern and peered into the water. It was dark as a nightmare, and he could see nothing of the rosette though he could hear it banging against the side of the boat. He reversed the direction on the winch, then turned it back on. First order of business was to get the equipment deep enough that it wouldn't damage the boat or have the line get tangled in the propeller.

Lily joined him at the gunwale, her gaze following the cable through the A-frame.

How the hell were they going to get the rosette out of the

water without the extra leverage the J-frame would have provided.

"As soon as we get it to the surface of the water," Lily was saying, "we can snag it with one of the outriggers."

"I've never tested anything this heavy on them," Quinn told her. "I'm not sure it will hold."

"You used to fish for halibut on this boat, didn't you, Rona?" Lily called to her.

"Sure did," Rona answered. "We'd haul up a barn door every once in a while."

"Barn door?" Quinn cocked an eyebrow.

Lily grinned. "As in the size of. If the outrigger will support a three-hundred-pound fish, it should handle the rosette."

They had a basic plan figured out by the time Will, finally clad in his wet gear, joined them. Lily turned on the winch. Slow as the speed was, Quinn cringed with every turn of the cable around the drum. Thinking about the way the equipment had banged against the hull, the boat would require a thorough check before they took it out again.

"Get over here, Will," Quinn commanded.

He came toward the stern, everything in his posture indicating he didn't like the request. Tough, Quinn thought. Getting the rosette out of the water was going to take all three of them, and if there was a way to do it without risking Lily, he'd do so in a heartbeat.

At last the rosette appeared.

"Winch off," Quinn called.

"Winch off," Lily repeated, instantly shutting it off. Will stood behind them, his arms loose at his sides as though he had no idea of how to help.

The swells were high enough to make grabbing hold of the rosette with the hook nearly impossible.

"Get out of the way," Patrick said to Will. "I'll help." Still looking as though he might throw up again at any second, he joined them at the stern.

"Help me hold the rosette still," Quinn said to Patrick, "so I can get her attached to the outrigger."

Quinn leaned far out of the boat, stretching, and still not able to reach it. Without asking, Lily was there next to him, stretching out behind the boat, her hands steadier by far than Patrick's. She seemed to realize the moment the swells lifted the rosette a little closer, and she made a grab for it.

The boat rode high on the swell for an instant, then made a slip to the bottom. Will slammed into Lily. She caught herself, but her arm skidded across the wet surface of the gunwale.

Before Quinn could catch her, she tumbled into the water and disappeared.

Chapter 8

Quinn stretched far over the side of the boat, searching the inky water for any sign of Lily's bright yellow wet gear. One second. A wave sloshed against the stern. *C'mon, Lily where are you?* Two seconds. He fought the urge to jump in after her. She was wearing a life vest, so she should have instantly bobbed to the surface. Three seconds. *Damn it, Lily, show me where you are.*

His heart crawled up his throat and choked him.

Behind him, he heard Will and Patrick arguing and Rona's curt, "Stuff it."

The boat slid into the trough of a wave, and another bitterly cold spray of water spilled over the gunwale. Black water and nothing, nothing, nothing…and then Lily popped to the surface, the yellow and orange gear bright as a beacon. Only she was yards too far away to reach.

His muscles coiled to jump in after her even as his mind cautioned him that that wasn't the best way to help her.

A life saver sailed over Quinn's head. From the corner of his eye, he saw Rona held the line attached to it.

Lily grabbed the lifesaver. Together, Quinn and Rona pulled her toward the boat. Lily's knit cap had disappeared, and her blond hair was plastered against her head. Her normally fair skin was white. She hooked her arms through the center of the donut and let them do the work. Seconds passed—decades passed—before she was close enough for Quinn to reach.

He leaned out of the boat and pulled her on board. She hadn't been in the water sixty seconds, but her teeth were chattering and her lips were blue. Cursing, he scooped her into his arms and carried her toward the bridge.

"I can walk," she was saying between chatters.

"Save your energy." Inside he set her down in the middle of the floor where a puddle immediately formed. He pulled the vinyl coat over her head. "Gotta get you out of these wet clothes and warm."

"I'll help her," Rona said, touching his shoulder. "Go get that damn rosette on board so we can head for home."

Ignoring Rona, he slipped the suspenders that held up Lily's vinyl pants off her shoulders. He couldn't leave her. Not until he knew—

"Go." This time Rona was more insistent, pushing him toward the door of the bridge.

His glance locked with Lily's.

"I'll be okay," she said. Her reassuring smile turned lopsided as she shivered again.

The fear uncoiled a little, making room for his temper. He turned on his heel and went through the door where the wind and a cold spray of water hit him.

Patrick and Will were squared off at the stern. Patrick was shouting, "You pushed her, you idiot."

"I slid. It was an accident."

"Like hell."

Quinn stepped between the two. "Save it." He looked from one to the other, Patrick's accusation echoing through his head. "You're going to do what I say, exactly as I say, and without one damn bit of discussion. Got it?"

Patrick nodded, and Will stuck out his chin, his expression making him look about twelve. About the age he was acting.

For the third time, they attempted to bring the water sampling equipment out of the water, and finally they were successful. The steel frame containing the Niksen bottles showed a couple of dents, but appeared to have done the job of protecting the bottles.

Step-by-step, Quinn instructed Patrick and Will. Of the two, Patrick was the most help. To his credit, Will followed instructions to the letter though he didn't have a clue about what needed to be done. Finally they got the rosette settled on deck and strapped down. As soon as they were finished, Patrick leaned over the gunwale, sick once again.

Normally, Rona would have had the boat under way as soon as they had all the gear on board. Instead they remained where they were, the boat rocking amid the swells. As they finished tying the apparatus down, rain began to fall. Quinn knocked on the bridge door and Rona opened it a second later.

"We're all set," Quinn said. "Anytime you're ready to head for home, let's go." His gaze went past Rona to Lily who had her back turned. She was dressed in a pair of faded jeans and a flannel shirt that were too big for her—evidently Rona's. At least they were dry.

He pulled his wet gear off, automatically hanging the pants and the jacket on a peg.

"You okay?" he asked Lily, who was briskly toweling her hair.

She turned around. Her skin had no more color than a sheet, her eyes were huge and dark. Her teeth were still chattering, but at least her lips were no longer blue.

"Thanks to Rona, I'm better." She wadded the towel.

"Good." He took it from her and flung it in the direction of the pegs that held their jackets and other gear.

Will came inside and shrugged out of his coat. Without saying a word, he retreated to a bench at the back of the bridge.

"Whatever the hell is going on between you and Patrick is affecting your work and everyone's safety." Quinn paused until Will met his gaze. "Solve it."

"Or what?" Will challenged.

"You'll be looking for a different job," Quinn said, striving to keep the irritation out of his voice. "Consider this a warning."

Will pulled a CD player out of his pack and snapped the earphones over his head. He jacked the sound up high enough that the driving rhythm could be heard over the drone of the motor.

Rona stepped behind the wheel and eased the throttle forward, and the boat began to move. She adjusted the direction until they were once again headed toward Kantrovich Island.

Patrick stood under the awning, protected from the worst of the downpour, but not from the gusts of wind.

Quinn opened the door. "Feeling any better?"

Patrick managed a grin. "Not much."

"Maybe getting warm will help." Quinn nodded for him to come into the bridge.

The kid met his eyes briefly, then ducked in and stripped off his wet gear. Closing his eyes, he settled on the opposite side of the bench from Will.

Quinn sat next to Lily on the bench. Despite the blanket she'd wrapped around herself, she continued to shiver. Without a word, he picked her up, sat in the corner where she had wedged herself, then settled her across his lap. When she glanced at him, he tried to smile.

"I'm sharing body heat," he said. "An old sailor's trick."

Despite her chattering teeth, she smiled. "Is that what you call it?"

She made no struggle to move away, but instead gradually relaxed, her body subtly heavier against his, though she still shivered. He braced one foot on the bench with his knee bent, then shifted her until he could tuck her bare feet under the blanket. The memory of warming her cold feet slammed through him and brought with it a rush of arousal. No way could he justify his body's reaction to her when he had insisted that she forget that they'd nearly made love.

None of them spoke for quite a while, the only sounds being the steady rumble of the boat's engines and the occasional chatter across the communications radio. Patrick and Will ignored each other, which made Quinn wonder what had been said before he interrupted them. Whether Will had pushed Patrick or not, the result was the same—Lily had ended up in the water. They were damn lucky things had turned out as well as they had.

The rain fell harder, and Rona switched on the wiper blades, which didn't do a lot to improve visibility. She glanced at Quinn.

"You two doing okay over there?"

"She's finally stopped shivering."

"*She's* also wide awake," Lily said, "so don't talk about me like I'm not here."

"Feisty, too," Quinn said, managing a smile. The awful constriction in his chest finally began to ease.

Rona's attention returned to the rain-slathered windshield. "I'd say she has a right to be."

Quinn bent his head, trying to see Lily's expression. "You're feeling better?"

"I'm warm for the first time all day."

"Then stay right where you are," he invited.

To his surprise, she did. He only wished he'd had altruistic motives instead of the simple need to touch her and to pretend that he had the right to comfort her, to protect her.

He held her for the next two hours, and at some point she fell asleep. When Rona guided the boat into the slip below the dock, rain still poured cold with the promise of winter, gusts of wind buffeting the craft. Quinn reluctantly let go of Lily and then went outside to lash the boat in place while Rona shut things down inside.

He had been right about one thing, Lily concluded as she watched him go about the business of securing the boat for the night. His body heat had warmed her, and as soon as he was gone she shivered. She slipped on her wet, clammy shoes, suspecting it would be days before they'd be dry enough to wear again. Worse than being cold, she felt totally wrung out. She'd love to go home, stand under a hot shower for about an hour, and do her best to banish those awful seconds in the water.

She reached for the vinyl jacket, then pulled it apart when she saw the tear across the back.

"Looks like somebody took a knife to it," Will said, his tone harsh. He put on his coat. "Pretty damn scary."

"Yes," Lily said, remembering the instant when the cable had struck her. Looking again at the jacket, she knew how lucky she was that the line hadn't caught her across the back of her head or on the face. That whipping cable could have seriously injured one of them.

"Since it was your fault, you might at least tell her you're sorry," Rona said to Will.

"How was I to know the cable would snap?" he asked.

"Common sense, maybe?" Rona said.

"I'm outta here." Will paused at the door and looked back at Lily. "You gonna be okay?"

"Fine."

"That one is pretty useless," Rona said after he left. She handed Lily a vinyl poncho. "Take this. It will keep you drier."

Lily slipped the garment over her shoulders. "Thanks."

She came out of the boat and stood under the awning for a second, watching Quinn work. His movements were controlled, efficient, done with the practiced ease of repetition.

During the last three weeks the man had been polite, professional, and friendly—big-brother friendly. Except, now and then she'd catch something in his storm-colored eyes so heated, so personal, she felt sure he hadn't been able to follow his own advice. *Forget this morning ever happened.*

Having him hold her the past couple of hours was the last thing she had expected. Given his clear ideas of what he wanted in the way of a relationship, she'd be a fool to read too much into that.

"See you tomorrow," she called to him.

"Hold on," he said. "I'm driving you home."

"You don't have to do that. I'm really okay." The truth was, if she was honest with herself, having him take her home sounded good.

"Maybe." He came toward her, his eyes intense. "But tonight, I'm driving you."

"But then my car will be here and—"

"Don't worry about it. I'll pick you up in the morning."

"Okay." She suspected some perverse sense of duty was motivating him, but she didn't care since spending a few more minutes with him was what she wanted.

"I can wrap this up," Patrick said.

"You're sure?"

The younger man nodded, his glance seeking out Lily. "I am sorry about the accident," he said. "Both of them."

"I know," she said, pulling the hood of the poncho over her head and wondering where Will had disappeared to. It wasn't fair that Patrick get stuck with all the work. "Get some rest. Tomorrow will be a better day."

"It sure as hell better be," Quinn muttered, taking her by the hand and leading her through the rain. "Today's nonsense could have gotten somebody killed."

"But it didn't." She squeezed his hand and stopped walking. When he looked down at her, she repeated, "It didn't."

"Who could have gotten killed?" came a male voice from the deep shadows beneath the warehouse eave.

She started, and Quinn pulled her closer to his side.

A man stepped away from the building, a trenchcoat belted at his waist, its collar turned up. Will Baker stood next to him. Lily glanced from Will to the man whose face was hidden by the bill of a baseball cap. He tipped his hat back, and Lily recognized him. The U.S. Marshal assigned to her when she had been in protective custody last spring.

* * *

"Cal?"

He smiled and extended his hand. "How are you, Lily?"

She shook it. "What are you doing here?" He'd been calling every few weeks since the trial ended, but she hadn't expected to see him. "When did you arrive? If I'd known you were coming—"

"I didn't realize the ferry came only once a week." Cal glanced from her to Quinn, then offered his hand again. "Cal Springfield," he said. "I'm a friend of Lily's from her days at the university."

"Quinn Morrison." He didn't release Lily's other hand as he shook Cal's. "You're not here to steal her back, are you?"

"I, uh, what?"

"To the university," Quinn supplied. "I don't think we can get along without her here."

"Glad to hear it," Cal said.

Lily studied him, wishing he had told Quinn that he was a U.S. Marshal. Since he hadn't…maybe there was another case he was working on. The instant that thought hit, she dismissed it. Lynx Point wasn't exactly the bustling center of anywhere.

"What are you doing here?" Lily asked.

"One of the students at the research station said you were doing fieldwork today, so I figured I'd hang out until you got back," he said, completely avoiding her question.

A chill crawled down her spine that had nothing to do with the rain. Now that the trial was over, he was her contact until they were certain the threats from last spring were all neutralized—Cal's word, not hers. He'd be here in person only if there was some kind of problem with Franklin Lawrence. And since he had just lied to Quinn about how he knew her, she couldn't ask him.

"So you like standing in the rain," Quinn said. He nodded toward Will, who still stood behind them. "I see you've already met Will. Patrick could use your help before you take off."

Cal turned around to look at Will. "I just wanted to make sure this was the right boat, so I asked the first guy who came by," he said to Quinn, his gaze remaining on Will. "Thanks."

"Sure. No prob." Will stuffed his hands into the pockets of his coat and walked back toward the dock and Patrick.

"So, what's this about somebody could have gotten killed?" Cal asked, repeating the question he'd asked earlier.

"An accident, that's all." Lily moved under the wide eave, which provided a bit more protection from the rain. "The storm was gusting up a bit, and I lost my balance and fell overboard. But enough about that. What brings you here?"

"I had business in Juneau and decided to come see you."

"Three hundred miles is a bit of a detour," Quinn said.

"Well, true, and I admit that I didn't figure on things being quite so spread out," Cal returned easily. "Or ferries that have this destination only once a week."

"Do you need a place to stay?" Lily asked.

"No, I've got a room above the Tin Cup." He glanced at his watch. "It's late, and I probably should let you go." Looking at her, he added, "See you tomorrow."

"Yes, sure." She watched him walk away and couldn't think of a single reason for him to be here except— "Cal, wait." Crossing the ten feet from the shelter of the warehouse into the pouring rain, she hurried to him. "What's really going on? Has something happened?"

"No."

Something of her disbelief must have shown in her face because he repeated, "No. I should have figured I'd worry you showing up like this. There's nothing that can't wait. Go home, I'll talk to you in the morning."

More worried than she wanted to admit, she watched him walk away. When she turned around, Quinn stood under the eave, dividing his attention between her and the two young men on the dock. As Lily turned around to look at them, the image of those seconds just as she fell into the water came back to her. Her and Patrick reaching for the rosette so Quinn could use his greater strength to hoist it high enough to attach it to the outrigger. Then a sudden jolt as Will slammed into her.

She shivered.

Quinn reached for her hand as she rejoined him. "Time to get you home and dry...again."

Reassured by his solid presence, she said, "You won't get any argument from me."

"And how do you know that guy?" Quinn asked, leading her toward his car. "You looked totally stunned to see him."

"Because I am. I thought—" She took a deep breath and wondered how to tell the truth without revealing Cal's lie about how he knew her. "That part of my life was behind me."

"The old lab, the old job?" Quinn questioned as they walked toward his SUV.

"Old life," Lily said. *Why had Cal come?* As Quinn had said, Lynx Point was a long detour from Juneau. And why stand out here in the rain waiting for her if whatever was on his mind could wait? And if it couldn't, why hadn't he called or hired a plane to bring him instead of taking the ferry?

"Ah." Quinn was silent a moment, then added, "Since you never talk about it, you make it easy to forget that you've been through a lot in the last couple of years." Another pause, then with a laugh he said, "A little like saying rain is wet."

"I didn't expect you to—"

"Remember?" He came with her to the passenger side of his vehicle and unlocked the door for her. As she climbed in, he said, "I should have Hilda check you out—make sure you're okay," he said after he had settled in the driver's seat.

"Nothing that a long, hot soak in the tub won't cure."

Their conversation turned to the things that needed to be done the following day, ordinary conversation that kept Quinn engaged with her. Sure, they had talked over the past couple of weeks, but until now he'd been distant. The difference between his friendly attitude of late and his now-concerned *friend* was subtle. But it was there.

And, in the process of talking, he drove right past the turn-off to the Ericksen house.

"Stop," she commanded.

He braked the car. "What?"

"I'm staying at the Ericksens'."

"I'd forgotten about that. Do you miss living with your sister?"

"No," Lily said with a soft chuckle. "And to be honest, I think Rosie likes this arrangement better, too."

Quinn backed up the vehicle, then turned into the tree-lined road that led to the Ericksen house. The headlights sliced through the shimmering rain and an occasional wet branch slapped against the vehicle.

"This road is dark as a tomb," Quinn said. "You're sure this is the right turn?"

She chuckled, then teased, "Do I strike you as the kind of person who couldn't find her own way home?"

"Who's watching the little munchkin when you work this late?" he asked instead of answering her.

"Sometimes she's at Rosie's. Tonight Hilda's daughter is watching her."

"She really does have four kids?"

"She really does."

"I heard that her husband was killed in a fishing accident," Quinn said.

Lily nodded. "Years ago, not long after Angela was born. After John died...since she'd been through it, too, she understood in ways that no one else did. Since she's been able to raise her kids by herself, she's given me faith that I can manage with Annmarie."

"I could tell you two were good friends."

"The best," she agreed. "And she never held it against me that I envied her when she began to have children. John and I wanted kids in the worst way, and it was a long time before we admitted that my having a child wasn't in the cards.''

Ahead the yard light flickered through the trees and an old VW Bug was parked in front of the garage.

"But you did. Annmarie looks like you."

"Actually, she looks like Rosie," Lily said as he brought the vehicle to a stop next to the other car. "Thanks to her, I have a daughter."

"I don't understand."

"Rosie is Annmarie's birth mother. John and I adopted her when she was a day old."

"She gave up her child?" His voice was sharp with accusation.

"She had a child for me—big difference. Every day, I'm grateful for the gift." She opened the door to get out. "Thanks for bringing me home."

Quinn opened his own door. "I'll see you in."

"Okay." Surprised again, she glanced at him. His expression revealed nothing of whatever was driving him.

She went to the back door behind the garage, which opened onto a mudroom. She slipped off her coat and hung it on a peg, then toed off her shoes, which she set neatly on a low shelf next to the chest freezer. She opened the door to the kitchen and called, "I'm home."

"Hey, Lily," Angela said, coming into the brightly lit room.

Lily glanced back to the mudroom where Quinn was also taking off his shoes, a slightly longer task than her own since his were lace-up work boots that came well over his ankles.

"Hey, yourself," she said, dropping a kiss on the young woman's cheek and tucking a strand of green-dyed hair behind her ear. "Say hi to Quinn Morrison."

She did and Quinn greeted her in return.

"New color this week," Lily said, touching one of the strands of hair again. "I thought purple was the thing."

"That was last week," Angela said, making it sound as though last week had been eons rather than days ago.

"And what did you and Annmarie do tonight?"

"Watched movies—and I made sure they were age appropriate."

Lily laughed. "Thank you. Since your mom's old Bug is outside, I'm guessing that she's letting you drive today." Lily pulled some bills out of her purse and gave them to Angela.

"Yeah. Good thing she didn't think it would rain. Like I wouldn't know to turn on the windshield wipers or something." Angela folded the money carefully, then stuffed the bills into her jeans' pocket and shrugged into a jacket.

"You're still available Monday after school?"

Angela nodded and headed out the door. "'Night."

"Call me when you get home," Lily called to her.

Angela shot her a disgusted look. "I'm not five."

"I know. Call me, anyway."

When the door clicked behind her, Lily glanced at Quinn, who had padded into the kitchen in his stockinged feet. This was the first time they had been alone since… That again. That thing she wasn't supposed to remember and couldn't forget.

"Make yourself at home," she said with a wave. "I want to go check on Annmarie."

Wondering what the hell he was doing here, Quinn watched Lily walk away from him. He should have stayed in the car. He should have bid her good-night and left her at the door. He should have…but he found himself following her through the house.

It was large, and though the furnishings were casual, he recognized they were also expensive. A huge leather couch flanked by big brass lamps faced a massive stone fireplace that dominated the living room. Quinn was sure the bank of windows with wood shutters closed against the night would overlook the inlet and the stretch of water that led to Foster Island.

"Nice place," he said.

From the hallway, she glanced over her shoulder. "A little

too much leather for my taste, and way too many dead animals on the wall.''

The wall above the fireplace held an assortment of mounted heads—an elk with an impressive rack, a bear caught in a snarl, and a bull moose, among others.

In the dim hallway, Lily pushed open a door and disappeared inside. Quinn passed another doorway and peeked in. The master bedroom, dominated by a king-size bed. Farther down the hall, he stopped at the doorway where Lily had disappeared.

Inside he could see her sitting next to her daughter on the bed. Annmarie was evidently sound asleep. Her cat was curled up next to her, and Lily petted her briefly before touching the child's hair. Lily's face went all soft as she gazed at her daughter. Quinn knew for certain that no one had ever looked at him like that. Feeling like the intruder he knew himself to be, Quinn retreated to the kitchen.

Make yourself at home, Lily had urged. He wasn't all that sure what she'd meant, but for some reason, making her something to eat seemed like a good idea. He opened the refrigerator door and peered inside. Within seconds he decided everything needed to make an omelette was available. A little more searching through cupboards and drawers turned up utensils.

He had whipped up the eggs and was halfway through warming a couple of slabs of ham when he remembered how good a cook Lily was. Again he asked himself what he was doing here, and reminded himself of all the reasons he needed to leave. She worked for him...cooking for her wasn't in the job description, so why was he still here? White picket fences...she was made for them. A saint of a dead husband...who the hell was Cal?

''Whatever you're making smells great,'' she said from the doorway. She gently pulled the door closed behind her. The telephone rang and she answered it. Quinn deduced from Lily's side of the conversation that the caller was Angela announcing that she'd made it home.

''You look better,'' he said when she hung up the telephone receiver. She had changed out of the baggy clothes that Rona had lent her into a pale yellow sweat suit and the lavender bathrobe he remembered. She had brushed her hair and pulled it away from her face in her California Girl look. There was nothing remotely suggestive about her purple slippers or her choice in clothes. But he remembered. The feel of her slim body in his arms. Oh, Lord, he remembered.

She grinned, moving toward him. ''Since I looked like something even a cat would overlook, that's not saying much.''

He didn't bother correcting her. ''That guy, Cal. Did you ever date him?'' Quinn realized how bald and rude the question sounded the instant the words were out of his mouth.

She laughed as though the idea of dating the man was beyond possibility. ''No.''

The flat denial relieved him.

''Hungry?''

She met his gaze, then held it. The oversize island housing a sink and cooktop separated them. Still, the air between them sizzled. He could have been swept away by her soft brown eyes, and he couldn't have broken that contact if his life depended on it. She worried her lower lip with her teeth, and he imagined kissing that very spot where her teeth had been.

''Starved,'' she finally said.

The oil in one of the pans on the stove popped, and he glanced at it. With more confidence than he really felt, he poured the omelette mixture into the skillet.

''What can I do?'' she asked, her gaze following his own around the kitchen, ending with the bare table. ''Set the table,'' she decided.

While she did that, he finished cooking the eggs—scrambled rather than the perfect omelette that he wanted.

''This looks good,'' Lily said when he set the plate in front of her.

''It's just eggs,'' he said. ''No big deal.''

She patted the chair next to the place mat she had set out. "Grab another plate, Quinn. You're going to eat, too, aren't you, since you've made more than enough food for both of us?"

To him, it looked like the amount he could have eaten alone, but he retrieved another plate and sat down. She divided the food, giving him most of it.

"You're sure that's enough for you?" he asked.

"It's plenty." She took a bite, then smiled. "Good. I really was hungry," she added, then put another bite into her mouth. "Where did you learn to cook?"

He laughed. "Frying an egg is about even with boiling water."

"Don't underestimate the importance of boiling water. What was your favorite food as a kid—the thing you most wanted your mom to make?" she asked. Then without waiting for an answer, added, "Mine was *lefse,* and though my mother gave me a griddle years ago, I don't make it as well as she does."

"What's *lefse?*"

"Traditional Norwegian food—"

"I thought that was *ludefiske,*" he said.

She laughed. "Also a traditional food. The one that almost no one likes. You'd like *lefse*—it's a crepe kind of thing, best right off the griddle with butter and sugar. Comfort food." With the same single-mindedness her daughter had shown, Lily asked again, "What's your favorite?"

"I don't have one." He took another bite of eggs. "I should have made toast or something."

"I don't need any," she responded. "What do you mean, you don't have one? C'mon, everybody has a favorite."

"Well, I don't. Did you want coffee or anything?"

She shook her head, her attention now on him instead of on the food, though she continued to eat. He wished he had something to tell her other than the ugly truth that he'd had no favorite because no one had ever made one for him—

maybe with the exception of Mrs. Perkins who had figured out his fondness for blueberry pancakes.

The inevitable comparisons that he always disliked marched through his mind, the ones that began with him being an outsider—always an outsider. He watched Lily eat a moment longer before setting his fork down.

This was why he had brought her home tonight. To make her understand he had no traditions where she had many. He had no roots. He had no blueprint for building a family and she had everything he'd always dreamed of. He had…no business being here and wanting things to be different than they were.

Unable to hold her curious gaze an instant longer, he pushed away from the table and stood. He wrapped his hands around the top rung of the ladder-back chair, then said, "I have to go." The words surprised him since he had intended to share a few choice truths with her, starting with the fact that he was no good for her, no matter how alluring the invitation in her eyes.

"Okay." When he headed toward the mudroom door, she followed. "Thanks for bringing me home."

"You're welcome."

"And making me dinner."

He shook his head. "Don't thank me for cooking you scrambled eggs."

"Okay."

There she was being agreeable again. Didn't she know that if she came another step closer his self-control would snap?

"I wanted to make sure you were okay." As if that somehow explained why he was torturing himself by being here.

"That's nice. Thoughtful. Thank you."

The door to the kitchen closed behind her, making the mudroom seem private and intimate instead of utilitarian. The room was illuminated by only the porch light outside and the light that came through the glass window of the door to the kitchen. The sound of the rain pattering against the roof was louder here, and the room was chillier than the kitchen, the white metal of the chest freezer gleaming coldly. Hot, wild sex filled his imagination. The urge to grab her and to hold on for all he was worth was about equal to his need to run.

"I'm not being nice, damn it." He jammed his arms through the sleeves of his jacket, then set his boots on the floor so he could step into them.

She nodded as though that answer somehow made sense, and he wondered what it would take to make her mad at him.

"What are you being, then, if not nice?" she asked.

Putting on his boots lost his attention, and he raked a hand through his hair. "Hell if I even know, Lily." He met her gaze. "I can't give you anything."

"I haven't asked for anything," she countered. "What's really going on?"

The only way to make her understand was to burn the bridge down so she knew how rotten he was at relationships. Maybe then, she'd be safe from him—a chasm separating them that couldn't be crossed. "I was raised in foster care. Some kids are lucky—and they get to stay with the same family for years. Some kids are unlucky—they get shuffled through the system and go from home to home to home."

"How many?" she asked, her voice quiet, instead of asking him if he'd been one of the unlucky ones.

"Nineteen," he said, meeting her gaze—her open, curious, interested gaze—with a challenging one of his own. It was past time that she understood he was no Boy Scout, no hero, no knight in shining armor. "From the time I was nine until I went to college, I never lived anywhere longer than a year. Ask any one of the shrinks who were in my head and they'll tell you that I have trouble with trust and I'm scared of being abandoned." He swallowed. "You want a guy who's rotten at relationships?" He tapped his fist against his chest. "Here I am."

"And since the last foster home?" she said in that unruffled way she had.

"I was married for a year. Right after I graduated from college." The lack of heat in her voice made his own more harsh. "Shelly will tell you that I made her miserable, and she'd be telling the truth. And it was no picnic for her kids, either. They hated me."

"Most kids hate their steps."

"My mom left me in a park when I was four years old—forgot about me."

Lily flinched as though he had hurt her. "I see."

The calm response made him lean toward her. "No, you don't see. That's the whole problem. My ex-wife deserved better. So do you. This chemistry between us—you don't think I feel it?"

Lily managed a smile. "I know you feel it."

He jutted his chin. "Getting involved with me would be stupid, Lily. You know what you'd have to look forward to? The honeymoon, and, lady, I'm good at it—I'll do anything I can to make you believe you're the woman for me for life. Then I'll find six zillion reasons to dump you."

She took a step toward him. "You would?"

He nodded. "In a heartbeat."

"Another first, then," she said. "I've managed to reach the ripe age of thirty-four without being dumped."

"You wouldn't like it."

She came closer. "No, I don't suppose I would." She stopped with only a foot left between them. She made a vague, airy gesture with her hand. "Given all that, why are you here Quinn? Why did you bring me home?"

Chapter 9

"Because…" Quinn's voice trailed away as Lily slipped a single finger between two buttons on the placket of his shirt and tugged. His throat couldn't have been drier if he had swallowed a mouthful of sand.

"Because?" she prompted, bringing him closer with that one slender finger until they stood a breath apart. She was so small standing there, and she didn't seem to have a clue about what she was risking. He hadn't driven her away…and now…she seemed bent on driving him out of his mind. If he was an honorable man, he'd walk away from the invitation in her eyes.

Somehow this deep, deep longing for her went beyond lust, though he wanted her. Somehow this threatened his heart, strange when he had no heart to share. The things she should have, he could never give to her. He dragged in a breath through the sand clogging his throat.

"This will never work."

"I'm pretty sure it will," Lily said, deliberately misunderstanding him, praying that her courage would stay with

her this time. Her gaze slanted down his body. His obvious
arousal made her own dance in response. "Even if you want
me to think the worst of you."

"I want you to see how things really are." He swallowed,
his Adam's apple bobbing. "You should send me packing."

"You should have thought of that before you brought me
home." Nobody's eyes should be so tortured, she thought.
Wasn't it the woman who was supposed to be this uncertain,
this afraid?

"I'm no good for you." He ducked his head toward her
even as indecision and regret lingered in his eyes.

"Then you'd better be very, very bad." And she lifted her
face toward his, standing on tiptoe.

Lily felt his breath merge with hers the instant before he
lowered his head and brushed her mouth with his.

The man's lips trembled, and she understood that he was
more vulnerable, even, than she was. Someone had to show
him he was worthy without him having to do anything at all
to earn it. So she kissed him chastely, silently comforting
him and letting him know that he didn't have to do anything
but let her cherish his mouth with her own. The most important thing…make sure he knew that she wasn't going anywhere, no matter how rigid his shoulders beneath her hands.
Long, heady seconds passed as she rediscovered the pleasure
of lips exploring lips.

His hunger kindled in a heartbeat, and he deepened the
kiss, impatient as he claimed her mouth. He swept his tongue
inside and demanded her surrender. His was what she
wanted.

His deep kiss was even headier than she remembered. She
moaned, or maybe he did. She wrapped her arms around him,
his neck hot against her cool fingers. Against her mouth, his
breathing turned ragged.

His fingers fumbled at the tie of her bathrobe and she gave
up hugging him to help loosen the knot. At last it was free
and he pulled her close once again, his warm, wonderful
hands sliding beneath her fleece top and touching her as she

had dreamed of for these three long weeks. Through the layers of clothes that separated them she could feel his arous:
pressing against her belly. All that power, all that strengtl
focused on her. She shuddered with desire.

She pushed his jacket off his shoulders, letting it drop t
the floor, and pulled his shirt free of the waistband of hi
jeans. At last she was able to reach the bare, hot skin of hi
back. He trembled beneath her touch, so she did the onl
thing possible—press even closer so he'd know there wa
nothing to fear, that she'd cherish him and keep him safe
Still…if this was too unbearable—and despite the kiss tha
was melting her to the core, she had the sense that it was—
he had to understand they could stop.

"If you don't want to do this," she whispered against hi
mouth, "you need to leave right now."

"Are you crazy?" Underneath her clothes, he cupped he
breast with his warm hand. Small as she was and huge as hi
hand was, it felt perfect to her. When he rolled her erec
nipple between his thumb and forefinger, her knees gav
way.

That was his invitation to lift her so she was sitting on th
lid of the freezer, the metal surface cool beneath her bottom
He stepped between her legs, so close she knew how mucl
he wanted her.

His kisses were everywhere. At her temple. Cherishing. A
the corner of her mouth. Teasing. At the base of her neck
Exciting. Cool air danced across her skin as he pushed up
the fleece shirt and ducked his head, kissing the valley be
tween her breasts, the swell above and below before pulling
her achy nipple into his mouth. Her arms became tangled i
the sleeves of her bathrobe and her shirt, binding her so al
she could do was endure the exquisite, sharp pleasure.

She had the fanciful thought that heated, fragrant oi
flowed through her veins instead of blood, bringing every
nerve ending to life. When he brushed her nipple with hi
tongue, tiny pulses shattered and left her in a thousand shim
mering pieces. As much as she had loved sex, it hadn't eve

been like this, taking her to the top of a mountain and plunging her off some dizzying height long before she was ready to make the leap.

She tried to reach for his belt buckle, and his warm, clever hands left her breasts to still her fingers.

"Protection," he muttered, his voice hoarse. "I don't have any with me."

She managed to touch his cheek and made sure he looked at her. "You don't have to protect me, Quinn," she whispered, fiercely wishing he did. Making babies with this man…was wishing for things that could never be.

"You're sure?" His eyes were so intense, so concerned.

She nodded. John had been tested and pronounced fertile. After trying for a baby for more than ten years, she was sure.

"Ah, Lily," he whispered against her mouth. His warm hands cupped her breasts once again. "To be naked inside you—do you have any idea how exciting that is?"

The words made her burn for him. She finally reached his belt, unzipped his jeans. With her first touch to his bare skin he tugged at her fleece pants and pulled them off her legs. Then he was back, stepping between her legs as he had before, only this time bare and hot and pressed intimately against her.

He stilled for an instant as if savoring the elemental brush of flesh against flesh. As for her, she was dying for the contact to be completed. At last her arms pushed through the constraints of her sleeves. She pulled his head toward hers, then took his mouth in a kiss intended to show him how much she wanted him. He pushed and was at last where she wanted. His throaty groan of satisfaction told her this was as good for him.

"Magic," she whispered, wrapping her legs around his waist.

"That good?" He gathered her close, his arms sheltering her in a tight embrace, and he began to move.

"More than good." She buried her face in his neck, nuzzling the collar of his shirt out of the way. The first shudders rippled through her, so intense all she could do was hang on to the solid anchor of him.

He own climax came in the next instant. His big body shuddered beneath her hands, and his groan of, ''Ah, damn, I'm not ready,'' in her ear was sexy beyond belief.

She held him fiercely until his spasms ended, his breathing slowed. To her great surprise, she found that she was in the cool mudroom when she opened her eyes. Who would have thought paradise could have been found right here?

Little by little, she became aware of their surroundings. The patter of the rain against the roof. The chilly temperature of the freezer lid against her skin. The porch light outside that lit the mudroom in a protective gloom.

He stood for long moments, resting his forehead against hers, his breaths at last coming normally.

''What you do to me,'' he whispered the instant before he caught her mouth in a kiss so full of longing that it made her soul burn. She held him with all her strength and wondered how she would ever convince him that he didn't have to be so scared of what was happening between them.

When he stepped away from her to pull his jeans back up and to tuck in his shirt, she wanted to experience that joining again, to feel him cradled by her body though he was no longer hard. He picked up her pants from the floor and thrust them into her hands. Then he swung her into his arms and carried her through the house to the master bedroom.

Efficiently, he swept back the bedspread and covers, and settled her on the bed. He kissed her cheek, then went into the bathroom where she heard running water. Though she wondered what he was doing, she lingered in the sweet haze of satisfaction, secure in the knowledge that he'd be back. A second later he was, carrying a washcloth. He sat on the edge of the bed, calmly parted her legs and cleaned her with the warm, damp cloth, his touch at once cherishing and unbearably intimate. The gesture was as unexpected as everything else about him tonight had been. Again, he left her without saying a word, turning off the bathroom light. When he returned this time he settled next to her on the bed, but on top of the covers.

"Are you going to stay?"

He didn't answer, but kissed her temple. His presence in her bed, even fully dressed as he was, was more than she had expected, less than she wanted. So she pressed her lips against his jaw and let her self sink toward sleep as she savored the feel of his warm body next to hers, the comfort of his strong arms surrounding her. She wrapped her own around him, as well, wanting him to feel as cherished as he made her feel. The man needed that, she was sure, even more than she did.

The following morning a brisk knock at the mudroom door interrupted Lily's breakfast with Annmarie. Hoping that Quinn had returned, Lily was smiling as she opened the door. When she had awakened without him, she thought that he'd probably left to avoid the morning-after awkwardness they'd had the last time and to avoid any questions Annmarie would undoubtedly present. Given the deep, deep wounds he had revealed to her last night, she now understood his need for self-preservation—even though she had wanted to awaken with him.

No Quinn, to her disappointment. Instead, Cal Springfield stood on the porch. The battered pickup that Frank Talbot rented out was parked next to the garage, explaining how he had gotten here from town without messing up the shine on his wingtips.

"Hello, Lily," he said, none of last night's pleasantries evident in his expression or his voice. "We've got to talk."

Lily glanced back through the mudroom to her daughter who was eating at the breakfast bar. Sure that she wasn't going to like anything Cal had to say, Lily stepped onto the porch and closed the door behind her.

This morning was one of the cool misty ones she remembered from childhood and had missed terribly when she had first gone to college in central California. Instead of the mist feeling like a welcoming blanket as it normally did, it chilled her. Much like Cal's presence.

"What's going on?" she asked, wrapping her cardigan more tightly around her body and moving away from the house to the edge of the porch. Through the trees, the water from the inlet slapped against the shoreline. Since she had been living with her sister until a couple of weeks ago, she gave voice to her second thought. "How did you know to find me here?"

He shrugged. "I followed you last night." When she looked at him, he added, "I was worried about you. How much do you know about your boyfriend?"

Embarrassment and anger surfaced in equal measure that Cal might have seen anything so private as what had happened in the mudroom last night. Granted, she and Quinn had both had their clothes on—mostly—but Quinn had bared his soul. His vulnerability was a private thing, too private to be seen by anyone. "If you had knocked on the door instead of skulking around you'd know that Quinn would never harm me."

Cal flushed and looked away.

"Why are you here?" she asked.

When he looked back at her, his gaze was troubled. "I've got bad news."

"What is it?"

Cal stared at the still water of the cove and the shrouded silhouette of Foster Island for a long minute. "Franklin Lawrence has filed an appeal."

"The D.A. already told me to expect that, so unless he's won it, that's not bad news."

Cal's expression became more troubled. "Lawrence still pulls strings, Lily, like I told you he would—no matter that he's in a maximum security prison." He stared down at her. "And he's put a contract on your life."

Lily heard the words, but they simply didn't register. "That's so stupid," she said, trying her best to ignore the cold trembling in the pit of her stomach. "Even if I was dead, he'd still be in prison."

A ghost of a smile flitted across Cal's face. "You underestimate him. If he's granted a new trial, and if the state's star witness was dead—"

"What good would it do him? They'd still have my deposition."

"Not as convincing as a live witness."

"I'm safe here." Even to her own ears, her insistence fell far short of convincing.

"Are you, Lily?" Cal held up a finger. "Based on what I've heard, there was an accident involving your car that is pretty suspicious." He held up a second finger. "While I was having breakfast at the Tin Cup this morning, the gal who skippers the boat you were on yesterday had some pretty definite things to say about a malfunctioning winch."

"It didn't malfunction—just a stupid accident because..."

"The kid on board was careless. Yeah, I heard." Cal held up a third finger. "And you fell overboard. None of that sounds very safe, Lily."

"You're adding two plus two and getting five." She hated that he was voicing her own fears out loud, hated even more the possibility that he might be right. All she wanted was a normal, ordinary life with her daughter. She had done her best to create that...and she hated that her best might not be good enough. "So you're here to talk about witness security. Again."

"Again," he agreed. "I know your family is important to you, Lily, but it's your best, safest option."

A lump rose in her throat merely thinking about it. The idea of walking away from her family...she couldn't imagine it. "You can't ask that of me."

"Staying for your boyfriend?"

Quinn. "He has nothing to do with this."

"I don't like you being here by yourself, but you make it easy to disappear, Lily. Say the word, and I can have you out of here within the hour," Cal said.

"Do you have any idea what that would do to my family?"

"That's not my concern. You are."

A year ago she would have assumed he was overstating the situation. But that was before Franklin Lawrence had gone after her family members to keep her from testifying. Still, the choice was unbearable. Disappear and have her family assume the worst. Or stay, only to have the worst happen. How could she do that to all of them?

"I know this isn't easy," he said. He sounded sympathetic enough, but she wondered how many times he'd repeated those same words. "I'll stick around for a few days until you decide."

"Oh, gee, thanks," she replied, unable to resist sarcasm. She took in his trench coat and dress shoes. "You might change the wardrobe to fit in a little more. Nobody around here wears a suit unless there's a funeral or a wedding, and sometimes not even then."

"Understood." He stepped off the porch. "And remember, Lily. I'm your good friend who used to work with you at the university."

She supposed his request was reasonable. She'd have to clue Ian and Rosie in since they both knew exactly who Cal Springfield was, and she'd have to come up with a convincing story. In a word, lie. She already hated it.

The sound of two cars coming up the tree-lined drive reached Lily. The first vehicle was Ian's pickup truck and the second was Quinn's SUV. Behind Lily, the door opened and Annmarie skipped down the steps. The instant Ian got out of his truck, she ran toward him.

"Uncle Ian." She lifted her arms with the expectation of being swung around, and she was.

"How's my petunia?" Ian said when he set her down.

"I'm fine," she told him with a grin, adding her usual retort to his pet name for her, "And I'm still not a flower." She turned her attention to Quinn. "Hi, Mr. Quinn."

"Hey, munchkin."

He tousled her hair, and after she tugged on his hand, his fingers closed around hers. Lily wondered if he had even been aware of that slight hesitation. His eyes, when they met hers, were warm, which gave her hope. His expression this morning was a far cry from the one he'd had that morning at Rosie's house.

Ian spared Quinn a glower before striding toward the porch. As soon as he reached the top step, he extended his hand to Cal. "Last time I saw you was at Lily's house before she moved."

"It's been a while," Cal said, a flare of surprise chasing through his eyes. "Stearne, if I remember right."

"Not that long. Just this past spring." Ian glanced over his shoulder. "This is Quinn Morrison. Lily works for him."

"We met last night," Quinn said.

"Right before you brought Lily home," Cal added.

That earned Quinn another frown from Ian. Folding his arms across his chest, Ian rocked back on his heels. "Why are you here, Springfield? Lynx Point isn't exactly a hotbed of crime and corruption that would require a federal marshal."

"I—"

"You're a cop?" Quinn interrupted. "You said were an old friend from the university, or did I miss something?" When he looked at Lily, his expression was irritated. "He lied and you went along with it."

Cal glanced back at Lily. "I was—"

"One of the marshals assigned to Lily when she was in protective custody," Ian said.

Cal nodded. "And like I said last night, I was in the area and decided to look her up."

"And like *I* said last night, getting here is a bit of a detour from anywhere." Quinn came to stand next to Ian.

He wasn't as tall, but his shoulders were broader. At this moment he was even more intimidating than her brother-in-law. That surprised Lily. She hadn't imagined Quinn in the role of overprotective warrior.

"Why lie?" Quinn asked Cal.

"To keep just this from happening. People hear U.S. Marshal and they tend to get a little uptight." Cal glanced back at Lily. "You didn't mention your neighbor had moved up here."

"He was your neighbor?" Quinn asked, jerking his head toward Ian. "Before you moved here?"

"He married my sister," Lily said, answering Cal's question first. "And yes, Ian was my neighbor and, after John died, my closest friend."

"That still doesn't explain what you're doing here," Quinn said, directing his focus back to Cal. "Or why you lied about working with Lily."

"I'd like to know that, too," Ian said.

"And who appointed you bozos to be in charge?" Cal stood to his full height, which was still inches shorter than either Ian or Quinn.

In his own way, Cal was as imposing. He made a point of letting his trench coat flap open so they could all see the weapon in his shoulder holster.

"Oh, please," Lily interrupted. "This is quite a lot more testosterone than anyone needs so early in the morning." She took Annmarie's hand. "Come on, sweetie. Let's finish breakfast and get ready for work." She opened the door to the house and paused to look back at Ian and Quinn who were providing a solid line of defense against whatever threat they thought Cal presented. "I'd appreciate it if you all didn't manage to kill one another before I'm ready to go. I'd have to call Hilda, and she's busy enough without having to put on her safety officer hat." She took a step inside, then turned back. "There's coffee in the kitchen if anyone wants it."

When she returned to the kitchen fifteen minutes later, Quinn sat at the breakfast bar with Annmarie, who had coerced him into coloring with her. Ian stood in front of the sink, his arms once again crossed over his chest, the scowl back on his face. Cal was nowhere to be seen. When she glanced out the window, the pickup was gone.

"What's he doing here?" Ian asked.

She poured a last cup of coffee into her travel mug and turned off the coffeemaker. She didn't answer until after she'd added cream to her cup. "Which 'he,' Ian? Quinn or Cal?"

Ian glared at Quinn. "Take your pick."

"Quinn brought me home last night, so I suspect he's back to give me a ride to work." She took a sip of her coffee. "And you know very well that Cal has been checking on me every couple of weeks since the trial ended."

"That doesn't explain why he popped out of the blue."

"You'll have to ask him." Lily looked away from Ian's penetrating glance and found Quinn watching her with just as much interest. With far greater care than necessary, she snapped the lid on top of her mug. The most important decision of her life loomed before her, and she had no one to talk to about it. Despite being surrounded by people she loved, she had never felt more alone or more adrift.

Avoiding Quinn's gaze, she asked, "Ready to go?"

Quinn nodded and stood.

Lily kissed her daughter. "You be good for Rosie today."

She grinned. "I'm always good. Auntie Rosie says so."

She patted Ian's shoulder as she passed him. "Lock up on the way out."

Quinn held the door open for her as she stepped onto the porch. She'd have to be blind to miss the wary exchange between Quinn and Ian. They might be united in their front about Cal, but it was clear they didn't think much of one another.

For as long as she could remember, the people she loved most seemed to think she needed a protector. Ian was like the brother she had never had, and Quinn...the feelings that had swept through her last night were once again right there at the surface, making her long for a future she had been so sure would be denied her after John died. She glanced at Quinn, a man so different from her husband, a man who had

somehow also cast himself in the role of protector. Not tha
she needed one.

She had carried around the burden of being a witness to
murder for months without help and had managed to keep
her life together. Not without a price, she silently admitted
But if things were normal—happy—for Annmarie, sleepless
nights were a smile price to pay.

As he had last night, Quinn held the car door open for her
When they were under way, he said, "Why'd you go along
with the lie last night?"

She met his gaze. "I assumed Cal had his reasons."

"One of the two things I hate most are liars."

"I didn't lie to you."

"Not if you don't count the lies of omission."

That covered way more ground than she cared to think
about. "Who lied to you, Quinn?" When he glared at her
she added, "Enough for you to hate liars and push me into
the pit with them."

"This isn't about me."

"No, I don't suppose it is," she agreed, turning her head
away from him.

A long ten seconds passed before he said, "Lies were
constant when I was growing up." Still she didn't say anything, and after another stretch of silence he added, "My
mom would promise to come visit, promise that she'd stay
sober. She didn't. The social workers would promise that the
next home would be okay, but they had no way of knowing."

"Those sound like broken promises, not lies."

"Same difference." He sighed, then flexed his hands over
the steering wheel. "Okay. Maybe you have a point."

"What's the other one?" she asked. "That you hate
most."

His gaze never left the road. "People who don't give a
rat's ass about their kids."

The vehemence in his voice and his choice of words gave
her pause. The magnitude of those nineteen foster homes
he'd so casually mentioned knifed through her, making her

che for the little boy who had suffered through years of broken promises. In his shoes, she'd hate liars just as much.

"Those lies of omission…" she finally said. "With Cal—"

"Things get a little complicated," Quinn concluded. "He's not trying to talk you into witness protection, is he?"

She glanced sharply at Quinn. "Why would you think that?"

"Simple. I asked Ian if you'd had any fallout from the trial. So is that why he's here, to talk you into witness protection?"

"He could try," she said, hating the lie of omission.

Quinn didn't reply, and she didn't dare look at him.

"Were the Niksen bottles damaged last night?" she asked.

"They looked okay," he said.

"Then we have a busy day."

"Let's hope," he said.

She managed to hold up her end of the conversation during rest of the drive into Lynx Point and up the hill to the research station that overlooked the community. Her attention, though, circled around Cal's announcement.

Franklin Lawrence wanted her dead. She wanted to believe that simply wasn't possible, but that didn't keep the icy knots from churning in her stomach. She couldn't imagine her life with the choice that Cal had put in front of her. Take Annmarie and live among strangers. Never again talk with her parents or her sisters or her best friend.

Lily glanced at Quinn. To leave this man she was pretty sure she was already in love with. A man who needed her despite everything he professed to believe about himself.

Give up her life? Walk away from everything and everyone important to her? How could she?

Chapter 10

From his seat on the steps of Lily's porch, Quinn watched her come down the shady driveway in Rosie's car which she'd been driving these past weeks. Only hours ago he had picked her up to drive her to work—hours that he'd been counting down all day as he mostly thought about making love to her again rather than doing the work—tons of it— that needed to be done.

Time for Plan A if little Annmarie was with her. They'd go for a sunset sail, eat the sandwiches he'd picked up from the Tin Cup. If Annmarie wasn't with Lily—and he didn't see her in the car—Plan B. He was crazy for thinking that Lily would fall for anything so obvious as a sail into the sunset. He was struck with the image of some Lothario giving her a leering grin and inviting her to see his etchings.

What he intended, though, was romance. After taking her like some hormone-crazed kid last night, she deserved that.

A smile on her face, she gave him a little wave as she parked the vehicle. Feeling awkward and unsure of himself—

and annoyed by the fact—he waited while she gathered her stuff together and then opened the door.

"Hey, you," she said casually, coming toward him, a jacket and tote bag in her arms. "I didn't expect to see you."

He stood, then jammed the tips of his fingers into his pockets so she wouldn't see how nervous he was. "Let's go for a sail." He nodded toward the powerboat he'd rented from Milt's Fishing Charter. He'd tied it up to the narrow dock that flanked the huge boathouse where Mike Ericksen stored his yacht.

"I—"

"Haven't picked up Annmarie," he finished.

Lily nodded.

"So, call your sister." He didn't add anything more. He wanted Lily alone, but if she wanted to bring her daughter... That wasn't as preferable as having Lily alone, but okay.

Lily climbed the steps to the porch, her gaze once again back on him—considering and wary, just as it should be. As he'd told her last night, he was no good for her. That didn't keep him from imagining her naked.

As if coming to some decision, she smiled at him, then touched his arm as she passed him. "All right." After she unlocked the door, she held it open for him. "Want to come in?"

Oh, man, was that a loaded question. Did he ever. Too much. "No." Grabbing the first excuse that came to mind, he added, "I've got a couple of things to double check on the boat."

"I'll be back in a couple of minutes." She let the door close behind her as she disappeared inside the house.

Quinn ambled toward the boat. If he had invited her to paddle over to Foster Island in his two-man kayak like he'd first planned, he'd have a way of working off all this nervous energy. Never mind that he would have been wishing that he'd rented the boat instead. Since she hadn't told him to take a flying leap for simply showing up...maybe she'd been thinking about last night, too.

He paced to the end of the dock and stared out at the water, which was beginning to smooth into a glassy surface as it often did this time of day. Remembering that he'd told her he had things to check, he boarded the boat. Except he'd already done all that, and everything was in perfect running order. A couple of minutes later, she came out of the house wearing jeans and a lightweight parka.

When she reached the craft, she shaded her eyes and said, "Annmarie is going to have dinner with Rosie and Ian. They'll bring her home in a couple of hours."

"So we're all set."

"Yes."

His hand was warm as he helped her step into the boat. Lily sure hadn't expected to find him sitting on her porch when she arrived home, and doubly surprising was his invitation for a sunset sail. She was glad, though, since she had used up all her courage last night. She'd half expected him to revert back to the friendly professional colleague, as he'd done after his concussion. She hadn't seen him all day, since they'd both had dozens of things that had taken priority.

She peeked into the doorway of the cabin. Even in the dim light, the tiny space looked inviting, made even more so by the mouth-watering aroma of food. A basket sat on the table.

"You brought a picnic," she said.

"Just sandwiches." He climbed the ladder to the flying bridge, and she followed him.

"That sounds good."

He turned the key of the ignition. "You haven't asked what kind."

"If the aroma is any indication, meatball with homemade sauce from the Tin Cup."

He chuckled. "Good thing I didn't want it to be a secret."

"If you've got some of their chocolate cake, I'm yours."

He slanted her a glance over his shoulder. "Promises, promises."

She grinned at him, a flutter of anticipation curling through her at those very ordinary teasing words.

He flipped switches and touched controls, indicating a familiarity with the craft. He chose to stand behind the wheel though he could have sat on the tall captain's stool.

Within seconds Quinn had them under way with a minimum of fuss and hardly a wake to mar the surface of the water. Once he was away from the shore, he opened the throttle and the powerboat picked up speed. The motor generated so much noise that they would have had to shout at each other to have a conversation.

Deciding that was okay since she didn't know what to say to him, Lily zipped up her coat and enjoyed the brilliant colors of the sunset despite the autumn chill in the air.

As if sensing her when she came to stand next to him, Quinn pulled her close so she stood between him and the wheel.

As happened every time she stood within the shelter of his arms, she felt protected and cherished in ways she was certain she never had. That always vaguely surprised her. Comparisons that were unfair to both Quinn and John—especially John—hovered at the edge of her mind. She pushed them away and focused her attention on the brilliant scenery in front of her—the landscape of her childhood that she had missed more than she had ever been willing to admit.

It was this kind of sunset she imagined seeing through the windows of her house, and she turned around to see if it was visible within the pines between the Ericksens's house and Rosie's place. It was, the newly installed windows reflecting the red glow of the sunset.

"Look," she said, nudging Quinn's arm. "See the place up there north of Mike's place? That's the house I'm building. Or rather, that Ian is building. He's my general contractor."

"You're going to have a great view."

"I have to be patient. It won't be ready to move into for months yet." Ahead of them the water was glassy-smooth. The sky and water caught fire. The incandescent sunset lit the scoured rock walls of Foster Island. Unlike most of the islands, it wasn't shrouded in trees, so the elemental shapes from the last Ice Age were still visible—mythic and mysterious. More distant islands marked the border between earth and sky.

"Beautiful," she breathed.

Quinn cut the motor. The silence that followed was broken only by the nearly silent slap of water against the boat as it rocked gently. He eased back until he rested against the seat behind the wheel. He crossed his arms around Lily and rested his chin against her temple.

"I love this so much," she said. "It makes me wish I had come home years ago."

"You're lucky that you have a place to come home to."

She turned slightly in his arms so she could look at him.

"Tell me what that's like," he said.

"All my relatives are great storytellers," she said with a smile. "First you have the Norwegian side of the family who have fish stories that are so big—"

"They'd sink a good-size boat?"

She laughed. "Something like that. And then you have the Tlinglit side of the family who can keep you entertained for hours with their stories. Hilda and I are cousins, you know."

"So that's where you get your dark eyes."

"Yes." She paused. "You're sure you want to hear about all this?"

He nodded.

While they watched the sun slowly sink beyond the horizon, she told him about her aunts and uncles, her life that embraced traditions from both cultures, and how she hadn't known how much she missed it all until she had returned home. Her thoughts strayed to Cal and the witness security program. That life sounded sterile and unbearable—more so now than ever.

"I always imagined what it would be like to have aunts or uncles," Quinn said when she fell silent.

"I'll share mine with you," she said. "They'd like you."

He didn't have anything to say to that, so he didn't try, but instead pressed a kiss against her temple.

"This is my favorite place," he said.

"Really?" She looped an arm around his neck. "That might give a girl ideas."

"About last night—"

"Don't you dare tell me that you regret it."

She stiffened slightly in his arms and not nuzzling her neck became impossible.

"I don't regret that," he murmured against her tender skin.

She relaxed within his embrace though her hands tightened around his arms. Her head fell to the side, offering him that smooth expanse of skin between the collar of her coat and her nape. The scent of her skin sank deeper into him.

"Careful," she whispered around a soft chuckle. "The last time you did that you left marks."

"I remember." He had a fleeting memory of biting her neck as he was now, branding her as his.

He felt her nod. "So, if you don't want people to talk…"

He didn't, but damn. Reluctantly he moved his lips from her neck to the side of her face. "I didn't intend to do this."

"Hmm."

He wondered if she was agreeing with him or gently mocking him. The latter he deserved.

Finally, "What did you intend?"

"This." He turned her in his arms so he could give her the kiss he'd been wanting all day. Kissing her, just kissing, was a thousand times better than sex had been with anyone in years. She kissed back without any sense of self-preservation. How could that be? he wondered. Didn't she know, didn't she understand that she was supposed to be building barriers between them? Instead she offered her vulnerability with such trust that she once again humbled him.

Letting go of her mouth, he steered her toward the ladder that led back to the deck. Clumsily, he descended the steps, turning instantly to reach for her. One more set of steps and he'd have her inside the small cabin. She followed him without hesitation, matching him kiss for kiss and heating his blood until it was molten like the sunset.

Inside the cabin, light blazed through the portholes, casting everything in crimson.

Her eyes crinkled at the corners as her gaze lit on the blanket he had laid over the bed tucked under the bow. "I can see that you've been planning a little more than dinner."

"A little," he admitted. "Your turn to say so if you want to go home." He pulled far enough away that he could see her face, praying she'd want to stay, praying that she'd tell him he was out of his mind and no way did she want this. If this ended right now, his battered heart might survive.

"To quote my good friend, Dr. Quinn Morrison—and a very bright man, I might add—'Are you crazy?'" She touched his face with the back of her hand, then began to unbutton his shirt.

He covered her hands with his own. "You're sure?"

She pushed his hands away and resumed unbuttoning. "I've heard sex is supposed to be fun." She tugged at his shirt, held firmly in place by his belt. "I've never made love on a boat."

He hadn't been aware that his heart had even stopped until it began beating again. "Me, either." Kissing her and unzipping her parka was easy enough. He could do that.

"And to think you were planning all this when I was so afraid you were already dumping me."

Those startling words shouldn't have been accompanied by her lifting her arms so he could pull the turtleneck over her head—but they were. She was teasing him, he realized, her lips curved in a smile, a come-hither expression in her eyes. His stomach tightened a notch as his gaze lit on the dark blue lace of her bra, then on her exposed skin—bathed in glowing light and so beautiful. The idea of leaving this woman didn't even compute.

He drew her close simply so he could feel the satiny smooth texture of her skin beneath his hands. She pulled his head toward hers so she could reach his mouth and bestow another of those kisses that reached clear to his soul. Beyond the arousal that had reached the point of pain, his heart felt as though it might crack open. Just kissing. She could do this to him simply by touching her mouth to his.

She tugged again at his shirt, and when it didn't come loose, her hands her were at his waistband, pulling open his belt, her touch inches away from where he most wanted and already so arousing he felt he might explode.

Remembering how fast things had been over last night, he dragged in a breath, willing his mind—and his libido—to slow down, way down. They had time, and he'd do this right or die trying.

"Shoes." He pressed a kiss at the corner of her mouth and pushed her back onto the bed. When he lifted her foot to take off her shoes, he discovered that she was wearing deck shoes that easily slipped off. His own were his usual hiking boots. So much for seduction planning.

"Need help?" Laughing, she arched a stockinged foot along his calf.

"All I can get," he said huskily. Sitting next to her, he made short work of the boots.

The instant they were off, she was back at his belt. When she was finally able to get it open and his shirt pulled from his waistband, he discovered her hands were trembling, too. He helped her push off his shirt and jacket. In a single, twisting movement he pulled the T-shirt over his head.

"Oh, look at you," she whispered, sliding her palms up the front of his chest. Within the hair that covered his body her hands looked impossibly feminine.

"I was a walking advertisement for a ninety-eight-pound weakling when I was in high school."

"A runt, hmm?"

"Yeah."

"But you grew." The satisfaction in her voice made him feel ten feet tall.

"Not until after my eighteenth birthday. Before that, I was barely taller than you."

She grinned at him. "*Was* being the operative word here. The next time there's a casting call for soap commercials, you should apply."

"And here I thought you wanted me for my mind." He reached for her, finding the clasp for her bra between her breasts. He was acutely aware of the lace brushing his knuckles as he worried the fastener open, then cupped her breasts with his hands.

"I like that, too." There was a catch in her voice and her gaze was on his hands touching her. He looked, then, discovering she was as small and delicately made as he'd suspected. Light gilded her body, searing his mind with images he'd carry with him until the day he died.

He came back for another kiss and she wrapped her arms around him, holding him as tightly as he needed to be held. Sensation replaced thought and in the next moment only one thing mattered. Having her bare. Somehow they got off her jeans and undergarments, then his.

In a haze of need and fractured memory, he ran his hand up the inside of her thigh searching for that softest skin that he'd found last night before touching her intimately. Ah, there it was, smoothest silk beneath his thumb.

She touched him on the same place and he shuddered, completely at the mercy of her tender exploration.

And higher, he brushed the curls that protected her. Even softer.

Her fingers skimmed his groin. So close. Not close enough.

His intimate touch of her silkiest flesh took him under when she quivered against his hand. Another time he was going to spend hours playing with her. But just now…

Her fingers closed around him…right there…in the way he liked best.

He kissed the nipple beneath his cheek, then pulled it into his mouth. The flesh in his hand throbbed, and his own arousal did the same against her palm.

She whimpered and fell backward on the bed, her delicate arms surprisingly strong, and she urged him closer, then closer yet. He positioned himself above her, reveling in the touch of her skin against his from thigh to chest.

Taking a deep breath, he forced himself to slow once again, taking time to frame her face with his hands and to push her hair away from her face. She smiled for him, then, and no one had ever been more beautiful.

"You're killing me, you know," she whispered.

"That's the whole idea." He lowered his body enough to tease them both with the intimate touch they each craved. This time, he wanted to watch her expression as he slid into her.

"Soon, Quinn."

Instead of complying, he kissed her and discovered the same rapture he'd had before. Then he gave her a little more of what they both so desperately wanted.

"Oh," she breathed against his mouth.

"Enough?" he teased gently.

Her eyes were nearly wild when she looked up at him. "You know it's not."

And then he sank into her the rest of the way, absorbing everything about this instant. The catch in her voice, the way her eyes dilated, the aroma of her body and their arousal. Beneath him, she felt so impossibly small.

Last night she had felt so wonderful. She felt even better now. He savored everything, noticed everything. She was soft, achingly tight, sheathing him in the most tender embrace. When he was buried to the hilt, they both stilled. She sighed as though nothing had ever felt better. He knew, because nothing had.

"You're okay?" he had to ask.

"Uh-huh," she breathed against his neck, wriggling beneath him and making him even more aware of her soft sheath hugging him so tightly he could forget to breathe.

Then she found his mouth with her own, her kiss searing him all the way to his soul. She moved that fraction of an inch that invited him to move with her.

He did, and she immediately climaxed, trembling so

greatly in his arms that he could only gather her closer, the endless kiss spiraling him ever deeper. When her spasms subsided, their pace went from languid to pounding. Like a man desperate for air, he clawed his way toward release that thundered through his body and was ever beyond reach.

She arched beneath him and he realized that she had climaxed again, her ragged breathing making him slow their pace, each stroke taking him to places he'd never been. And there it was…rushing toward that final, deep chasm where his blood roared in his ears, where all his emotions poured through him and rushed to the precipice. He fell into her, spent and empty and lost, and somehow *home* because of the amazing woman in his arms. His embrace tightened, and he decided he never wanted to be anywhere else.

Somehow he forced himself to shift to the side so he wouldn't be so heavy on her. She seemed as reluctant to give up touching him as he was, and she curled close, her hand coming to a rest on top of his thundering heart.

Wide awake, he watched the light shift inside the cabin as the sunset faded. Their breathing slowed, and he watched her watch him.

Within minutes he knew they were going to do this again, but their touches remained languid. With a finger he traced the curve of her cheek, moving from one freckle to the next, pausing now and then to kiss her. She traced the outline of his ear, then followed some imaginary line down his arm. A nonsexual touch that shouldn't have made him hard, but it did.

He pressed his lips against each of the freckles he had traced on her cheek, ending at the corner of her mouth. Her breath caught and she stilled as they both waited for him to finish the contact. Waiting was unbelievably erotic, a game he discovered that he liked. Her breath merged with his as she laced her fingers with his. As the anticipation stretched taut, she touched her tongue to the bottom of his lip, and he was gone.

Fusing his mouth to hers, he lifted her over him. Relinquishing control to her and rewarding himself with the pleasure of touching her breasts and sliding his hands across her body, she sank over him and began to move despite the shudders that racked her body and the convulsions that squeezed tightly around him.

Nothing had ever been more exciting or satisfying than the knowledge that his body gave her pleasure. Again, all thought was swept from his brain and he rode a towering wave toward completion, knowing that when it crested, he'd be lost in the undertow…he was, and somehow, it didn't seem to matter.

When the looming outline of Mike Ericksen's boathouse came into view a couple of hours later, Lily snuggled closer to Quinn, where he once again held her between the wheel and himself. "Do you want to stay the night?"

He pressed a kiss against her temple even as he shook his head. "You okay about that?"

"I have to be, huh?" She tipped her head against his shoulder so she could look at him.

"You don't want to have me in the house when your daughter gets up or ask me to sneak out before she awakens."

"You're right." The invitation had been an impulsive one, and she had to admit to herself that he was right.

The house beyond the narrow dock and the boathouse came into view. The lights were on inside. Since Rosie had said that she and Ian would bring Annmarie home, Lily wasn't surprised.

Quinn throttled down, and eased the boat toward the dock with the same skill he'd shown in everything he'd done this evening.

"I could make some coffee," she said.

"I should take Milt's boat back," he countered.

She nodded toward the house. "You're just worried about explaining to my brother-in-law why we're so late."

Quinn's eyes were bright as he gazed down at her. "I have

the feeling he knows.'' He looked toward the house, then shut off the motor, as if he'd come to some decision. ''I'll walk you to the porch.''

She put her arms around his waist. ''Or you can kiss me right here.''

He grinned. ''I can.'' And he did. ''I'll still walk you to the house.''

''Promise me one thing,'' she whispered against his mouth. When he didn't answer, she added, ''Don't tell me that I need to forget about this.''

He smiled back, but it didn't reach his eyes. ''That would be sort of like telling the tide not to come in tomorrow, wouldn't it?''

''Exactly.''

''So we'll play this out.''

As commitments went, his wasn't much of one, but she sensed it was honest.

Lily helped him tie the boat up to the dock, and they walked hand in hand to the house. Since he'd promised only to see her to the door, he surprised her when he followed her into the mudroom. Swamped with memories of last night, she squeezed his hand, then called, ''I'm home.'' She took off her jacket and hung it on one of the pegs.

When there was no answer, she called again, ''Rosie? Ian?'' Seeing movement in the living room, she headed toward the door. ''Hey, you guys.''

The man standing at the window of the living room wasn't her brother-in-law. A cold knot of fear expanded in Lily's chest and she backed up a step, coming to a stop against Quinn's reassuring presence.

Cal Springfield turned from the window. ''Do you have any idea how stupid not locking doors is, Lily?''

Lily pressed a hand against her chest. ''And you might have answered when I called instead of scaring me half to death.''   '

''What are you doing here?'' Quinn asked.

''Same as you,'' Cal said. ''Checking on Lily.''

He was dressed in a sweat suit and athletic shoes. If she had still been living in California, she would have assumed he'd been out for a run.

"As you can see, she's fine." There was no mistaking Quinn's tone for anything other than what it was—territorial.

Cal opened his mouth to answer just as Lily heard the door to the porch open.

"Mommy, guess what?" Annmarie called from the kitchen.

"In here, sweetie." She gave Cal a long look. "You've got some explaining to do. Even around here, most people don't barge in—even if the house is unlocked."

Annmarie ran into the kitchen, her face lit in a smile. "Aunt Rosie said that I get to help when the baby comes." Her smiled grew wider when she saw Quinn. "Hi, Mr. Quinn."

Behind her, Ian and Rosie followed, and Annmarie continued to chatter about the various tasks required to care for an infant.

"What are you doing here, Springfield?" Ian asked, echoing Quinn's question, adding, "I didn't see a vehicle. How did you get here?"

"I was out for my run," Cal said. "It's not that far."

"In daylight," Quinn said.

Annmarie tugged on Lily's hand. "Mom, I'm trying to tell you about all the stuff we did today."

She smiled at her daughter and from the corner of her eye watched Quinn and Ian close in on Cal much as they had this morning. Had that been only this morning?

Quinn nodded his head toward Lily. "Must have been important to make you come all the way out here."

At the same time Annmarie was saying, "We had the most fun. We made baby clothes and planted little baby trees in the greenhouse and played with little baby kittens."

Rosie caught Lily's eye and grinned. "Her very fave."

"Don't I know it." She chuckled. "Go get ready for bed now, sweetie."

Annmarie did, though she continued to dally, stopping first to give Rosie a lengthy good-night hug followed by another with Ian, then Quinn. By then, Cal had picked up his jacket from the back of the sofa and was putting it on.

"You never did tell me what was on your mind," Lily said.

"Finding your door unlocked so anyone could come in got me distracted," he said.

"I'm duly warned," she responded.

"And I'm going to Anchorage, then Juneau for a few days. I have some things to check out there."

Quinn's scowl deepened. "You walked all the way out here to tell her that?"

Cal gave him an easy smile in return. "Kill two birds with one stone—get a little exercise and see Lily, too." He glanced at his watch. "And I do need to be going."

"I'm headed that direction," Quinn said. "You walked out—you can sail back."

"I don't mind—"

"Now that it's dark, you never can tell what you might find on the road," Ian said. "Skunks or—"

"Bears?" Cal asked.

"Every now and then," Ian said blandly.

"Let's go," Quinn said, heading toward the kitchen and waiting for Cal to precede him through the door. "See you tomorrow, Lily."

"Yes."

Ian crossed the room and dropped a kiss on Lily's cheek. "Cal's advice about locking up—it's good advice, little sister."

Rosie rolled her eyes as Ian snagged her by the hand and led her toward the door.

"There he is, in protector mode, again," Rosie said. "And before I get the full scoop on your date."

Date? Lily hadn't thought of her time with Quinn as a date, but she supposed it was.

"You can talk to her tomorrow," Ian said, and then threw

over his shoulder her nearly exact words to him of this morning. "Lock up, Lily."

She followed them to the mudroom and watched through the window. Cal and Quinn were on board the powerboat; she watched as it moved away from the dock. A second later Quinn throttled up the motor and the boat sped away from the shore in a wide arc. Ian and Rosie climbed into his big pickup, and as they drove out of the driveway, he beeped the horn once.

As instructed, she locked the door. Then she felt for the house keys in the pocket of her jacket hanging in the mudroom. Locking the door was a habit so deeply ingrained, she hadn't given it up after moving back here. As a child, the doors had rarely been locked. As an adult in California it had taken only one theft to teach her the lesson that you didn't leave doors unlocked.

Her fingers closed around the keys and she tried to remember. Had she been so anxious to be on her way with Quinn that she had forgotten to lock the door? She didn't think so, but if Cal had found the door unlocked, what other explanation could there be?

Chapter 11

"Mr. Quinn, are you a husband?" asked Annmarie nearly two weeks later.

"No, I'm not." The innocent question brought Quinn's head sharply up from the clipboard on which he was making notations. Sure as he was standing here in the lab, she was going to lead him into her quagmire about babies. Just once he'd like the simple questions, like how to determine the subunit molecular weight of a protein.

She had been to work a few times with Lily this week, here this morning because Mama Sarah wasn't able to watch her until the afternoon. His time alone with Lily had been far less than either of them wanted, though they had made love again—in the back seat of his SUV.

How they got from their discussion of the pricey equipment required to maintain the barophiles—to having their hands all over each other, Quinn wasn't too sure. All he knew positively was that each time he made love with her the sex was just as hot as the first time and left him wanting more.

Since then, he reminded himself a dozen times a day not

to touch her on the back or squeeze her shoulder or wink at her or any of the other dozen proprietary gestures that would have announced to everyone that she was his woman.

His house was five minutes from the lab. He'd thought about taking her there over lunch all week. Walking her through a living room filled with weight-lifting equipment, two kayaks and a rowing machine on the way to his bedroom, however, sounded anything but seductive. A closer truth he reluctantly admitted. He didn't want her to see how sterile his house really was. She already knew too much about him.

Forcing his attention back to the work at hand, he came to halt in front of the tank of bay ghost shrimp that one of the graduate students had collected a couple of days ago.

Annmarie stopped a few feet away in front of the crab habitats. "What's the name of this purple one?"

He grinned. Maybe he'd have a reprieve, after all. "Purple shore crab."

"Not that name. The other name, you know, the science one that you and Mom always use."

"Hemigrapsus nudus."

Annmarie giggled. "Grape soup. And that's purple, huh?"

"If you say so. Personally, I've never had grape soup."

"But you could. Sometimes you have tomato juice and sometimes tomato soup. I bet that's how it works."

Quinn laughed. Another example of her free associations that expanded his world. Grape soup. It sounded terrible, like something a wizard might serve an unsuspecting apprentice. Except where Annmarie was concerned, he was often on the learning end of things, especially where her family was concerned.

A couple of days ago she had explained to him with matter-of-fact acceptance how her aunt Rosie had given birth to her and how her mommy was still her mommy and what a lucky girl that arrangement made her. Personally, he couldn't make the whole situation jibe with his own experiences. His mother had never wanted him, which she had proven in spades the day she'd left him at a park and never returned for him. Instead a cop had picked Quinn up, and the next few days had worried him to death.

Years later he had read the reports. Learned that his mother had been found near the apartment passed out drunk, and that his father had been in prison for car theft since Quinn was a toddler. He'd never heard from the man, had long since given up the fantasy that someday his dad would come looking for him.

In the beginning, there'd been supervised visits with his mother that she missed more often than not. Quinn had coped with being shuffled through a system he didn't like and didn't understand the only way he knew how—by acting like he didn't give a damn and keeping to himself. If he had ever been as secure and as open as Annmarie, he didn't remember it.

At the next display case, yet another variety of crabs inside, these brick-red, she paused and he dutifully said, *"Cancer productus."*

"I like the grape ones better." She followed Quinn across the room to where he checked the gauges for the pressurized tanks that held specimens collected from the vent site. "I asked my aunt Rosie what a munchkin is."

"Yeah."

"She says it's a special little girl. That's right, huh?"

Though Quinn felt her looking at him, he kept his gaze safely on the notations he was making from each tank. "Yep."

"And you like my mommy, too, huh?"

Like? Oh, yeah. "I do."

"I've been thinking," Annmarie said.

He had the feeling that spelled trouble, so he didn't ask what about. If she ran true to form, she'd tell him and there he'd be—flopping around like a fish caught on the beach after the tide went out.

"Uncle Ian says husbands are forever and ever, but I don't think that's right."

Husbands again. He had been a husband once—a long

time ago—and he'd been so bad at it that he didn't care to repeat the experience. Husbands weren't forever—in fact, just the opposite, at least in his world.

"And Aunt Rosie says that for mommies to have a baby— not dogs and cats, of course, just people—you have to have a husband to be the daddy."

Quinn stared hard at the numbers on the clipboard. His stomach sank toward the floor. He wanted to run right now. Kayaking over to Foster Island during a storm would be easier than facing this little girl and her plans for that baby brother or sister that she would never have. His boat was lashed to the top of his SUV—all he had to do was cut her short and leave.

"Annmarie—"

"Uncle Ian is a husband and so is Mr. Mike," she rushed on as though sensing that he was about to bolt out the door. "And Mr. Max, he's too old." She sighed. "You're just right. You could be the husband," she said. "It doesn't have to be forever. Just until there's a baby."

He could sense her looking at him, but he didn't dare meet her gaze. Nothing had ever been more terrifying than this child's simple trust. Even if she had no idea that she was asking the impossible—not only for him, but for Lily, as well.

"Mr. Quinn." Her voice was impatient. "Did you hear me?"

"I did, munchkin." He dropped to one knee so he was at eye level with her. When you couldn't avoid a situation, the best tactic was to face it head-on and get it over with. "You want a husband for your mom."

"No." She shook her head. "I want a baby brother or a baby sister. A daddy would be nice, too, but I really, *really* want a baby." She took a step closer. "So, what do you think?" Her big brown eyes were so uncertain that he wanted to gather her close and promise her anything. "Would you?"

The outright denial he had to give her stuck in his throat.

He swallowed, then said as gently as he knew how, "I was a husband once, a long time ago. I didn't do it very well."

She took another step closer. "Maybe you just have to practice. That's how I got better at riding my two-wheeler."

If only it were that simple.

As if sensing he was about to turn her down, she whispered, "It can be a secret. I won't tell Mommy. You can think about it—that's what grown-ups say. They have to think about things."

"Annmarie…" When she bit her lip to keep it from trembling, the outright no that he had to tell her became impossible. Sighing, he said, "Okay. No promises, but I'll think about it."

She grinned as if he'd given her presents, leaned forward and kissed him on the cheek, and then skipped away. "I'm going to go find Thad now."

Hilda's son had also come with Annmarie and Lily this morning. The last time Quinn had seen him, he was peering intently through the lens of a microscope.

Quinn watched Annmarie dance across the room, her pigtails bouncing. He touched his cheek, possibilities he didn't want to think about tantalizing and tormenting him. Being a husband…being a daddy…being part of a forever family. The lyrics from a song he couldn't quite remember flitted through his head—something about little girls growing up and dads who were lucky enough to be given butterfly kisses. Oh, man, was he in trouble.

Fifteen minutes later Annmarie came back through the lab, this time with Thad, who announced that he'd seen hairy monsters in the microscope that Lily had let him look through and that they were on the way to his house for lunch.

"You told your mom you were leaving, didn't you?" Quinn said to Annmarie. Lily had somehow struck a balance keeping a close eye on Annmarie and enough freedom to be a child.

"Yep," she replied. "And she said to stay on the road

and to go straight to Hilda's house.'' She grinned. ''And she said to tell you thank you for putting up with me.''

He laughed. ''Any time.''

Will glanced up from his task of cleaning beakers as Quinn came through the door, his expression vaguely like someone with his hand caught in a cookie jar. He often had that expression, come to think of it. Quinn frowned, wondering what the guy was up to his time.

''I thought you were supposed to be helping Patrick or Max this morning,'' he said.

Will shrugged. ''Max said he could handle things alone.''

''Where's Patrick?''

Will shrugged again. ''Like I would know.''

After the incident on the boat, the friendship between Will and Patrick had dissolved into an uneasy truce. Will did just enough to get by, and Patrick was preoccupied. The two of them were beginning to drive Quinn crazy.

Lily was on the phone, a conversation that let Mama Sarah know the kids were on their way. Given Lily's protectiveness about her daughter, Quinn wouldn't have been surprised if she had been determined to walk down the hill with the kids. She glanced up and the smile she gave him was the friendly one she gave everyone at work. If there were rumors about any involvement between them—and he suspected there were based on his experience with small towns—nothing in her behavior was the cause. He told himself he was relieved about that even as Annmarie's heartfelt request tightened his chest.

Being a husband to Lily…no way did he want to go there. A guy like Saint John—as Quinn had begun thinking of her dead husband—that's the kind of man she needed. As long as Quinn kept telling himself that, he could avoid admitting the idea of spending his life with her sounded great. A fairy tale that would never come true, a fantasy.

And then the thought of someone else touching that soft, warm skin on the inside of her thigh flashed through him, followed by an even stronger surge of jealousy. He bit back a curse and found himself glaring at Will.

"The big pressure tank closest to the door has had some strange readings this morning," Quinn said to him, handing over the clipboard that he'd nearly forgotten was tucked under his arm. "I want hourly readings the rest of the day."

"Okay."

When Will just stood there, Quinn added, "Start now."

Without a word, Will ambled toward the door, shaking his head as he went.

"Everything okay?" Lily asked.

"Fine." Nothing was, Quinn decided. Not the slow pace of the repairs on the submersible, not the decision he'd made to hire Will, and certainly not this urge he had to get Lily naked and tucked beneath him every time he saw her.

"Fine, hmm?"

Something in her voice made him look more closely at her. She waited until the door had closed behind Will, then smiled and crooked her finger at him in a "come here" gesture.

He didn't dare—not while she had that particular expression on her face.

She slipped off the stool and came toward him. The white lab coat mostly hid another of those sheer blouses she liked—this one pink, buttoned to her throat, and making her skin glow. She didn't stop until she stood a breath away from him, and then she took both of his hands within her much smaller ones.

The flirtatious smile became a more genuine one. "You don't have to tell me things are fine when they aren't." The smile widened a fraction. "Even for me, the eternal optimist."

"Things are fine," he insisted.

She squeezed his hands. "Now they are." She gazed up at him. "You have only one thing left to do."

"What's that?" He realized he didn't care. She could ask anything of him.

"Kiss me, then go take care of whatever it is that has you so preoccupied."

He could hardly tell her she was the reason for his pre-occupation, so he did the only thing possible. Lowering his head, he brushed her lips with his own, then kissed her as she had requested, savoring the lush heat of her mouth. She held on to his hands as though they were a lifeline. For him, that touch was… It kept him anchored to the kiss—a simple kiss, though Lord knew there was nothing simple about this one.

Gradually, it ended, and her smile was brilliant when he lifted her head. "My mom always said, 'Kiss it and make it better.' She was right."

Better so long as he didn't count the uncomfortable fit of his jeans. "You're going to be the death of me."

She let go of his hands and took a step away. "Go away now, or I won't be able to concentrate."

Quinn laughed. She wasn't the only one. He turned on his heel, deciding that he'd check on Max and the progress on the submersible's repairs. As he came through the front offices, the main door opened and Cal Springfield came through.

Quinn had heard he was back from Anchorage, and based on the brand-new jeans and waterproof slicker he wore, he'd evidently done some shopping while he was there. The guy had "cop" written all over him, which made Quinn wonder why he'd ever believed the story that he'd worked with Lily.

"What's up, Springfield?" Quinn asked by way of greeting. According to the gossip at the Tin Cup, he was hunting someone on the FBI's Most Wanted list. Evidently he had given up the lie he had told Quinn the night he had arrived in Lynx Point. Helping to catch a criminal was one thing. Ratting on your neighbor was something else—and by breakfast time this morning, Springfield had managed to erode any support he might have had from nearly everyone.

"I'm trying to find that handyman of yours." Cal flicked his thumb against a folded sheet of paper that he took out of his pocket. "There's a mistake on his social security number."

"Yeah?" If there was, it was undoubtedly some glitch with the accounting department in Anchorage.

"Yeah." Cal dropped into a chair next to Quinn's desk even though Quinn had remained standing. "Things are quiet around here this morning."

Quinn made a point of glancing at his watch, hoping the man would take the hint and leave. "Personally, I like it that way. Makes it easier to get things done."

"If you say so." He put the sheet of paper back in an inside pocket of his windbreaker, folded his arms across his chest, and stretched out his legs.

Quinn took a couple of steps toward the door. "Anything else you need? I'm kind of busy here."

"No. Just thinking."

Quinn raised an eyebrow. "You need to be here to do that?"

Cal grinned. "You're a little testy this morning, Morrison. Relax." He shoved out of the chair. "Just wondering where your handyman would be, since he's not at home and I haven't found him around here."

"The island isn't that big. He'll turn up." Quinn supposed he could guide Springfield toward the workshop where Max was probably hard at work. But he didn't.

"He'd better," Cal said, heading for the door. "I've got a few things to ask him."

"Hope it goes well for you." Quinn shook off the irritation Springfield always raised. Quinn wasn't adverse to him checking people out if that would keep Lily out of harm's way. That night Springfield had ridden with Quinn back to the marina on Milt's boat, he had made a big point of that— Lily's safety was his only concern.

Max was right where Quinn had expected to find him, in the large heated workshop that had double doors opening out to the driveway behind the center. As usual, Max had on a radio, classical music playing loud enough that it could be heard outside the room. From the looks of things, he had made a lot of progress on those final few repairs since Quinn had checked earlier in the morning.

"Springfield catch up with you?" Quinn asked.

"You mean the U.S. Marshal who's been asking questions all over town?" When Quinn nodded, he added, "Haven't had the pleasure of meeting the man."

Quinn grinned. "And you'd like to keep it that way."

"Heard he's a pain in the butt, so what do you think?" Max looked up from his task long enough to grin. He was installing a new headlight on the submersible, the final thing required to complete the repairs. Since the light was housed behind a pressure shield, the installation wasn't as quick and simple as it might have been. He had his tools laid out on a cloth in precise order, and screws and other parts neatly set alongside.

"It will sure be something to see this baby in the water," Max said as Quinn stepped up to help him, handing over a screwdriver.

"I keep hoping. It seems like everything that could go wrong has, and I sure never figured I'd have it for three weeks without ever having it in the water."

"This weekend, maybe."

"If the tech from N.O.A.A. gets here in time to inspect our repairs," Quinn said.

After another twenty minutes Max had finished and he and Quinn had moved onto the checklist of things to test.

Someone cried out. At first, Quinn thought the voice was one within the opera playing on the radio. A second later Thad burst through the connecting door to the lab yelling Quinn's name. The kid's face was flushed, his eyes frightened.

"Gotta come quick," he said between gulping breaths as he came to a skidding halt in front of Quinn. "Annmarie is trapped."

"Where?" Quinn demanded, following Thad to the exterior door on the other side of the lab, Max right behind them.

"The Hollywood Bowl."

Quinn's blood froze. How the hell had the kids gotten from the safety of the road clear down the beach to the old collapsed mine shaft? It was no place for a couple of young kids. And the tide was coming in.

Thad pulled on his hand. "We've got to hurry."

Quinn grabbed him by the shoulders. "Go tell Lily—"

"She told me to come get you." Thad waved toward the hillside that lead to the beach. "She's on her way and said she'd meet you there."

Of course she was already on her way. Images of her being battered by the surf raced with chilling clarity through Quinn's head. He had to get there first.

"Be faster if we drove," Max said. "What do you need?"

"Hell if I even know." The tide was supposed to be high today. Since there was another storm headed in, the surf would be huge. Assessing possibilities, Quinn took his keys out of his pocket and headed for his vehicle. "You coming?"

"If you need an extra pair of hands—"

"Let's go." Quinn ran toward his SUV, figuring it was a piece of luck that he planned to paddle over to Foster Island later in the day. His kayak was tied to the roof the vehicle. Thad and Max climbed inside.

"What the hell were you two doing there?" Quinn asked Thad. "I thought you were on your way to your house."

"We were," Thad said, a quiver in his voice. "We were near Old Lady Harrison's house, and a guy said that he'd seen a black-and-white cat down here."

"Annmarie's isn't the only black-and-white cat."

"He said it looked like hers."

"He?" Quinn glanced from the road to the boy. "Who?"

Thad squirmed. "I dunno. A guy I've seen before."

"What happened next?"

"I told Annmarie 'no way,' but she started to cry, so I told her we'd go look. We got down there, and we could see the cat. And it *was* Sweetie Pie."

"And you went in to get her." Of course they had, Quinn thought. Annmarie loved that animal.

"Where'd you leave Annmarie?" Max asked, giving voice to Quinn's question.

"We climbed up. You know, that place that looks like stairs at the very, very back?"

Quinn knew the place. The "stairs" were rotted timbers that had once supported the walls and ceiling of one of the shafts. Who knew when the next tide would yank them loose? Annmarie would be out of the water...temporarily.

At the bottom of the hill where the road forked to the village or toward the beach, Quinn brought the vehicle to a skidding stop. "Go get your mother and any other help she can round up," he said, lifting Thad out of the vehicle.

Thad nodded his understanding and took off at a run, and Quinn jumped back in the vehicle. He put the vehicle into four-wheel drive and left the road, maneuvering around the boulders. Already his focus was on the best approach into the cave. If he was lucky, he could wade in, retrieve Annmarie and be back out before Lily showed up. If he wasn't, he'd have to go in on the kayak. He mentally rehearsed the entry into the cave, moving through the churning surf between huge boulders that stood like sentries at the entrance.

The short drive took forever to him. He knew this was faster than running here but every second seemed liked ten, every foot like a hundred. The breakers at the beach seemed bigger than ever today. Lily was nowhere to be seen. He could only pray they were far ahead of her.

"I've only been down here once," Max was saying. "And it's sure no place for a couple of little kids."

"You got that right." All for a damn cat.

Quinn went as far as he dared with the vehicle, leaving it parked above the high-water line. From where they were they could see the wide opening of the cave, and each wave brought a huge swoosh of water that came in then sucked back out.

The water was too deep, too treacherous to make his way into the cave on foot. He looked back up the hill for Lily.

"She should be along any minute," Quinn said as he began unfastening his kayak from the top of the SUV.

Without a word, Max helped him pull the boat off the vehicle. He carried it toward the waterline while Quinn put on a waterproof jacket, his life vest, and the kayak skirt that slipped over his shoulders and fastened like overalls. Slapping the helmet on his head, he grabbed the oar and followed Max.

"You make sure Lily stays here," Quinn said over the roar of the surf.

Max nodded his understanding.

Within seconds Quinn was in the water and securely fastened in, thanks to Max's surprisingly expert help. Quinn paddled into the surf, using the swells and the breakers to carry him out far enough to make the turn and come back in toward the cave. When he made the turn and headed in, each crash of the surf against the walls looked huge to him.

He tracked through the sentry boulders and focused his attention on the back of the cave. To his complete dismay, Lily had beat him here. She was standing in waist-deep water and holding Annmarie on one of the timbers above her head.

Waves battered Lily's legs. The surf swept out and left her in less than a foot of water, but he could see that she had climbed up three or four feet from the floor of the cave. The surf crashed back in and swept Quinn toward them. The wave reached Lily's chest before it receded. The next breaker or the next, and she'd lose her balance.

He'd never been as scared. He called her name. She was soaked, and the sweater she'd thrown on would do nothing to keep her warm.

She glanced over her shoulder, her eyes dark, frightened. Her skin had about as much color as salt.

"Mr. Quinn!" Annmarie called.

"Hey, munchkin," Quinn called, hoping that he sounded

more reassuring than he felt. "You doing okay?" he asked Lily, somehow holding the boat still.

She nodded.

There was no way to get Lily and Annmarie out of the cave at the same time. The knot in his stomach grew tighter.

"Annmarie, can you hang on a little while longer by yourself?" Quinn asked. He didn't like leaving the child here, but she could climb up a little higher. She, at least, was dry.

Lily sent him a fierce look over her shoulder. "I'm not leaving her in here."

"The water is getting higher by the second, Lily. I can't get you both out at the same time." He didn't add that hypothermia scared him as much as the prospect of drowning.

"Annmarie first."

Quinn shook his head. "Lily—"

"I can climb up higher." With her free hand she gestured toward the narrow ledge where Annmarie perched.

"Okay," he agreed after deciding they had no other option. When the next wave ebbed, he rammed the paddle into a crack between two of the timbers, which gave Lily something to hang on to as she scrambled beyond the water's reach. Shivering, she reached down and helped Quinn pull the paddle free.

"That was a stupid stunt," she said to him. "What if it had broken off?"

"It didn't, so don't think about it."

Quinn stripped off his life vest and handed it to Lily. She took it and started to fasten it around Annmarie.

"No," he said fiercely. "If I don't get back here as fast as I'd like, you're going to need that."

Lily had one concern only: her daughter's safety.

"Put it on, damn it, Lily." A muscle ticked in Quinn's jaw. "I'm not leaving here until you do."

"You're taking Annmarie—"

"And you're wearing the damn vest if I have to get out of this boat and put it on you."

It was a threat he couldn't carry through, but given the

terrible risk he'd taken with the oar to get her above the water, she had the awful feeling that he'd try.

"Anybody ever tell you that you're a hardheaded man?" With shaking fingers she stripped off the sodden sweater that clung like slime to the sheer fabric of her blouse, then put on the life vest. It was miles too big for her, but it was warmer by far than the sweater and still held Quinn's body heat. She pulled the zipper to her chin, then glared at him, her imagination kicking into overdrive on a dozen horrible outcomes because she had the vest instead of Quinn. "Happy?"

"Not even close, darlin'." His attention shifted to Annmarie. "When I say go, you're gonna jump into my arms."

She opened her jacket and Sweetie Pie poked her head out. Quinn swore.

"What if I drop Sweetie Pie?"

Quinn extended his arm. "Hand her down."

She did, and the cat made the transfer with all four legs and claws extended, announcing her displeasure with an unhappy yowl. Quinn slipped the cat beneath the skirt around the opening of the kayak.

He glanced back at the wave, and Lily could see he was watching for that moment when it would lift him higher toward her and her daughter.

"Now!" he commanded. "Jump, Annmarie."

She did while Lily's heart stopped beating.

Quinn's arms closed securely around Annmarie. With no fuss he settled Annmarie in front of him and fastened the top of the skirt back up, cinching Annmarie close to his body and sealing the boat. Then he took off his helmet and put it on her.

He looked back at Lily, his hair plastered against his head and his dark eyes intent. "I won't let anything happen to her. I promise."

Lily believed him. "I know."

He glanced at the timbers above Lily. "You climb up another four or five feet."

"Get going," she countered.

"Now, Lily," he said. "I need to know that you're beyond the water's reach until I get back."

Acutely aware of him watching her, she did as he asked, the wood feeling sticky beneath her hands, the smell of seawater and creosote clogging her throat. She reached a perch wide enough to sit on, and looked back at Quinn.

He winked. "Stay put, darlin'. I'll be quick as I can."

Lily wished she felt as confident as he sounded. Now that she was out of the water, the surf seemed even more huge.

He turned the boat around, every move demonstrating strength, finesse and his confidence in his ability. His attention focused on the incoming breakers, and as soon as the next one hit the wall, he paddled toward the opening of the cave, the water carrying the kayak away at a dizzying speed.

Scared as Lily was, she deeply inhaled her first real breath in what seemed like hours. Quinn had Annmarie, and they were on their way to safety. That was the important thing.

The next breaker broke against the cave wall and showered her in spray that felt as cold as the fear coiled in her stomach. All she had to do was to stay put and wait.

The next set of swells beyond the cave opening took on gargantuan proportions. She could see that despite Quinn's strength and skill, he was fighting to get beyond the surf into deeper water. Strange that they'd be safer farther away from the shore, but she knew that they were.

Finally they were out far enough that Quinn made the turn toward Lynx Point. Too soon he vanished from sight. To pass the time she counted the breakers, each one a little higher than the last. Beyond the cave, what little of the water Lily could see was marked by rank after rank of whitecaps. The sky grew darker—undoubtedly rain was on the way. Just what they didn't need today. The churning water was so noisy she couldn't hear anything else, and her world was reduced to her worry and her view of the ocean beyond the mouth of the cave. The surf pounded against the timbers beneath her, and the old wood quivered and groaned, the sounds too human for comfort. With each creak of surf against old wood her fear grew.

A fear that made her want to scream when another boat finally appeared beyond the opening of the cave...and it wasn't Quinn. Where was he? Dear God, was her daughter okay?

Chapter 12

Two men were paddling the kayak, Lily realized. This one was a sit-on-top inflatable and it resembled a canoe. As the craft drew closer, she recognized Max. The man with him was Dwight Jones—the geologist who worked for Anorak Exploration, a man she knew only casually.

They rode the incoming breaker into the cave, both of them paddling like mad and working together to avoid the huge rocks at the opening of the cave. She watched the water as it shot to the right, then tipped on itself to the left, all in a rush of foam that in the next instant would spray over her. It did, the drops of water feeling like needles. Now that she looked more closely at the water swirling within the cave, she realized it was deeper and a lot more turbulent than it had been when Quinn was here.

"Heard you called for a taxi," Max shouted over the roar of the surf.

She appreciated the attempt to reassure her, but she had only one thought. "Where's Quinn? Is he okay?"

"He and your daughter are fine," he said. "Dwight

showed up with another kayak, so we got a head start on getting you out of here. It looked to us like the tide was coming up fast, and there's a storm squall on the way.''

"And, if I know Morrison, he's probably on his way back.'' Dwight paddled much as Quinn had, doing his best to hold the craft steady as the wave receded. She wasn't at all sure how she was going to manage to get into the boat without capsizing it.

"Since you're already wet," Dwight said as she crept down the rotted timbers, "it will be safest if you get about level with the boat, then let us haul you onboard." He motioned with his hand, "Catch on to the grab loop right here."

Humiliating as being hauled anywhere sounded, she knew he was right. She climbed down, until the waves were once again around her feet. However cold she had been before was nothing compared to the water swirling around her legs. Another wave broke against the back of the cave, and at once, she was in water up to her chest. She reached for the boat, and the receding wave swept her toward it.

She made a grab for the inflated hull and missed.

"I've got you." Max grabbed her arm. Somehow he and Dwight pulled her aboard, the boat pitching this way and that. She grazed her cheek along the rough surface of the inflated hull. Now that she was in the boat, it no longer seemed like such a good idea. But then, neither was staying in the cave. Especially with a storm on the way, which would only make the surf more turbulent, the tide even higher.

"You okay?" Dwight asked.

She nodded and he gave her a reassuring grin.

"Okay. We're outta here."

The boat lurched against another wave, and Lily reached for something—anything—to hang on to. She caught a grab loop.

Max and Dwight fought through the unpredictable currents. Wild as their paddling looked, she instantly realized they weren't a bad team. Surprisingly, Max's finesse nearly matched Dwight's. One more thing in the man's surprising repertoire of skills. But it wasn't easy. With each twist of the boat she was sure they were an instant away from a disaster.

As if responding to her fear, the kayak careened across the surf toward one of the huge boulders at the front of the cave. Lily had never felt more helpless, and she bit back a cry. Max and Dwight paddled hard. At the last possible instant, the boat swerved and somehow missed slamming into the boulder.

The kayak slid through the water in the opposite direction, the roar of the ocean loud around her, the water spraying across them. Each second stretched into endless minutes as the surf churned this way, then that like a roller coaster gone mad. Hard as Max and Dwight worked, they had too little control over the boat, and Lily was sure in the next second…or the next…they'd overturn and be dumped into the water where they would be pounded against the unforgiving rocks.

She looked up in time to see a huge swell rush toward them. It crested and charged, a mythic beast with wide-open jaws. The bitterly cold wave crashed over the top of them, and the boat floundered.

One instant Max was in front of her. The next he was gone. Simply gone. Lily screamed. The front of the boat went up and up and up; she was sure it would flip back on itself.

Somehow, though, they rode over the crest, and dropped with dizzying speed into the trough at the bottom of the wave. Out of the corner of her eye, Lily saw the oar Max had been holding pop to the surface. She leaned out of the boat, her coordination leaden, and grabbed for it. To her enormous surprise, she actually caught it.

She knew less than zero about paddling a kayak, but she scrambled into the spot where Max had sat, and then paddle she did, all the while looking for Max. Then she saw him, swimming yards away from where they were. His movements were awkward. She began mentally counting the seconds they had to get him out of the water before hypothermia set in.

Despite her efforts and Dwight's greater strength and skill, they made no headway toward Max. Incoming waves once again pushed them back toward the shoreline. Her fear for Max grew with every stroke she took.

Through the pounding surf, Quinn came into view, paddling his kayak for all he was worth. He headed for Max and threw a rescue bag. Max made a grab for it and managed to slip an arm through one of the loops. Quinn hauled in the line.

Lily could hear Quinn and Dwight shouting at each other, but over the roar of the ocean, she couldn't make out what they were saying. With each paddle her arms hurt more. Max was clearly in trouble. Eventually, Quinn pulled him close to his boat.

"He's got a broken arm," Quinn shouted to them. Then to Lily, "Rest a minute."

She braced the paddle across the middle of the boat and took in a huge gasp of air. Dwight and Quinn shouted back and forth to each other and decided that their best chance was to get Max back on the kayak with her and Dwight.

The process of getting Max on board was even scarier to Lily than her getting into the boat. As soon as Max rested against the hull, the boat leaned in that direction. With sheer brute strength Dwight hauled him up while Quinn held the two boats steady. Even as Max tried to help them by throwing his leg over the hull, lines of pain bracketed his mouth. Lily threw her weight to the other side of the boat, but even then it tipped over and over… At last he was in; he collapsed in the middle of the boat. Then they were on their way again.

At one point they seemed miles from the shore, and she was sure they'd never arrive. Time blurred after that, and suddenly they were riding the incoming current, which seemed far too fast to safely make the shore. Ahead, half a dozen people converged toward them. Dwight threw the tow line toward the shore, and at once willing hands pulled them in.

Lily's throat clogged and tears burned her eyes. As if by magic, Hilda was there reaching for her.

Lily nudged her friend's arm. ''No, take care of Max. He's been hurt.''

Hilda gave her shoulder a reassuring squeeze. From the corner of her eye, Lily watched as Dwight and Hilda half carried Max out of the boat, his feet barely touching the ground as they hurried him above the high-tide line. Soon, Lily thought, very soon, she'd get out of the kayak when she had energy to stand. All she wanted, though, was to lie down and sleep. A little nap, and then she'd feel better.

''Had enough excitement for one day?'' came Quinn's voice, as if in a dream. She felt herself lifted out of the kayak and held securely against his surprisingly warm body. He couldn't be carrying her—the man had paddled to hell and back. He should be taking care of Annmarie—

''Where's my daughter?''

''In my car.''

Lily twisted in Quinn's arms, looking for his vehicle. When she saw through the window that Annmarie was sitting in the back seat with Thad, her relief was so great that tears sprang to her eyes, and her breath caught on a sob.

The sob erupted into a wail, and she clung to Quinn while the fear poured out of her. What if she had lost her daughter? It had nearly killed her when John died, and she had only loved him with all her heart. But Annmarie was her very life. To lose her daughter…she couldn't bear that.

Lily relived those moments when she had run headlong down the steep hill, fear keeping pace with every single step. Her heart had nearly stopped when she'd reached the cave and saw how close the water was to Annmarie. Lily hadn't cried then, but the torrent of tears now had no end. She held on to Quinn, crying as she never had before. The storm spent itself little by little, and she realized that Quinn was cradling her close, his cheek pressed tightly against hers.

A final shuddering sigh racked through her and she absorbed that his face was wet—whether from the water or her tears or...

She leaned back far enough to look at him.

He smiled down at her, but the look in his eyes was kind, fathomless, gentle...and he softly said, "So you're the kind of girl who's a rock during a crisis and turns into pudding when it's all over."

"I guess I am." She hadn't known that about herself until about a year ago, but then, she'd had no one to hold her.

"Annmarie is okay, darlin'." He shifted Lily in his arms so he could open the door. "Hey, munchkin." He set Lily on the seat.

"Mommy." Annmarie was wrapped inside a blanket.

"Your upholstery is going to be soaked," Lily said to Quinn.

"Screw the upholstery."

Lily turned on the seat so she could see her daughter's precious face. Annmarie held Sweetie Pie in one arm. With her other hand she held Thad's, whose regard was even more serious than Annmarie's. She might not realize how serious all this had been, but Thad probably did.

Lily didn't even realize Quinn had stepped away until he was back, pulling at the zipper for the life vest and slipping it off, then folding a thick blanket around her.

"Mom, can we—Thad and me—"

Lily turned around to look at her daughter. Annmarie's chin quivered and tears rolled down her cheeks. She handed Thad her kitty, then scrambled over the seat and threw her arms around Lily. Once again crying, Lily held her daughter, fear and relief and thanksgiving all wrapped up together.

Lily pulled the blanket more firmly around the two of them, and Annmarie burrowed closer, her tears gradually subsiding. Lily watched Quinn outside the car as he stripped out of his waterproof gear, Gortex pants and a blousy over-shirt that had kept him mostly dry.

Her gaze strayed across the shoreline, which was still filled with activity. A couple of people were carrying Max on a stretcher toward one of the other vehicles. Dwight and another guy were headed in their direction, carrying Quinn's kayak.

Quinn came back to the open door and briskly rubbed up and down her arms and back as though the blanket was a towel. Then she became aware that the engine was running and heat was blowing full-blast out of the vents. Oddly enough, a chill coursed through Lily's body, and she admitted she was colder—far colder—than she had been earlier. The only place she was warm was where Annmarie was cuddled next to her.

"That's my girl," Quinn murmured as Lily began to shiver. "You're warming up."

"That's not what it feels like," she said, her teeth chattering. Far preferable was the sleepy lassitude than these shivers that made her feel as though she might shake out of her own skin.

Someone thrust an insulated cup into her hands, the scent of the coffee heavenly, the warm liquid feeling good as it went down.

Dwight Jones set the kayak on the ground near the car and came to peer inside at her and the kids.

"You did great out there," he said. "If I ever need a new paddle partner, you're my first choice."

"Pull the other leg," she replied between shivers. "Thanks for coming to get me."

"No thanks needed." He slapped Quinn on the shoulder. "Want your baby lashed back to the roof?"

Quinn nodded. "I'll give you a hand."

Lily brought the blanket more closely around herself and watched Quinn through the windshield. He handled the kayak with such ease, she was sure that he'd lifted it on top of his car many times. When he and Dwight were finished, they both leaned against the driver's side fender, facing the surf.

"Her bad luck keeps piling up," Dwight said, the breeze carrying his voice easily inside the car.

"Yep," Quinn replied.

''First there was the accident with the car and then that whole thing with the boat. Somebody lured those kids down here, Morrison. It's a damn lucky thing somebody didn't get killed today.''

''I've been thinking the same thing,'' Quinn said after moment, his answer slicing through her.

This thing today had been deliberate? A faceless man setting an irresistible trap for her daughter? Lily sorted through the possibilities, and only one made sense. Her daughter had been bait to lure Lily into the cave. If the incoming tide had been a little higher, if Quinn hadn't arrived so quickly, if his skill with a kayak had been less, if she had lost her balance…

She began to tremble. She'd had the stupid idea that she would recognize if a villain was after her and Annmarie. Only she hadn't. If Franklin Lawrence wanted her dead, and if he wanted to make sure no fingers were pointed his direction, it had to come in the form of an accident. And what better accident that being killed by a runaway car or drowning while trying to rescue her daughter.

In that moment, she could have swept down like an avenging angel herself and taken his life. Certainty flowed through her that as long as Franklin Lawrence was after her, the people she loved would never be safe.

The only way to make them safe…was to leave them.

Lily bit back a sob, and Cal's voice echoed through her head as she remembered him telling her how it would have to be when she went into the witness security program—and from the beginning he had been so sure that sooner or later she would do it. No goodbyes. No out-of-the-ordinary phone calls or conversations. No one could suspect she was leaving. No one could know when or how she'd leave to enter her new life.

Could she do it? Lily wondered. Always looking over her shoulder, always worried about her little girl, always afraid the next stranger might be the one sent to kill her. She shuddered and her arm tightened around Annmarie, who curled more closely into her.

Could she deny her daughter all the family who loved her? Lily knew losing them both would kill her parents, would devastate Rosie. What right did Lily have to take her daughter away from Rosie?

Tears seeped from under Lily's eyelids as she concluded there was only one thing to do. Protect her daughter, who would eventually recover from losing her mother…just as long as she had aunts and grandparents and cousins who would all love her and take care of her. The pain of losing a mother would scar, Lily knew that it would. Better a scar, though, than the open festering wound they'd have if Lily took her daughter into a new life where they'd always wonder if they had been found out. How could Lily take Annmarie away from everything familiar to her? Because she'd remember Rosie and Ian and her grandparents and Dahlia and Jack. And Annmarie wouldn't understand.

Lily bit back a sob, sure this was the right choice, but sure of something else, as well. No matter where the witness security program settled her, no matter her new job, her new life, she'd never again be fully alive.

"Hey, girlfriend," came Hilda's voice from the open door.

Lily opened her eyes, and she lost sight of her best friend beneath the stream of tears.

Without a word, Hilda leaned into the cab and enveloped Lily in a hug. One more loss. They had been best friends since they were seven and had been thrilled when they learned they were cousins. That had made Hilda as much her sister as Rosie or Dahlia.

"You're safe," Hilda was saying. "You're going to be okay. Annmarie is okay. You made it."

Lily leaned back far enough to meet Hilda's concerned gaze. "Find Cal Springfield, okay? I need to see him."

"All right."

Quinn joined Hilda at the car door and Lily saw that Dwight was walking away. Lily wiped her tears and tried to smile when Quinn ducked down to look at her.

"You want me to take Lily to the clinic?" he asked Hilda.

Lily met Hilda's gaze. "We don't need to do that."

"You've got a scrape on your cheek," Hilda said. "Did you hit your head?"

"No."

"Are you hurt anywhere?"

Lily shook her head. "I'm cold and I want to go home."

"Then go home," Hilda advised, opening the back door and helping her son out of the car. She glanced at Quinn. "Just keep an eye on her. She got pretty chilled out there today."

"More than she's willing to admit," Quinn said.

"I'm warmer now, honestly," Lily said, another rack of shivers coming in the middle of her defense. *Normal.* Good God, somehow she had to figure out how to act as though nothing was wrong until the plans were made.

Old cautions from when Cal had first approached her echoed through her head. *Until the second you're in a U.S. Marshal's custody, you go about your life and make plans for tonight, tomorrow, next year.*

"Like I said." Quinn's gaze rested on her.

"Nothing to be done except getting her warm," Hilda said. "Rosie and Ian are in San Francisco, so there's nobody else."

"Consider it done."

"I can't impose on him like that," Lily said to Hilda as another thought slammed through her. Would she ever see Rosie again?

Hilda grinned. "Then talk to the man, girl, not me. Unless you really want to spend the night with my brood."

Lily shook her head, and Hilda's smile grew wider.

"So, let him take care of you." Hilda stepped back from the car and closed the door. Through the window, she waved at Lily.

Quinn slid behind the steering wheel. "Ready to go home?"

"I am," Annmarie said.

"I don't have my keys," Lily said.

"Then we'll go get them." Quinn put the car in gear. "Second honeymoon for your sister?"

"You mean, because of the trip to San Francisco?" Lily shook her head. "They went back to finish moving out of Ian's house."

Quinn brought the car to a stop in front of the research center. Annmarie handed the cat over to Lily and insisted on going with Quinn when they went inside to get her purse. She watched them go, a worry eating away at the edge of her mind. How could she act as if everything was okay when her nerves were scraped raw?

Quinn and Annmarie reappeared at the front door, and the two of them came down the walkway toward the car hand in hand. As usual, Annmarie seemed to be chattering up a storm, and Quinn appeared to be listening intently.

When they got back in the car, he said, "One more stop."

"Where are we going?" Annmarie asked.

"My house. I'd like to get into some dry clothes."

"Good idea," the child agreed.

A couple of minutes later Quinn parked the SUV in a driveway next to a small modular house. "Want to come in?"

"Yes," Lily said. It wasn't that much farther to home, but she needed to go to the bathroom. She and Annmarie followed Quinn to the door. He held it open as they went inside.

She wasn't at all sure what she had expected from his house, so the living room contents were both a reflection of the man and a surprise. No couch, no television. There was exercise equipment, and a kayak—smaller than the one he'd used today—rested against one wall. She peered into the kitchen and decided the man must eat while standing up because there were no chairs, much less a table.

"Be back in a minute," he said, heading for the bedroom. The instant before he closed the door, Lily caught sight of a king-size bed, which was unmade.

"He sure does have a lot of stuff," Annmarie said, looking

around the living room. "But there's no place to sit, is there?"

"Not that I can see." Lily headed for the bathroom, which was cluttered but clean. The aromas she associated with him were stronger here—soap and shaving cream. The towels might have been white at one time, but were the color of gray that suggested they had been washed with blue jeans and dark socks. Utilitarian and no fuss—as she had discovered the man to be.

Exhausted as she was, the remembered sensation of him moving inside her came with the aroma of his toiletries. Remembered sensation…and remembered want. Tears threatened again. She had wanted this new relationship so badly, and as it turned out, she'd be abandoning him just the way everyone else in his life had. That thought nearly sent her to her knees.

When she came out of the bathroom, Quinn and Annmarie were waiting for her. He'd changed his clothes. Another pair of jeans, another dark flannel shirt that made his shoulders look impossibly broad. The attire made her smile.

"What's funny?" he wanted to know.

"You," she said with a gentle wave that encompassed both him and the living room. "You're such a bachelor."

"I suppose there's a point to this."

"No real point," she said, heading toward the door and trying to memorize everything about it so she'd have it all to remember later.

Quinn held open the SUV doors and waited until both Lily and Annmarie were inside before he closed them. When they were under way again, he squeezed Lily's hand. "The Ericksens wouldn't happen to have a hot tub in that fancy house of theirs?"

Lily shook her head. "No hot tub. But a nice, deep, old-fashioned soaking tub."

"You'll feel better after a bath."

"And dinner," Annmarie said from the back seat. "I'm hungry, and so is Sweetie Pie. Then we can watch videos."

"No videos tonight," Lily said.

"Mom." Annmarie's voice had gone from subdued to whiny.

Lily turned around and caught her daughter's glance. "Cool it. You don't want me counting to ten. Not now."

Annmarie squirmed on the seat and her glance fell away. Lily caught Quinn winking at her daughter.

"Don't you encourage her, either," she said. *Normal,* she reminded herself.

They fell silent until they arrived at home. Lily fished her keys out of her purse and handed them to Quinn.

When she stepped out of the car, her legs felt like rubber. She was grateful for his steadying arm. She savored his touch and had the fleeting thought that maybe this was what it was like when you knew you were dying. Each moment, each touch, each word, became memorable.

As if sensing how close to the end of her reserves she was, he whispered against her ear, "Hang on, darlin'. We're almost there."

The next few minutes blurred together as Lily allowed herself to be steered toward the master bedroom. Annmarie chattered away, helping Quinn find bubble bath and open the faucets on the huge tub. All the while, Lily stood there, feeling more bemused by the two of them by the second.

"Mom likes candles," Annmarie said as the tub began filling. She opened a drawer. "The matches are in there. I'm not allowed to light them, did you know that?"

He took the small box from her. "That sounds about right." He dutifully lit the candle that sat on the tile-covered shelf above the tub. "I guess all that's left for us to do is to leave your mom alone and go find some dry clothes for you."

Annmarie glanced down at herself. "Okay. Then I think we should make dinner." She peered up at him. "Can you cook?"

The seriousness of her question made Lily laugh. Quinn shot her a dirty look. "Yes, I can cook." He glanced down at Annmarie. "I bet your cat is hungry. She's had a busy day."

"That's my job, feeding Sweetie Pie."

Quinn winked at her. "Then you'd better get to it."

When Annmarie skipped away, he said, "I'm a little worried about leaving you in here alone. Once you get warm, you'll probably fall asleep." He came a step closer. "If I stay here like I want, I'm going to have the most ungentlemanly thoughts."

"You are, hmm?"

He lifted his hands as if to unbutton her blouse, then dropped them. "I am." He took a step backward. "I'll send your daughter back in a minute."

"You're running again," she teased even though she knew having him stay wasn't a good idea. She was tired…but not *that* tired. Tired enough her judgment was seriously addled, though, as she remembered her daughter.

"With reason," he said. Quinn turned on his heel and closed the door behind him as he left. He leaned against the door a second, too aware of Lily taking off her clothes on the other side of that door.

Though thinking about her all naked made him erect, he was mostly concerned that she was okay. Judging by the abrasion on her cheek, she had hit her head somewhere along the way. Since he was likely to be sore from the day's activities, he could only imagine what it would be like for Lily.

He found Annmarie in the kitchen. She was sitting on the floor next to the cat, who was eating and purring at the same time. Quinn looked beyond her to the windows framing the sunset view and looking across the water. The storm that had been threatening all afternoon had finally arrived. This day there would be no glorious sunset—just gray rain that would likely fall much of the night.

He turned his attention back to the kitchen and clapped his hands together. "Okay, what should we make for dinner?"

"I like pizza," Annmarie said.

"Unless you've got a frozen one in the freezer, I think that's a little more than what we can do tonight," he said.

"Let's see what else there is," Annmarie said, leading him toward the freezer in the mudroom.

Quinn followed, once again swamped with memories of Lily. The night they'd first made love.

He opened the freezer and peered inside with Annmarie. An assortment of frozen meats met his gaze—nothing that looked like a thaw-and-eat kind of meal. In the pantry, though, he found the makings for chili, which, combined with the frozen hamburger, would do just fine.

He'd never had a helper before, but Annmarie stayed right with him, asking her usual dozen questions a minute and showing him where the various utensils he needed were kept.

As he had promised, he sent Annmarie in to check on her mother. She was gone a long time, long enough that Quinn got worried and finally went down the hall to the bedroom. The door was closed, but inside he could hear the two of them talking. Breathing a sigh of relief that they were both okay, he listened a moment, enjoying Annmarie's giggles and Lily's soft laughter. Ah, to be part of that—to have the right to go inside and be a part of the family they were.

Troubled by that thought, he went back to the kitchen. Annmarie arrived minutes later. Pink and scrubbed. Clearly fresh from a bath, too, she was wearing fleece pants and a top and the fuzzy slippers he remembered.

"Mom says she's hungry enough to eat a whole whale," Annmarie said.

"Good thing we cooked," he said.

When Lily came into the kitchen a few minutes later, Quinn figured they'd done okay. He'd managed to cook without turning the room into a disaster area and, thanks to Annmarie, they'd set the table with all the requisite stuff, including place mats. If he'd ever set a table with place mats, he didn't remember it.

Lily had left her hair down. Thanks to the bath, her skin was once again pink instead of the color of chalk. He'd figured she'd be wearing the lavender bathrobe like she had the other night, but instead she wore a dark blue scoop-necked tunic and charcoal-colored leggings that looked both warm and comfortable—and as suggestive as the more intimate bathrobe.

Annmarie skipped over to her and took her by the hand, leading her toward the table. "Mr. Quinn and me, we cooked. It smells pretty good, don't you think?"

"I think so," Lily said with a smile, sitting in a chair. She met Quinn's gaze. "Thanks." A dimple appeared at the corner of her mouth. "Unless you made eggs again and I'm not supposed to thank you for that."

He laughed, remembering that night perfectly. "Chili, and whether you thank me depends on whether you like to sweat while you eat."

The dimple deepened. "Get the inside *and* outside warm."

"Something like that." He ladled soup into the three bowls and carried them to the table. "Nothing fancy."

Lily smiled up at him. "If I'd been left to my own devices, we'd be having toast and tea."

He didn't believe her, but that didn't keep him from enjoying the compliment. She waited with her napkin in her lap until he sat down. He would have had to be a blind man not to notice Annmarie beaming at him as he sat between them.

"It's just like a real family, Mom," she said. "Isn't it?"

Chapter 13

A real family?

Quinn's head came up, and he looked from Lily to Annmarie, whose smile was huge. To give Lily credit, her smile looked only a little forced as she nodded her agreement with her daughter, her gaze avoiding his. As for himself—he had fallen into a trap of his own making. He knew what this looked like to Annmarie.

That little girl was hoping—believing—he had agreed to her outrageous request. A husband for Lily…just for a little while…just until there was the baby that would never be.

His chest tightened, and in front of him were Shelly and her kids instead of Lily and Annmarie. That had been a real family, too. Complete with crying kids and shouting between himself and Shelly. He'd forgotten about that. Not only had he been an insensitive husband, he'd been an uncaring, rotten stepparent. He'd wanted the forever marriage, and he'd bailed before even a year was up. And, like this…it had begun perfectly.

At the time he'd made every excuse in the book. The pressures of working full-time and going to graduate school and trying to make a go of a marriage and get along with children who saw him as the obstacle keeping their mother and father apart. The truth was a lot more simple. He didn't have what it took.

"Something wrong?" Lily asked.

Quinn gave himself a mental shake. "No. The day is catching up with me, that's all." The day, hell. His life was catching up with him. Sure as he was sitting here, one thing he was positive of. He'd never wanted anything more than to be here like this with Lily and her daughter. The knowledge that he would surely, surely screw it up was a thousand more times scary than it had been to see the surf pounding around Lily's slim body this afternoon.

He ate his meal in silence. He could have been eating sand for all he tasted. Through the meal, Annmarie chattered, to the point he wondered how she ever managed to get anything eaten. All he wanted was for her to be quiet so he could think. So he didn't look at her when he responded to her questions, and he ground his teeth together to keep from telling her to be quiet. Lily wouldn't appreciate his scolding her child any more than his ex-wife had.

"Annmarie, eat your dinner," Lily said as if she had somehow read his mind.

"But, Mom—"

"Enough. I know it's a challenge, but be quiet for the next two minutes."

Annmarie shot her mother a glare, swinging her feet to some internal beat and tapping her spoon against the edge of the bowl.

One thing was for damn sure. He couldn't stay.

He finished eating and looked up to find that Lily was watching him. She'd eaten less than a quarter of her chili. She was either a slow eater or he'd wolfed down the food. "You must have been hungry," Lily said.

"I was." Quinn seized the excuse like a man reaching for a lifeline and pressed a hand against his middle.

He sat for a moment watching her, then abruptly stood and headed for the kitchen sink where he rinsed off the dishes and put them in the dishwasher.

He came back to the table and wrapped his hands around the top of the chair. "You're feeling okay now?"

"Fine."

"Good. Uh, good."

"What's the matter, Quinn?"

"I've got to go," he said.

"I wanted to watch videos with you," Annmarie said, her voice whiny—an additional signal that she was tired. Even he recognized that symptom.

He managed a smile. "Another time, munchkin."

Lily stood up from the table and followed his retreat across the room. "Are you okay?" She detoured by the stove, where she grabbed the teakettle, which she filled with water, then put back to heat.

"Fine," he said.

"Not that again." She folded her arms over her chest and her chin lifted in the first display of any temper that he'd seen in her. It wasn't much of one, but he had the feeling that for Lily, even this much was a lot.

"What?"

"Fine," she said. "The word you always use when things are *not* fine."

He put his jacket on and opened the door to the mudroom. Just like he'd done before, sooner or later he'd make Lily hate him. He had to get out of here, and right now. "There's nothing complicated. I left some things at the lab that I need to take care of."

"What things?" she challenged.

He scowled at her. "Things. That's all. Things."

"You're running again," Lily accused. At once her conscience pricked her. Fine one she was to accuse him of that when she was planning to do the very same thing.

He put a hand behind her head and pulled her close, pressing a kiss against her forehead. "I'll call you in a couple of hours." Then he did just as she had accused him of—he ran, though on the surface the pace was a saunter.

And at the bottom of the porch steps, there stood Hilda. "Leaving?" she asked mildly.

He nodded. "Lily's doing fine. There's no reason to stay."

"If you say so." She climbed the steps, and as Quinn got into his car, he looked up to find the two women watching him.

"What was that all about?" Hilda asked, following Lily into the mudroom. She tossed her jacket on the freezer and slipped out of her shoes.

Lily watched Quinn drive away, then carefully closed the door instead of giving it the slam she was tempted to. She ought to be thankful the man was leaving since they had no future. Her throat tightened unbearably. *Normal.* What would she normally say? "He'd risk his life to help, but if a simple word like 'family' comes up, he runs like demons are after him."

"Maybe they are."

After all that Quinn had told her, she knew that Hilda's assessment was dead-on. Maybe more demons than she'd be able to overcome. What was it going to take to convince the man that he was far more capable of loving and being loved than he gave himself credit for? Tears she couldn't afford threatened as she realized that she'd never know how things turned out for him.

"Something smells good," Hilda said.

"Chili," Lily said, instead of demanding to know if her friend had found Cal. "Quinn cooked, and it's very good. Would you like some?"

"The man cooks?" Hilda said. "Since he ran out of here like he was being chased by a swarm of mosquitoes, are you sure it's safe to eat?" Despite the teasing, she got a bowl out of the cupboard and dished the chili into it.

The water on the stove came to a boil and Lily poured water into the teapot she had prepared, then carried it to the table with cream and sugar and a pair of mugs.

"Impressive." Hilda took another bite of the chili. "This is really good."

"I've tried calling Cal," Lily said. "And I keep getting his voice mail. Have you seen him?"

Hilda shook her head. "Milt rented him a boat a couple of days ago, and he still has it. Maybe he went to Wrangall or someplace else."

"How's Max doing?" Lily asked.

"He's going to be fine," Hilda said, tucking her hair behind her ear. "He's going to sleep in the clinic tonight so I can keep an eye on him."

"You didn't come out here to give me that report unless the phone lines are down," Lily said.

"I came for the chili."

"Sure you did. How long did you ground Thad for?"

Hilda's indulgent smile lit on Annmarie. "Until he's old enough to enlist in the Marines. I don't want another scare like that for as long as I live."

Lily's gaze went to her daughter. "Amen to that."

While they ate, Hilda related Thad's summons for help and how everyone who was around had instantly responded, how there'd been a real panic when they realized the engine for the boat normally used for rescues wouldn't start, how relieved they were when Dwight showed up with another kayak. Through it, Lily kept wondering why her friend was really here. Everything they were talking about could have waited until tomorrow.

"Are you finished eating?" Lily asked Annmarie a little while later.

The child nodded.

"Then go brush your teeth."

"I'm not sleepy yet." Annmarie stuck her chin out. "It's too early to go to bed."

"It is," Lily agreed. "So, after you're finished, you can pick out a story for me to read to you and your teddy bear while Hilda and I talk."

Annmarie slipped off her chair, folded her arms over her

chest, and made a point of sighing before she headed toward
the bedrooms. A second later she reappeared at the door.
"Mom?"

"What, sweetie?"

She fidgeted a minute, plucking at the sleeve of her shirt.
"Am I going to be punished, too? Like Thad."

"Yes."

"But, Mom, it was Sweetie Pie."

"You should have come to get one of us," Lily said.
"And next time, that's what you'll do." She simultaneously
wanted to punish Annmarie for being so foolish and to hold
her close and to closet her away for the next fifteen years so
she could never, never be hurt. "As for your punishment…"

Annmarie's chin quivered, and she bit her lip to keep it
steady. As had been the case since Annmarie was an infant,
Lily wanted to scoop her up and promise her that everything
would be okay. Today had proven beyond any doubt that a
few lessons had to be reinforced no matter how much she
wanted to shelter her daughter. Maybe the last lessons.

She cleared away the lump in her throat. "This was a very
serious thing today, don't you think?"

A single tear rolled down Annmarie's cheek, and she nodded.

"I think…I think that I need to give this a lot of thought,"
Lily said. "We'll decide in the morning."

Annmarie watched her a moment, the quivering of her chin
killing Lily. She held out her arms. Annmarie ran into them,
and buried her head against Lily's chest. Lily's arms con-
vulsed around her little girl, and she absorbed the warmth of
her child.

"I'm sorry," Annmarie sobbed. "I didn't mean for bad
things to happen."

Lily kissed the top of Annmarie's head. "I know." She
continued rocking the child until her tears subsided. She gave
Annmarie another kiss, then said, "Go brush your teeth now.
Pretty soon, I'll come sit with you."

"And hold me until I fall asleep?"

Lily closed her eyes against a new rush of emotion and had to clear her throat before she said, "Sure." She watched her daughter walk away, then asked Hilda, "Are you ready for tea?"

"Please," Hilda said. "What's Cal really doing here, Lily?"

Lily swallowed the hysterical laugh that threatened. What was the *normal* answer for that question? Opting for as much of the truth as she could, she said, "There are some things that had to be taken care of for Franklin Lawrence's appeal."

"Are you in protective custody? Like you were for the trial?" Hilda asked.

Lily sorted through the gradations of truth. "He's making himself available if it looks like that is needed."

Hilda surged to her feet. "I knew it. All those questions he's been asking all over town didn't make any sense. That's just a cover. To give him a reason for being here."

Lily nodded.

"Where in the hell is the man? Because it sure looks like you do need him." She sat back down and leaned across the table to Lily. "I think somebody was in your house. It's the only thing that makes sense. How else would the cat have ended up miles from here?"

Lily's eyes burned and she bit her lip against the need to tell her best friend everything. "I think you're right."

Hilda sat up. "You do? You believe me?"

Lily nodded and managed a smile. "No rose-colored glasses tonight." She couldn't afford them. Not if she was going to save her own life.

"The guy Thad described sounds like one of the university students—skinny guy with a ponytail and a beard."

"That could be Patrick," Lily said. "A couple of the other guys also have beards, but Patrick is the only skinny one."

"It's time he and I had a talk," Hilda said, then asked for his last name and if Lily knew where he lived.

A knock at the outside door interrupted whatever Hilda was about to say. Lily went to the door. Quinn. Her heart lurched as she unlocked the door and let him into the mud-room. "You came back."

"I couldn't stay away." He pulled her toward him. "I'm no damn good for you, but I had to come back."

"You hurt me." Her breath caught as she gazed at him. The man looked none too happy about being here, even as he laced his fingers through hers. Harsh lines bracketed his mouth, but it was his eyes that drew her—intent on her as though she was the center of his universe.

"I'm sorry," he instantly said. He cupped his hands around her face then, and captured her mouth in a deep hungry kiss that bordered on desperate.

Against her face his skin was cold and scented with night air, but his mouth was hot and fueling everything needy inside her. She gave herself to the conflagration, her blood roaring in her ears. Realizing she had the power to hurt him as much as he had hurt her, she knew she should send him away. But she couldn't. Whatever happened tonight would have to satisfy her for the rest of her life. Selfish as that was, she wanted it, needed it.

"Hilda's still here," he said against Lily's mouth. He gave her another kiss, then stepped away. "Hold that thought."

Taking her by the hand, he led her into the kitchen. Hilda still sat at the table.

"I'm glad you came back," she said. "Otherwise, I was going to talk Lily into coming into town with me."

Quinn's gaze rested on her. "I always forget that you're also the town safety officer." He cleared his throat. "Putting on that hat—today wasn't an accident. It couldn't have been." He glanced down at Lily, his eyes full of apology. "Somebody deliberately lured those kids—"

Lily pressed her fingers against his lips, unwilling to hear him say the words out loud. "I know," she said. "I've already talked to Hilda and she's checking into it."

"That's right. I'm on my way to have a talk with a couple of the students—especially Patrick Riggs." Hilda stood, taking her dishes to the sink. "You're going to stay tonight, right?"

"Yes."

"Good." She grinned and patted his arm as she headed for the mudroom. She looked at Quinn a long moment, then back at Lily. "I'll call you the minute I know anything more."

He locked the outside door after Hilda, then came back into the kitchen and closed the door between it and the mudroom.

"Why did you come back?" Lily asked.

"Because staying away was impossible," he simply said, reaching for her.

She held her arms out to keep him from hugging her and instead cupped his cheek with her palm. "I want you. I really do. But I've got to spend some time with Annmarie first."

He nodded. "That's fine." He dropped a kiss on her cheek without otherwise touching her. "I'll be right here when you're finished."

"Promise?"

"Cross my heart," he said, making an X over his chest.

She went down the hall and pushed open the door to her daughter's room. Annmarie was sitting in the middle of the bed with an assortment of stuffed animals piled around her, the cat in her lap, a book in her hands.

"Would you read to me, Mommy?" Annmarie asked.

"Of course." *Mommy.* Not Mom, but Mommy—as Lily was when her daughter was at her most vulnerable. Lily settled herself carefully within the nest of stuffed animals. Annmarie climbed into her lap, and Lily turned the picture book back to the first page. The story was a well-loved and familiar one about a little boy whose magical crayon drew pictures that became real, all because of a wish he had made.

When the story was finished, Annmarie tipped her head back and said, "Does wishing make things come true?"

Lily traced the edge of her daughter's bangs with a finger. "I guess it all depends. What are you wishing for, sweetie?"

Annmarie turned around so she could face Lily, crossing her ankles under her knees. "A baby. But I've been wishing for a long, long time."

"I know you have."

"Maybe my wish went to Aunt Rosie and Uncle Ian."

Lily nodded. "Probably. Since you'll be right here, it will be as good as having a baby brother or sister." It had to be since that child would, in reality, be her brother or sister. Lily closed her eyes against another sharp edge of pain. Rosie and Ian would become Annmarie's legal guardians.

Normal, Lily reminded herself, then whispered, "Are you ready to go to sleep?"

"I guess so."

Lily tucked her in, as she did every night. As she did every night, she wound the music box that played Schumann's *Traumerei.* Lily lay next to her daughter on the bed and held her. And as happened every night, Annmarie fell asleep before the music box wound down.

In the dim light Lily studied her daughter, memorizing each feature, praying she'd be strong enough to do the right thing to keep her safe. Praying that the choices she made over the next few hours or days would be the right ones. Imagining the changes as Annmarie grew from child into young woman. And Lily's heart broke that she wouldn't be there to see it.

Her emotions too shaky to face Quinn just yet, she quietly left Annmarie's bedroom and went to her own. She sat on the edge of the bed and stared at the wall above the small desk. The picture on the calendar above the desk caught her eye—a gift from Dahlia, the pictures ones taken during her visit the year before. This one was of Annmarie and Lily's mother, the two of them planting flowers. She hadn't changed the month, Lily realized. She flipped up the page and stared a long moment at the next photograph, this one of Annmarie with Uncle Ross and his family at the potlatch given in her grandfather's honor on his eightieth birthday. A date caught her eye, as did the tiny X in the corner of a box four days earlier. Her period was late.

Lily pressed a hand against her stomach, remembering all the times she had prayed to be late when she and John had been trying to have children. She hadn't been. Not once. Annmarie's longing for a baby zapped through her mind and left Lily trembling. She didn't dare hope for the impossible. Not after having been disappointed so many times before.

She must have miscounted. She flipped the calendar back to the previous month, and unless she had miscounted then, too, her period really was late.

Lily sat in the chair and stared unseeingly into the room. She was at once terrified and exhilarated, and her thoughts raced. Quinn's baby. A brother or sister for Annmarie. The contract against her life. The need to leave before someone got hurt or killed. Her already impossible choice became even worse. If she was pregnant, what did she do about Quinn?

She flattened her hand against her belly, unable to wish she wasn't pregnant though that certainly would be the best thing in this difficult, awful situation.

The telephone rang, startling her out of the turmoil of her thoughts. She crossed the room to the nightstand and picked up the phone.

"Hello, Lily," came her mother's voice on the other end of the line.

"Mom." Lily sank onto the bed, tears springing to her eyes at the mere sound of her mother's voice.

They talked for ten or fifteen minutes, and through it, Lily kept thinking of all the things she wanted to share with her mother, but couldn't. *Normal,* Lily reminded herself, trying to keep tears at bay. She wanted to tell her mother about the possible pregnancy, but how could she? Lily wouldn't be here, and the knowledge would be one more unbearable loss for her mother. Lily hated the possibility this might be the very last time they ever talked. Even more, she hated that she couldn't say anything that would seem out of the ordinary. So she made plans for a visit that would never happen and let the conversation end as it always did.

"I love you, Mom."

"And I love you, my daughter."

Lily pressed the disconnect button on the phone and held the receiver against her chest for a long time.

When she finally felt more in control of her emotions, she went back to the kitchen. To her surprise, Quinn had done the dishes and the kitchen was spotless. He stood at a window in the living room where he had opened one of the shutters and was staring at the rain beating against the window.

He turned when he heard Lily.

"I didn't mean to be so long," she said, stepping into his arms. "Annmarie wanted a story and then my mother called."

"The family thing," he said, leading her toward the over-size chair, which was large enough for the two of them.

"Yes."

He sat and pulled her with him. "You deserve to know why I ran tonight."

"I—"

He pressed his lips against hers, but didn't take the kiss any deeper.

"I met Shelly when I was in graduate school—she was a secretary to the dean." He took a breath and settled his cheek against the top of Lily's head. "It's totally uncool to tell you that she was terrific, but she was even though she was seven years older than me. She had a couple of kids from a previous marriage, and I didn't really spend any time with them until after we were married." He glanced down at her. "I know, big mistake."

"Big," she agreed, taking his hand within hers.

"They hated me." He took a deep breath. "It would just about kill me to get into that pattern where you and I fight all the time because Annmarie hates me."

"That's not going to happen," Lily said, wondering if he realized he was making plans for their future. "You've already spent time with her, and she thinks you're okay.'' For the moment, she allowed herself to believe this conversation was a foundation on which they could build a life together. For the moment, she wanted to pretend that she didn't have to leave.

''That could change.''

''Maybe.'' She studied the hand she held, liking the strength she found there, but also liking the way he had always, always been gentle when he touched her. ''I was reminded tonight that right now is the only sure thing.''

''The only sure thing about right now,'' he said, ''is that I want you.''

She tipped her head back and smiled at him. ''Really?''

''Really.'' His arms tightened around her and he lowered his head and kissed her, first on her cheeks, then at her eyes, and finally on her mouth. She kissed him back, trying to convey everything she felt for him in that one caress. If this was all they had… *Don't think about that, or you'll cry.*

Though she poured her longing into the kiss, fragments skittered through her. *I think I love him… I'm no damn good for you… You came back.* It all burned into fluttering ashes as she responded to his need and her own hungry heart.

He scooped her into his arms, stood and carried her toward the master bedroom. There, he locked the door behind them, then turned to her, pulling at her clothes and his own until they were skin to skin. Urgent need erupted, taking her again to places she'd never been before, his body so hot against her own that she was ignited and consumed in the fire of his hands and mouth on her body.

Her feelings flowed like molten lava and spilled as tears were too intense, too painful to bear. Fear and love and need and want all flowed together and shattered her until there was nothing left but him. At his first touch of her most private flesh, she climaxed. Somewhere in the distant corridors of her mind was the absolute wonder of it—that it always happened like this with Quinn when it had never been this way before.

Quinn fought to slow down, fought to find some semblance of control. Both were lost to him. The slide of her hot, silky skin against his pushed him over the edge into a free fall that would surely destroy him. The touch of her hands stroking him as though she found him worthy made him soar.

He wanted to touch her everywhere, kiss her everywhere, and he did. She clung to him through each caress, her needy whimpers and the aroma of her heated body erotic beyond anything he'd ever known. Her slender arms brought him close, then closer yet as though being separate from him hurt.

Shared kisses turned fierce. She bucked against him, seeking the joining she needed more than air. At last it was there, and they stilled.

Quinn lifted his body away from hers, absorbing the pulse that fluttered at her throat. His gaze raked her body, utterly feminine and so beautiful to him.

Finally he bracketed her hands with his own above her head, so he could watch her from the point of their joining to her beautiful eyes. He gazed down at her, lost himself within those fathomless eyes. Without warning, the sensation rose to a plateau where joy exploded through his veins. It was more intense than anything he'd experienced in his life.

Lily gazed up at him, caught in the eye of a storm where everything was reduced to this one man, this one moment, and the shattering climax that pulsed endlessly through her before capturing him in the same vortex.

And when they were spent, she wondered how she would bear leaving him.

Chapter 14

Quinn watched Lily sleep, the fear for her that had driven him back here surfacing once again. She was in terrible danger, a gut level certainty he didn't question.

In the illumination from the bedside lamp he should have turned off a long time ago, her pale hair tumbled around her shoulders and softly curled over the curve of one beautiful breast. Small, perfectly shaped, the dusky nipple was soft now, it would become a tight bud in an instant if he touched his tongue to it. He hardened at that thought. Tempting, but he was content—at least for the moment—to simply watch her.

The haze of satisfaction that enveloped him gradually gave way to his need to do something to eliminate the threat, to make sure she was safe.

Pulling the bedcovers over her shoulder, he gently slid from bed so he wouldn't awaken her. He pulled on his jeans, turned off the light, and left the bedroom. He checked on Annmarie, who was sound asleep and watched over by the cat. That damn pampered cat that had ended up more than four miles away in that cave.

Too many things didn't add up, starting with the U.S. Marshal. He'd made it clear from the first night that he was interested in Lily's safety. But today, when a dozen or more people had turned out to help, Cal Springfield hadn't been among them. Quinn wondered if the guy had taken off for Anchorage or someplace else again. Quinn had never been the least interested in law enforcement, but he'd give a lot to know how you went about protecting someone without being joined at the hip.

Next…the deal with her car and her keys being locked inside was maybe an accident. *Maybe.* If today had never happened, he might be convinced. But today *had* happened, and Lily could have died. She was the target—he knew it to the marrow of his bones.

The whole idea had been to lure Lily into…what? A trap? The cave was surely that. Its dangers were endless, from being battered against the rocks to drowning. As it was, they'd been lucky and gotten out of there with only Max's broken arm and Lily's deep chill.

Somebody had deliberately set up both things. Since the U.S. Marshal was here, it seemed logical to Quinn that "somebody" was the guy she'd put away. Following his hunch, Quinn went into the study, another room filled with hunting trophies, plus a locked gun safe. Quinn powered up the computer, then returned his attention to the safe. Much as he appreciated Mike Ericksen's attention to safety, at the moment, Quinn would prefer easier access to a weapon.

As soon as the computer was up, he logged on to the Internet, and soon found what he was looking for: a whole series of articles about Franklin Lawrence. His activities as a businessman, his arrest for suspicion of murder, the accounts of the trial, his conviction, and the date for his appeal.

Quinn shut down the computer and stared at the blank screen, concluding Franklin Lawrence had to be the key—he had a lot to gain if the state's star witness died—especially in some tragic accident that looked like something other than murder. Admit it, Quinn told himself. He knew squat about the tactics required to keep someone safe from a determined killer.

The last time he'd dealt with any personal threat, he'd been a runt. His answer to that was a weight-lifting regimen that had put on more pounds than he had hoped for and had the desired effect of giving him enough size and strength that most people didn't mess with him. This situation required finesse rather than strength.

He prowled through the house, double checking that windows and doors were all closed and locked. Returning to the living room, he turned off the light, then settled into the oversize leather chair that faced the window where he had opened a single shutter so he could see outside. Beyond the window, the night was as black as his worry for Lily. Twice he thought he saw the silhouette of a man in the shadows beneath the trees, and he watched, looking for anything that would suggest someone was really out there. The storm had finally moved on, leaving behind a midnight sky sprinkled with stars. No moon illuminated the landscape, which was varying shades of black.

Movement beyond the window caught his eye, and he sat up in the chair to watch the shadows beneath one of the pines. A black bear waddled across the yard then disappeared within the woods once again. A soft swish of sound caught his attention, this inside the house. He turned his head and found Lily coming toward him, her nightgown sliding softly over her skin.

"What are you doing up?" she asked.

He reached for her. "Couldn't sleep."

"With me?"

Especially with her, since sleeping was a thousand times more intimate than sex. But she didn't need to know that. "With all that was running through my mind."

"That bad, huh." She perched on the broad arm of the

chair and ran her fingers through his hair. He pulled her onto the chair and across his lap.

Now that the moment had arrived for him to confess his suspicions, he wasn't at all sure how to go about it. One thing was certain: the baldly stated, direct approach he usually took wasn't the way to go. So he simply held her and tried to ignore that he wanted her again, nearly as much as he had when he had come through her door a couple of hours ago.

"It would be beautiful out there," she said sometime later, "if I didn't think someone was watching me."

So, she did suspect. "When did you come to that conclusion?"

She rested head against his shoulder, as though she was seeking comfort. "Consciously? Today. Unconsciously? I think I've had that feeling for a while."

His arms tightened around her. "I think someone is, too."

"That's why you came back?"

"Partly." He took one of her hands within his, smoothed his finger across the surface of her fingernails. "I was worried about you being alone."

She traced a line down the center of his bare chest. "And here I was hoping you wanted me for my body."

His breath hitched when her hand reached the waistband of his jeans. "That, too." He pulled her close for a kiss, the need thrumming through his veins and demanding attention.

Her breath was as hot as a fantasy when she whispered, "I thought you'd need some recovery time."

He'd thought so, too, as she helped him unbuttoned the fly to his jeans. Then it was simply a matter of her straddling him. Languid, this time. Peaceful, like the glistening mirror of the water's surface beyond the window, and a profound sense of being home.

"I keep thinking," he said, relishing the sheer pleasure of her sliding over him, "that one more time and it will be enough." He pressed his lips to her neck and shoulders above the scooped neck of her gown. "And I keep being wrong."

Her breath caught, and when he eased his hands into her hair, he discovered tears at the corners of her eyes.

"Lily?" he questioned. He pressed one hand against her hip, stilling her movement, wishing a light was on so he could see her expression, needing to know what he had done. "What's wrong?"

In answer, she wrapped her arms around his shoulder and pressed her cheek against his, her tears scalding him.

"Love me," she whispered. "Just love me." Then she pressed her mouth against his, and the kiss swept him away. Nothing mattered except the feel of her breast beneath the silky fabric of her gown, the heat of her mouth, the undulation of her body moving against his. When he came, he admitted to himself that having enough of her wouldn't happen in the next day or even in the next century.

She collapsed against him, her legs around his waist. "Tell me if I'm too heavy. Otherwise, I may never move again."

He chuckled. "Not moving…that sounds fine."

Sometime later she whispered, "My leg has gone to sleep."

So he helped lift her until she stood next to the big chair, shaking her leg to get the circulation back. He scooted to one side when she sat back down, resting her legs next to his on the ottoman. He loved having her back in his arms, the intimacy of the dark reminding him of the night she had repeatedly checked on him.

"Can I ask you something personal?" she asked, resting her hand over his heart.

"More personal than what we've just done?" He looked down at her, her expression indiscernible in the darkness.

"Maybe. How old were you when you got married?"

He drew a blank. "I'd just graduated from college."

"Twenty-two or three?"

"Twenty-one," he said.

"And you mentioned something about your wife having kids."

"So?"

Against his side, he felt her shrug. "Color me curious. I wondered how old they'd be now."

He stared out the window into the black night, thinking back and discovering the memories weren't as clear as he'd thought. "Ryan had been ten, I think," Quinn said, thinking out loud. "Eleven, maybe? And Rachel was a year younger. Which would make them twenty something." That didn't seem possible.

"You sound surprised about that."

"Stunned, actually." He shook his head. "They're older than I was when I married their mother. How the hell did so many years go by?"

"One at a time," Lily said, her voice oddly gentle.

He rested his cheek against her hair. "And your point to all of this is?"

She took his hand within hers, and even in the dark, hers looked so small, as did her feet next to his on the ottoman. He tipped her head toward his so he could kiss her. She kissed him back, open and giving, as she always was, and as always, his defenses were breached.

"Maybe," she said when the kiss ended, "fitting into a family is a bit like trying to make yeast grow. Dump it into hot water and you'll kill it, into cold water and it won't grow. Give it the right environment, and it can turn flour, water and salt into bread."

Quinn stared at the top of her bent head feeling as though he'd been given irrefutable proof the sun was the center of the solar system after believing all his life the earth was. He'd been twenty-one, for God's sake. Just a kid, self-absorbed and selfish and with no clue about being an adult in an adult relationship, much less a father.

Touching his face, Lily said, "If I go back to bed, you're not coming with me, are you?"

He shook his head.

"Okay then." She went to the couch and lifted the lid of the chest that doubled as a coffee table, bringing out a quilt.

Returning to the oversize chair, she sat on his lap with her legs dangling over the arm of the chair. "We'll sleep here."

And she covered them with the blanket, once again resting her head on his shoulder.

"Are you okay?" she asked a while later.

"Fine." His arms tightened around her, and he stretched his legs out on the ottoman.

Her soft laugh vibrated against him. "Oh, no, not that again. Fine."

He pressed his lips to her hairline. "Believe it or not, this time it's true."

"It better be." She relaxed against him, her head resting on his chest. Within seconds she fell asleep. And he realized he didn't know why she had cried.

Over those next hours, he divided his attention between the woman in his arms and the night beyond the window. Not until the landscape outside began to change subtly from black to gray did he carry her back to the bedroom where he tucked her in. Then he returned to the living room and stretched out on the couch. He was exhausted and his body hummed with sexual satisfaction. Sleep should have come easily. But it didn't.

The phone ringing early the following morning woke Lily up. The instant she realized she was in bed...and alone...her heart sank. Was Quinn still here? She could only hope.

She picked up the phone and scowled at the clock—after seven, so not as early as she'd thought.

"I was afraid I'd wake you," Hilda said.

"What's going on?" Lily asked, sitting up.

"After our conversation last night, I knew you'd want to know...one of Patrick Rigg's roommates found him on their front steps about an hour ago."

The silent second that followed was one of the longest of Lily's life.

"He's been beaten as badly as I've ever seen anyone,"

Hilda said, her voice emotionless—that in itself telling Lily how serious the injuries were.

"Oh, God." Tears sprang to Lily's eyes. Suspicious of him as she had been, she hadn't imagined this. "Is he going to be okay? Is there anything I can do?"

Hilda's voice sounded tired. "It's not good, Lily. He's unconscious, and without a battery of neurological tests, who knows how much damage there is. I've ordered a plane from Juneau to come get him. If we're lucky, it will be here within the next couple of hours."

Lily glanced outside. Last night's storm was gone, so the medical rescue plane would be able to land.

"One more thing," Hilda said. "Is Quinn still with you?"

Lily glanced toward the doorway and found him standing there, still in his jeans, shirtless and barefoot, but most important, here. Relief shuddered through her. "Yes."

"Cal Springfield showed up a little while ago," Hilda continued, "and he seems to think Quinn might have something to do with—"

"Quinn would never—"

"How can you be so sure?"

"Because I've seen him angry. Do you remember me telling you about the night I fell overboard?" Without waiting for an answer Lily added, "Quinn was furious—and completely appropriate in his handling of the situation." She took a breath. "Cal didn't happen to say why he hasn't called me back—I've tried to reach him several times."

Hilda sighed. "He's on his way out."

"Good," Lily said, feeling as though it was anything but. If Patrick had been involved with yesterday's near disaster, it stood to reason his beating also had something to do with that. One more thing that proved to Lily her faceless stalker was getting closer. When Cal arrived, she'd have to tell him of her suspicions and her agreement to go into witness security. Would she have another day, another week? The uncertainty of it tore her apart.

Go about your normal business, she had been coached by

Cal months before. Since this whole mess was anything but normal, how in the world was she to do that?

"Just so you know, Lily, Cal is as positive as you are about what Quinn is capable of—only he's drawn a very different conclusion."

"I'll talk to him," Lily said, then asked, "Are you okay?"

Hilda's answer was a long time in coming. "Patrick wasn't home when I went by there last night. I keep wondering if I'd tried harder to find him…"

After her voice trailed away, Lily asked, "Do you want me to come to town? I can be there in fifteen or twenty minutes."

"No. There's nothing you could do right now, anyway."

"And what is it that I would never?" Quinn asked, moving into the bedroom as Lily hung up the phone.

"Beat Patrick Riggs within an inch of his life."

"What?"

She related what Hilda had told her, and realized how much had been left out. As if he sensed how much the news had upset her, Quinn sat on the edge of the bed and drew her into his arms. Awful imagines flashed through her head, reinforcing just how foreign violence was to her even though she had once witnessed a cold-blooded execution.

"I should get dressed and go see what I can do to help," he said. "Since that boy is a student—"

"You feel responsible," she finished, standing when he did and pulling on her bathrobe.

"I *am* responsible," he corrected.

"What happened isn't your fault." When he didn't answer, she said, "I'm going to check on Annmarie."

Lily pushed open the door to her daughter's bedroom and found her sound asleep. Images from the previous day left Lily gripping the doorjamb. Though it was long past time to get their day under way, she was loathe to wake the child when sleep was what she clearly needed.

She felt Quinn behind her, and his hand came to rest on

her shoulder. He took her hand and led her toward the kitchen.

"Let her sleep," he said.

"But I know you're going to be antsy until you've checked on Patrick and called his parents." She went through the automatic motions of making coffee.

"It will have to wait." He finished buttoning the flannel shirt he had grabbed from the bedroom.

Lily finished making the coffee, thinking about last night and how he'd run. How he had come back when his worry for their safety overrode his fear of letting them get too close.

She walked around the island and pushed him into one of the stools at the breakfast bar, then stepped between his legs.

"Admit it, you're afraid to leave me here alone."

After a second he nodded, looping his hands at the small of her back.

She made a point of glancing around the kitchen and what was visible from the living room. "I love that you care about me enough to worry about me."

"You have no wheels and—"

She pressed her fingers against his lips. "You need to go call the university and Patrick's family, right?" When he nodded, she continued, "And the phone numbers are in your desk at work, right?"

Again he nodded.

"And it's making you crazy to sit here."

He brought her head toward his until their foreheads rested together. "It will make me just as crazy to be gone and worrying about you."

"I know." She stepped out of his arms and went back around the island. She opened the cupboard above the coffeemaker and pulled a stainless-steel travel mug from the shelf, which she filled with coffee. "But you need to go. The sooner you go, the sooner you can come back."

"You're not kicking me out."

She set the mug next to him on the counter. "Oh, but I am. It's daylight. There are locks on the door and a phone right over there. Plus, I have that grant proposal I'm working on, so I'll have things to do until Annmarie wakes up.''

''You make it sound too logical,'' he said.

''You can't be with me every minute of every day.''

He stood and came toward her. ''You're sure about this?''

''Positive.'' She wasn't, but she gave him a gentle nudge toward the door, anyway. Besides, Cal would be here soon, and the things she had to tell him had to be done in private. ''I can't live my life being afraid,'' she said, a pep talk for herself as much as for Quinn.

In the mudroom, he put on his boots, then his jacket, and Lily handed him the cup of coffee.

He gazed down at her a long moment, then finally kissed her. ''I'll be back as quick as I can.''

''I know.''

He kissed her again. ''Lock up.''

''I will.'' She opened the door. ''Now go take care of things for Patrick. We're going to be fine.''

He stepped off the porch, aware of her watching him. Without turning around to look at her, he waved. The whole thing felt oddly surreal and totally right. Having someone to kiss as he went out the door in the morning. He liked that. Even if he didn't like leaving her behind. As she had said…the sooner he took care of things, the sooner he could come back.

Halfway to town, he met an oncoming pickup that made no effort to move to one side of the narrow road. Undoubtedly the U.S. Marshal, Quinn decided when he recognized Frank Talbot's truck. Quinn inched his SUV to the side of the road and stopped.

''I've been looking for you,'' Springfield said, pulling even.

''You've found me,'' Quinn returned. ''What's up?''

''Patrick Riggs.''

''I'm on my way to the clinic now.'' Quinn motioned down the road. ''How about you follow me?''

After a second, Springfield nodded.

Five minutes later Quinn pulled his car to a stop in front of the clinic. He was acutely aware of Springfield following him, but didn't wait. Finding out if there was anything he could do for Patrick was far more important.

He walked through the door and called for Hilda. She answered from the examining room, and he went back.

"Figured you'd show up," she said. She had a stethoscope to her ears, which she methodically moved across Patrick's bare, battered chest and abdomen. Numerous dark splotches and abrasions marred his skin, especially around his ribs.

Quinn bent over the young man, scarcely recognizing him. Despite being cleaned up, there were still traces of blood in his beard, and his cheeks and nose were scraped and swollen. "Looks like someone took a board to him."

"That would be my guess."

Even his arms were bruised. Quinn had been on the receiving end of beatings by a couple of bullies years and years ago, and he recognized the defensive nature of the wounds. Shaking his head, Quinn asked, "How did this happen?"

"That, we don't know. Not yet."

Her reply was a long ways from the sassy ones she had always given him when he'd been injured. She'd never before struck him as a vulnerable woman, but she did now.

Her gaze focused behind him and Quinn turned around. The marshal stood in the doorway. "His roommates said he never came home last night. One of them heard something outside a couple of hours ago, got up to see what the commotion was, and found him."

"You've had a long night, then," Quinn said to Hilda. "First Max. Now this."

"A regular crime wave." She pulled the sheet back over Patrick's chest.

"Where is Max?" Quinn asked.

"He helped me with Patrick until about the time I called Lily—broken arm and all. Clearly, a man together enough to help with this kind of emergency situation isn't suffering any lasting effects from a concussion, so I sent him home."

"That tells us where your handyman spent the night," Springfield said. "And you say you were at Lily's."

Quinn stared at the man without answering.

"All night?" the marshal asked.

"Yeah," Quinn said. "If there's an accusation in there somewhere, spit it out."

"No accusation. Just trying to get it all straight in my head. It would appear Patrick here is the guy who told the kids about the cat in the cave."

That news stunned Quinn and he glanced at Hilda, who again shrugged. "It could have been. Thad said it was a guy with a beard and wearing a plaid flannel shirt."

"That describes most of the men on the island."

"It's no secret that you had an ax to grind with him," Springfield continued. "Everybody in town from the skipper on your boat to Patrick's roommates have said you think the kid is a screwup and that you've been riding him hard for weeks."

Quinn nodded. "Like you said, no secrets. Thinking he's lazy is one thing." He waved toward the young man's still form. "This is something else, and I didn't do this."

"I saw your car in front of the Tin Cup last night."

"You keep acting like I'm a suspect."

Springfield smiled. "Nope. Just shaking the tree and seeing what falls out."

"You guys can take this outside," Hilda said.

"When the plane gets here, I'll come back to help you load up." Quinn shouldered his way past the Springfield, who followed him out of the clinic. After Quinn reached the street, he faced the marshal. "You're here because there's a threat against Lily, right?"

Springfield's gaze sharpened. "Is that what she told you?"

Quinn snorted. "Since she's not a prisoner waiting for an escort and since she was in protective custody while she was waiting to testify, what else would it be? This isn't exactly brain surgery."

"Get to the point, if you have one."

"Maybe you ought to be figuring out if Patrick has an accomplice," Quinn said. "Did you stop to think how the cat got to the Hollywood Bowl?"

Springfield gazed down the deserted street.

"So instead of accusing me of a crime you known damn well I didn't commit—"

"Like I said, I'm trying to nail down the pieces from last night."

"Yeah, I went to the Tin Cup," Quinn said. "Ordered pie and coffee. I didn't finish either one, because I was worrying—"

"About Lily?"

Quinn nodded. "Tell me what kind of help you need and I'll get it. These accidents targeting Lily have got to stop before somebody gets killed. That's what matters here."

"We don't get civilians involved."

"It's a little late for that."

"Let's suppose for a minute that I believe you—you had nothing to do with that boy's beating." Springfield met his gaze. "Who are the suspects on your list?"

"Patrick. Will Baker." Quinn met Springfield's gaze. "You."

Springfield stared at him, then shook his head. "I'll say one thing for you. You've got nerve." He headed for his truck, then turned around. "You've heard that thing they always say in the movies. Don't leave town. Don't do anything stupid." As intimidation went, he had it down pat. "It's good advice, Morrison. Follow it."

Chapter 15

The collect call Max had been waiting for came about an hour after he got home from the clinic.

"It's done," said the voice on the other end of the line.

"As soon as it hits the news, I'll make the deposit," Max said. He disconnected the phone. He allowed himself a moment's satisfaction—Franklin Lawrence was dead and would never again blackmail anyone.

Surprisingly, the feeling that came over him wasn't relief, but worry. For months, he'd had one goal—revenge for the double cross Franklin Lawrence had pulled on him last spring. The mess Max had found himself in with the Jensen sisters all stemmed back to being blackmailed into kidnapping Dahlia Jensen.

Thanks to that, his face and fingerprints were now on file with the FBI, something he'd managed to avoid for more than twenty years. No matter how careful he'd been, there was always the possibility that one of his earlier jobs could now be traced back to him. Even though he had planned to retire, he could no longer do so with the assurance that he couldn't be tracked down. His younger sister believed he was a man who lived well because he had invested well. Max wanted to keep it that way.

Worse, somewhere along the way, he had grown to care about the two women—first Dahlia, now Lily. Ensuring her well-being had gone beyond a matter of professional pride to caring about her. And she was in far more danger than she imagined.

Thanks to Patrick's whispered confession during the night, Max knew that Will had orchestrated the accidents and that he had stolen Lily's keys so he could get into her house and take the cat. Patrick fulfilled his end of the bargain by luring Annmarie and Thad to the cave. A stupid idea that had damn near worked. That might have been the end of it for Patrick if he hadn't had an attack of conscience. For that he had been beaten and left for dead.

Franklin Lawrence always had a backup plan, and since the planned "accidents" had failed to take Lily's life, a new plan was now in play. Never mind that he was already dead.

Max packed his belongings, a task made more awkward because of the cast on his broken arm. Not that there was much to pack—only what he could carry in a duffel bag. He cleaned and loaded his Glock, and put two extra clips in his vest pockets. Then he systematically wiped down every hard surface in the house where he might have left a fingerprint. He didn't figure anyone would bother to check, but just in case, he wanted to make damn sure there was no connection between Max Johnson and the assassin he had once been— Max Jamison.

Will Baker figured this plan had to work. It had to. This was his last chance. It had been made clear to him that he'd suffer Patrick's fate if he failed.

Will double checked the readings on the one pressure tank that had been worrying Morrison. A little more heat and a lot more pressure was the answer, so Will turned up the thermostat well beyond the temperature Lily had said was needed for the organisms in the tank. Give it a couple of hours and the tank would blow. All Will had to do was to make sure she was here when it happened.

Jimmying the lock on the supply cabinet was easy, and he found the final ingredient for his planned accident—elemental sodium. His favorite experiment in chemistry had involved elemental sodium and water, and he had always wondered what it would be like with gallons of water rather an a few ounces in a beaker. He imagined the direction the water would take when the pressure tank exploded and made sure the sodium was sprinkled in its path out of the lab and into the office area in the front of the building.

He was just finishing when he saw Morrison drive up. Will retreated to the lab, closing the door and turning off lights. To his relief, Morrison didn't come into the lab. After a couple of seconds, Will heard him on the telephone. Quietly he crept across the room and peered through the cracked door. Morrison sat with his back to the lab door, hunched over his desk. He stayed maybe ten minutes, then left. Will breathed a sigh of relief.

Time to go let Lily know there was a big problem that required her immediate attention.

"Mom, are you still going to punish me?" Annmarie asked while Lily got dressed. "I sat in the car with Thad for a long, long time. Like a very, very long time-out."

"That wasn't a time-out." Lily zipped up the jeans and pulled a sweater over her head. "As for your punishment, I'm still thinking about it." She sat on the edge of the bed and reached for her daughter, rubbing their foreheads together. "Unless you want me to think of something awful right now."

Annmarie giggled. "What if I promise to be very good?"

"Hmm."

"I'll make my bed every day," she said, "and help you empty the dishwasher and feed the cat and keep my toys picked up and—"

"Bribes might work." Lily gave her a smacking kiss on her cheek. "Let me finish getting dressed."

"Okay." Annmarie ran out of the room and a moment later Lily heard the chorus of a children's song on CD-player in the living room, Annmarie's voice singing along.

Lily went into the bathroom to give her hair a quick brush, her survey of herself in the mirror critical. This day she had given up her tailored clothes for jeans and a burgundy sweater. Practical, she told herself, for whatever might happen later. Never mind that she was really proud she looked good thanks to the ten pounds she had lost over the past few months. She absolutely was not dressing to look good for Quinn when he returned. *Liar.*

The decisions she had to make washed through her and she stared into the mirror. It was so easy to forget her vow, to pretend the biggest worry on her mind was whether Quinn liked her as much as she liked him.

Her temporary good mood squashed, she dialed Cal's number once more, and once again there was no answer. If Hilda hadn't said that she had talked to him, Lily would have been tempted to think the man had left. He had said he was on the way out here—so where was he?

"Can I have some cheese?" Annmarie asked a few minutes later, poking her head into the bedroom.

"Sure," Lily responded.

"Good." Annmarie ran back toward the kitchen and Lily could hear the refrigerator door opening. She grinned. Slices of cheese for breakfast wouldn't have been her first choice, but at least Annmarie was hungry enough to eat this morning.

Shoes in hand, Lily headed for the kitchen. When she didn't see her daughter, she called, "Annmarie?"

There was no answer, and from the living room, a familiar song played.

"You didn't take food into your bedroom, did you?"

Still no answer. Lily sat at the table and put on her shoes. She was heading back toward the hallway when movement outside the huge living room window caught her eye—a skunk followed along by several of her kittens. In the next instant she realized she was looking at a small—very small— black and white dog and her puppies. Annmarie was outside with them, kneeling down and holding out a piece of cheese.

Had it been any other day, Lily wouldn't have questioned the need to rescue the animals. Instead fear wound through her in the scant second she took to scan the copse of trees that surrounded the house. She rapped on the window. Annmarie looked up with a grin, and the dog ran.

''No. Come back.'' Lily couldn't hear the words, but she could read her daughter's lips. Annmarie ran after them, the mother dog leading the way and the pups strung out behind her.

Lily rushed to the mudroom. She flung open the door to the porch. ''Annmarie!''

The child didn't answer.

Her heart in her throat, Lily yanked her keys off the hook and pulled the door shut behind her. She automatically locked the door and dropped the keys into her pocket, then took off at a run after her daughter.

An overriding fear rode her. What if the dog was a lure to get her and Annmarie out of the house? If she called to her daughter, ''they'' would know they had succeeded. So, Lily didn't call out like the panic in her chest demanded.

The undergrowth of the forest grew exponentially thicker the farther away from the house Lily got. Her mind went wild and her hands went cold and her chest went tight and she couldn't hear anything except the warning bells clamoring in her head.

A bright blue flutter caught Lily's eye—the same fabric as Annmarie's jacket. Fear overrode caution. ''Annmarie.''

The only answer was her own thundering heartbeat.

Finally she heard Annmarie somewhere ahead of her, calling to the dog.

Sure that every snap of a branch meant that someone was after them, Lily plunged headlong through the forest, following the sound of her daughter's voice. At last, there she was.

"Annmarie," Lily called.

The child immediately stopped and waited for her. "Oh, Mom, you should see the babies and the mommy."

"You should have waited for me." Lily dropped to one knee and pulled her daughter close, hugging her hard.

Lily scanned the forest around them expecting to see some nightmarish abductor pop from behind a tree.

"But, Mom."

"You remember the rules." Fear still riding her hard, she resisted the urge to shout at Annmarie for scaring her so.

"Put on my shoes before going outside." She stuck out a foot for inspection. "I did. My coat, too. See?" This time an arm went out, the sleeve missing the ragged tear that Lily clutched in her palm.

"What else?" When Annmarie didn't answer, Lily said, "What about staying in the yard?"

"I forgot."

"No running off on your own," Lily added. "Not even for a dog and her puppies." Lily's grip around her daughter's shoulders tightened. "What if you had fallen down and hurt yourself?" Lily waved at the brush around them. "How would I find you?"

"I don't know."

Lily glanced around the underbrush. "Which way is home?"

Annmarie pointed behind her, then frowned and turned in another direction.

Lily pressed a hand against her chest, willing her heart to stop racing. "That's the most important reason why you can't run off like this. You don't want to be lost, do you?"

Annmarie shook her head. "But what about the mommy dog and her babies?"

"They'll manage on their own." Lily glanced around the brush, then said softly to Annmarie, "See that log right over there? We're going to go sit there for a minute. Then, we're going to listen to the sounds of the forest."

Annmarie smiled. "I remember this game. Then I tell you what I heard."

"That's right." The log was mostly concealed from view and deep within shadows. A plus if you wanted to hide. And Lily did. They sat behind a log as deep within the shadows as Lily could manage, which was only a little damp from the previous night's rain.

Every time Annmarie started to speak, Lily touched her fingers to her mouth and shook her head. She listened. Little by little, she heard the sounds of the forest around them. The occasional chirp of birds and the more distinctive call of a blue jay. No sounds of anyone moving through the forest. Not that she necessarily trusted that. Her uncle Ross had been able to move through the forest like a shadow.

"Are we done yet?" Annmarie whispered.

Lily nodded.

"I heard birds," Annmarie said. "And the wind and a boat. And, Mom, I heard the puppies, too." She took Lily by the hand. "Can't we go find them?"

"Not right now," Lily said firmly, standing and heading back through the brush toward the house. She had also heard everything Annmarie named, except the puppies.

As they got to the edge of the woods, Lily heard the rumble of an engine—one that belonged to an ATV or a motorcycle rather than a car. Still worried the dog had simply been a mechanism to lure them outside, Lily motioned for Annmarie to be quiet and led the way around the yard, well within the shadows of the trees. When she could finally see all the yard from the driveway where it came out of the woods to the porch, she stopped cold.

A battered all-terrain vehicle was parked near the porch. In the next instant, she saw Will Baker. Thinking that Quinn might have sent him because she hadn't answered the phone, she was about to call out to him when Will casually put a rock through the window of the mudroom door, reached inside and unlocked it. Lily covered her mouth to stifle the gasp that sounded as loud as an eagle's cry to her. Pulling her daughter deeper into the shadows, Lily watched as he walked into the house.

"Mom, that's a man from your work. What is he doing?"

"I don't know, sweetie." A part of her wanted to believe that he was looking for her out of concern. But she didn't trust that enough to come out of the shadow of the trees.

Wishing there was some way of knowing Will's intentions for sure, Lily knelt and pulled Annmarie farther into the underbrush with her.

"Mom, it's wet in here."

"I know." Lily squeezed Annmarie's shoulder. "We've got to be very quiet for a minute."

"Okay," she whispered back. "I know how to do this 'cause this is what happened when the bad mens came to Aunt Rosie's house. Remember?"

Lily did remember. Though it had been weeks after the fact when she learned about it, she had been terrified her plan to remove Annmarie from harm's way had backfired. Rosie and Ian had literally been chased from Rosie's house, and they had taken Annmarie into hiding until after Lily had testified. Looking back, she was positive that she would have succumbed to the pressure if she had realized how great a danger she had put the members of her family in.

And here they were again.

Moments later Will came back outside and stood on the porch looking around. He pulled a hand-held radio from his belt, and began talking into it. She couldn't make out the words. Was he talking to Quinn or someone else? She wished she knew. A second later he clipped the unit back to his belt and stalked toward the boathouse. It was also locked, and he was close enough that Lily could see he was irritated.

He brought the radio to his face again and said, "I'm telling you, she's not here." He listened a moment, then said, "You've got to be kidding. She's not an outdoorsy kind of person. If she went to her sister's house, she took the road." Another silence. "Okay, I'll go there. But if her car is still in town, I'm betting she's here somewhere." He listened an instant longer. "If you say so... I'll meet you here."

Meet who? Quinn? She wanted to ask Will, but she still couldn't decide if she trusted him or not.

She watched as Will climbed onto the ATV and turned the ignition. The vehicle roared to life and he zoomed down the driveway.

"What now, Mom?" Annmarie asked.

"I'm going to go call Quinn," she said, just then deciding. She caught Annmarie by the shoulders. "I want you to wait right here for me, okay?"

"And be real quiet," Annmarie added. "In case that bad man comes back."

The statement gave Lily one more glimpse into what her daughter had gone through last spring when Ian had brought her to Rosie for safekeeping. Lily took her daughter by the shoulder. "Promise me."

"I promise, Mom."

Swiftly, Lily crossed the yard, paused only a second when she reached the edge of the trees, then ran the remaining distance to the house. In the kitchen she dialed the number to the research center. When the phone was finally answered, it wasn't Quinn, instead his voice asking to leave a message. If Will had been talking to Quinn, wouldn't he still be there?

"It's me, Quinn, at about nine. Call Hilda. Right away," Lily said, opting for careful and deciding that she really didn't want to be here when Will came back.

Then she dialed Hilda's number. It, too, rang without being answered. When Lily looked at the clock on the wall, she saw it was about the time for the evac plane from Juneau to arrive. That might also explain where Quinn was.

Lily hung up, then dialed the law enforcement number that she knew would send Hilda a voice page. At the beep, Lily said, "It's me." She glanced at her watch, then added, "It's about nine and I bet that you're busy with Patrick. Will Baker—you remember him. He's the lab helper who came to work at the center. Anyway, he's broken into the Ericksens' house. He's talking to somebody on a walkie-talkie, Hilda, and he's gone to Rosie's house, looking for me. I've called Quinn to see if he sent Will out here, but he's not there. I need—''

Her voice broke off. Just what did she need exactly?

''Help,'' she said. ''And I can't stay here because somebody else is coming and I don't know who.'' The panic in her chest rose a little with each passing second. What if Will came back before she got out of the house? What if whoever he was talking to showed up? What if… ''I know I'm rambling, and I'm sorry. But…I'm taking Annmarie to my house. Come get us there, okay?'' She disconnected the phone and then dialed Cal's number, and then she heard it— the sound of the ATV returning. She was out of time.

She hung up the phone and ran out of the house. She raced across the yard faster than she had run since she was a girl, her lungs feeling as though they would explode. She jumped over a log and scrambled down the shallow embankment where she had left her daughter hidden.

Annmarie gave her a reassuring smile. ''You run very fast, Mom. Almost as good as Aunt Rosie.''

High praise since Rosie was in much better physical condition.

The sound of the ATV grew louder.

''Come on, sweetie,'' Lily said, once again leading the way into the thicker brush, looking back one last time. The ATV skidded to a halt in front of the house. Curious as she was about Will, her overriding instinct was to get as far away as she could in as short a time as she could. Since Will had said she wasn't an ''outdoorsy'' sort of person, she chose a route that took them through the thick undergrowth.

''Where are we going?'' Annmarie asked.

''To our house.''

''Oh, good.'' She slipped her hand inside Lily's. ''And maybe that's where the little dog is going, too.''

''Maybe.'' Within a hundred yards Lily decided that Will had been dead-on. She was a city girl, and she would have given a lot for a nice groomed trail that led through a post-card-perfect forest rather than tangle of primeval wilderness that made each step a battle.

Twice she was sure that she'd heard vehicles on the road. She hoped they belonged to Quinn or Hilda. She feared they belonged to Will and his unknown buddy. Lily heard the unmistakable sound of a seaplane revving up its motor while taking off, and a minute later the plane itself appeared above the trees. It had the distinctive logo of the evac planes, which confirmed Hilda's whereabouts.

Lily trudged along, holding branches to the side for her daughter, her thoughts circling from yesterday to Patrick's beating to Will's breaking in. She frowned, remembering that she'd seen the two of them arguing a couple of days before.

They hadn't walked much farther when she became aware that Annmarie kept digging into her pocket. Lily stopped and saw that Annmarie was dropping something on the ground. A closer look showed that it was a piece of cheese that she had torn off one of the slices.

"What are you doing?" Lily asked.

Annmarie grinned up at her. "I'm leaving a trail so we don't get lost. Just like Hansel and Gretel."

"I see." Lily glanced back in the direction they had come. Now wasn't the time to be reminded that Hansel and Gretel had ended up as the witch's prisoners. "We're not lost, sweetie."

"But just in case," Annmarie said, holding up the entire package of sliced cheese.

Lily didn't think it was likely that Will would follow them by a trail of cheese, and it had the benefit of keeping Ann-marie's mind occupied with something other than the danger that marched step-by-step with Lily.

It took nearly an hour to reach the house. Had they taken the road, it would have been an easy walk. When they reached the clearing, she once again decided that staying hidden within the protection of the trees made the most sense.

"Aren't we going inside?" Annmarie asked.

"Not yet," Lily said.

"'Cause we're still hiding from that bad man."

"Yes." Agreeing was easier to explain than that Lily wasn't sure if he was, especially since she had just put them through an arduous walk. So they sat on a log and played the guess-what-I-am game that soon had Annmarie in giggles and kept Lily's mind off the fact that she hadn't put on a jacket and was once again cold.

As the minutes dragged by Lily worried that Hilda had gotten her message, that Quinn had returned to the house and found them gone or, worse, mugged by Will and his unknown partner, that Will had somehow found Annmarie's trail of cheese and would find them.

A little while later Annmarie whispered, "Mom, look."

Less than ten feet away was the little black-and-white dog—a cocker spaniel mix, Lily decided, based on her huge floppy ears and the shape of her face—nibbling at the last piece of cheese Annmarie had dropped. She promptly sat on the ground and took another slice of cheese out of her pocket and broke a piece off, then held it out to the animal.

Quinn arrived at Lily's house later than he'd intended. By the time he had made the phone calls to the university and to Patrick's parents, the evac plane had arrived. As promised, he'd gone to help. His only other stop had been to pick up new locks from the general store.

Whistling under his breath as he came up the porch steps, glass crunched beneath his feet. He looked down, then up at the door. The gaping hole in the bottom pane of glass next to the doorknob made his heart stop.

Quinn went inside, calling Lily's name, then Annmarie's. Neither one answered.

Cursing himself for leaving them alone, he dropped the sack from the general store on the freezer top and rushed through the house. Stupid. He should have never let himself be talked into leaving. Within thirty seconds he knew they weren't in the house. He came back to the porch and again looked at the glass and the fist-size rock that had been tossed onto the porch floor. Other than the glass, there were no signs of a struggle.

Where the hell were Lily and Annmarie? He strode down the path to the boathouse. It was locked, and near as he could tell, nobody had been inside. In the next instant he decided that near-as-he-could-tell wasn't enough. He had to know for sure. He remembered seeing keys in one of the drawers in the kitchen, and headed back there to find them.

Halfway back to the house, the telephone started ringing. Quinn sprinted toward the house and made it inside to the phone just as it rang for the fifth time.

"I was hoping you'd answer," came Hilda's voice on the other end of the line.

"And I'm hoping you know where Lily is," he said.

"Her house."

Fear clutched Quinn by the throat. "I'm here, and she's not."

"Not the Ericksens' house," Hilda said. "The one she's building." Then she explained about the message that Lily had left on her answering machine, including Will's break-in, ending with, "Lily was trying to figure out if you'd sent him out."

"I haven't seen him today," Quinn said.

"One more thing, Quinn. I just went by Max's house, and he's not there."

"Maybe he went to work."

"No. I mean he's not there. His place is cleaned out—no clothes, no toiletries, nothing but the furniture that was in the place when he rented it."

Quinn's gut knotted. "I have a bad feeling about this."

Somehow Hilda laughed. "I'd be real worried about you if you had a good feeling. Go get Lily."

"I'm on my way."

The turn off to Lily's new house was little more than a two-rutted track, and he nearly missed it. None of the underbrush had been cleared away from the road, and it scratched against the sides of the vehicle, the sound grating on his nerves like fingernails scraping across a chalkboard.

The road curved left, then right, and then up a final incline. The house sat on a promontory and looking vaguely obscene with the plywood exterior uncovered yet. A dark bottle-green roof, windows, and doors gave the house at least some protection from the rain. Quinn noticed and cataloged all that while he looked for any sign of Lily and her daughter.

"Lily," he called. "Annmarie."

"Over here," came Lily's answering yell.

He turned in the direction of the ocean and started down the incline, still not seeing them, a thousand different awful possibilities racing through his head.

Then he spotted Lily on her hands and knees, and he was sure that she had been injured. Except that conclusion totally didn't fit when Annmarie looked up, a big smile lighting her face. In her arms were wriggling puppies. When Lily turned around, he saw why she was on her hands and knees—she was gently petting a dog whose soulful eyes pierced right through him.

"God, but you scared the life out of me," he said, dropping to one knee next to Lily and putting his arms around her. "When I got to the house and couldn't find you, and then Hilda called."

Lily hugged him back. "You think you were scared."

"So what happened?" Seeing that she didn't have a jacket and was shivering, he took off the micro fleece vest and dropped it over her shoulders, reminded of that very first day.

"We found puppies," Annmarie said. "Lots of 'em."

Quinn grinned as one of them licked her face. "I can see that, but what happened?"

While she continued to pet the mother dog, Lily related the morning's adventure, ending with, "You didn't send Will?"

Quinn shook his head. "Nope." He stared at the scenery without seeing it. The whole thing was like setting up a chemistry experiment without knowing whether the combination would blow up the lab or make table salt.

"Maybe some other emergency came up."

"If you trusted that in your gut, you wouldn't have run. That's good enough for me." He stood, taking in the bouncy puppies who seemed as enamored with Annmarie as she was with them. "I suppose they're going, too."

"Yes," Annmarie said. "I think they will be very cold and scared and hungry if we leave them here."

"Let's go." Quinn scooped up one of the wriggling puppies who barked, then licked his face.

Lily gathered up two of the others, leaving Annmarie to carry one. "Come on, Duchess," Lily said to the mother dog. "We don't want to leave you behind, either."

The dog watched them with her big sad eyes, then followed.

"She's yours," Quinn said, watching the dog follow Lily. When she lifted an eyebrow in question, he added, "You've named her already."

She chuckled. "My dad used to say the same thing. 'Don't name the strays. Please don't.'"

"Can we keep her, Mom? And the babies, too?"

"I'm—"

"Thinking about it," Annmarie finished with a sigh.

"We have to find out if they're lost, first," Lily said. "And if they are, they are going to need a forever family."

"Like us," Annmarie said.

If Quinn hadn't been watching Lily closely, he would have missed the shadow that chased across her face.

"Like us," she agreed.

As Quinn helped Annmarie and Lily into the car, he thought about that—a forever family and Lily's comparison last night of growing yeast to growing families.

Was it possible that finally, after all these years, he had what it took to be part of a forever family? A painful buoyancy filled his chest. Did he have the guts to go after it?

Chapter 16

They had pulled onto the road running between Rosie's place and Lynx Point when a battered ATV roared up beside them.

"It's Will," Lily said.

Deciding he looked frantic with all that waving of his arms rather than threatening, Quinn pulled to a stop and rolled down the window. "What's up?"

"The one pressure tank that you were worried about—the gauge is sky-high. I can't figure out how to shut it down," Will said.

"That's why you came to see me this morning?" Lily asked.

"Well, yeah." He flushed. "You didn't answer the door."

"I was out for a walk, and I watched you drive away."

"Sorry about the window," Will said. "I just was trying to find you."

"Who were you talking to on the radio?" Quinn asked.

"Kev," he said, naming one of the students.

"We're on the way," Quinn said.

"Okay." Will revved up the ATV and took off ahead of them.

"Do you believe him?" Quinn asked when they were under way.

Lily took her time before saying, "Yes. Now that I'm not scared out of my mind and imagining the boogeyman jumping out, it all makes sense. I feel so stupid—"

"Don't." Quinn covered her hand with his own. "I'd rather you be safe—"

"Than sorry?"

"Yeah. I was going to stop and board up the window."

"It doesn't sound like there's time," Lily said. "We can take care of it after you've checked on the tank."

"If the pressure's too high, your barophiles are—"

"Cooked," Lily finished. "Let's hope that's the least of the problems."

Quinn wished he shared her perspective, though he supposed if equipment had to malfunction, better to be at the beginning of a project rather than later when the loss of specimens would also mean the loss of months, possibly years, of research.

At the center Quinn parked the car. He rushed inside, leaving Lily and Annmarie to follow along behind. The munchkin was doing her best to convince her mom the dogs needed to be with her, and Lily was equally adamant they'd had enough excitement for one day and probably needed a nap in the back of his car. Will zoomed around the building to the workshop.

Argument won and the dogs settled in the cargo area of the SUV with partially opened windows, Lily set her daughter down at the empty desk in the office with pencils and crayons and said, "You stay right here, sweetie." When Annmarie didn't quite meet her gaze, Lily added, "I mean it. No visits with the dogs in the car, no coming into the lab. You sit here."

"Is this my punishment, Mom?"

"Yes," Lily said, then headed for the lab and propping

the door open so she could see Annmarie from inside the lab. Quinn was on the floor under the tank.

"What can I do to help?" she asked.

"The damn valve is stuck, so I'm trying to shut off the backup," he said. "There's a set of allen wrenches in the workshop that I need—somewhere over by the window."

"I'll get them." She headed for the door that led to the back of the facility and the workshop.

"Lily?"

She glanced back.

He'd stood up and was reaching behind the tank. "Do you really know what an allen wrench is?"

She grinned at him. "You'd better be teasing me or I'll bring you a crescent wrench, instead."

"One more thing." He waited until she turned around to look at him. "I get what you were saying about the yeast."

"Good." She went through the door, smiling. In the next instant she remembered. Unless the threat against her went away right now, helping Quinn to see they could be a family wouldn't matter. Instead she had just set him up for heart-break, and that was unbearable.

She pressed a hand against her belly again thinking about her period that still hadn't come. If there was a baby…wouldn't that be a miracle? What was the right thing if that were so?

She opened the door to the workshop and, to her complete surprise, there stood Cal. With a gun pointed toward the floor.

"Cal?"

He motioned, and her shocked gaze lit on Will who lay sprawled on the concrete—his eyes sightlessly fixed on the ceiling, a neat little hole in his forehead and a pool of blood under him. Will…who had just waved at them as he drove the ATV around the building. She glanced through he open garage door where a truck was parked next to the ATV.

She went numb. Instead of seeing Will lying there, she too vividly remembered another man. A man in a conservative suit—the assistant D.A., she had learned later—caught in the obscene glare of headlights. Standing one instant, then toppling over, that same awful hole in his head. Standing over him, two others. Men with the guns and cold, blank eyes. Like Cal's.

"This is the guy behind the accidents," Cal said. "He tried to kill Patrick after he got remorseful—"

"Why?"

"Drugs. Patrick needed them and Will supplied them."

"I...see." But she didn't. What she really wanted to know...and perversely didn't want to know...was why had Cal killed Will. Lily took a step back, her gaze fixed on the gun. "You killed him?" Surely the most stupid question ever. Finally she realized what looked strange—inexperienced as her eye was, she recognized the silencer on the end of the barrel.

"It was him or me."

Lily looked around, trying to clear her head, trying to remember why she had come here, trying to stuff down the panic bubbling through her chest, trying to imagine Will being threatening enough that it really was "him or me." She swallowed when she looked down at him, and tears filled her eyes.

"You're not going to cry over that scum, are you?"

"His name was Will Baker." A low rumble filled the air. Or maybe she felt it. Or maybe it was her own panic trembling through her chest.

"And he was trying to kill you," Cal said. "All those accidents. Your car, the snapped line on the winch, the kids being lured—"

"You've made your point." Recognizing the adrenaline rush didn't do a thing to make it better. Except she could swear the floor was vibrating. She had to—God, what had she come here for? It was important.

The allen wrenches. The pressure tank.

An explosion knocked her to the floor, and she realized too late that she had been smelling propane. She screamed, her thoughts fighting through the encroaching black cloud of unconsciousness, for Annmarie, for Quinn. Cal reached her as her last thoughts stretched toward Annmarie and Quinn. Oh, God, please let them be okay.

About thirty seconds after Lily went to the workshop, a seam on the tank gave way with a tremendous pop and a geyser of water shot from the ripped opening. In the next nanosecond the tank split down the side as though it had been unzipped, the pressure of the escaping water as intense as a fire hose. The force of it threw Quinn through the open doorway into the office. He slid across the floor on his back.

Godawful ringing pounded through his head. A torrent of water spewed into the office, soaking everything in its path. He scrambled to his feet. Annmarie, looking dazed, sat on the floor near the window. He sloshed through the water toward her and scooped her up.

"Are you okay?"

She nodded, her lower lip trembling.

Quinn headed for the outside door and pulled on the fire-alarm handle as he passed by. No fire. Simply a gush of water pouring out of the once-pressurized tank. But the alarm would bring help. He had to get to the gate valve in the rear hallway near the workshop and shut off the water. As soon as Annmarie was safe. She clasped him tightly around the neck.

His mind raced. Gate valve first. Shut off the gas. Next the breakers. He glanced back toward the lab and the godawful mess they'd have to clean up, the loss of equipment and experiments and research piling up and weighing him down.

Under one of the desks in the office, bright fire flared suddenly and danced across the top of the water the way it did when elemental sodium melted and produced burning hydrogen. Odd, he thought. With the flash of igniting hydrogen came the realization this was very, very deliberate...and dangerous. Small explosions burst through the water here and there, and then flames spread over the surface of the water. Horrified, Quinn watched as the water and the flames spread. If the fire reached the gas line, all hell would break loose.

He ran from the building, his first thought to get Annmarie as far away from it as he could, his second to warn Lily before she returned from the workshop.

Halfway to the parking lot, an explosion ripped through the building. Quinn heard it the instant before he felt it. He fell to the ground, sheltering Annmarie with his body, a single thought chanting through his head—Lily was in there.

When Annmarie cried out, his arms tightened around her.

"I've got you, munchkin," he whispered. "You're okay."

Another explosion tore out of the building and a fireball bloomed out of the roof accompanied by the awful odor of hot metal, raw propane, and his own choking fear. Barely comprehending, he rose to his feet. He couldn't see the back of the building—the workshop where he had sent Lily.

"Mommy!" Annmarie screamed.

The sound reverberated to the bottom of Quinn's soul, and he did the only thing he knew how—hold her. Simply hold her.

A truck with its siren shrieking came up the road. Even before it stopped, men piled out of the cab and out of vehicles that followed.

Hilda appeared at Quinn's side, and he thrust Annmarie into her arms. Then he raced into the building. Everything beyond the lab door was engulfed in flames. He couldn't get to the workshop from there.

Shaking off hands that would have stopped him, he ran back outside and around the perimeter of the building. The size of the building seemed monstrous to him as he ran flat out and with each step his heart thundered and his fear grew and he ran faster feeling the burn in his lungs and ignoring it while his heart cried out for Lily and the first prayer since childhood passed his lips. *Lily be safe. Lily be safe.*

Fire roiled out of the open doors to the workshop, licking around the ATV parked right next to the building.

The heat was so intense, his body simply would not obey the command of his mind to go in, to find Lily.

Again and again, he rushed toward the flames, and again and again the fierce heat drove him back. Someone tackled him. Quinn fought to escape.

"Where's Lily?"

Quinn focused and Dwight Jones stood in front of him.

"Did everyone get out?" he asked with the thin patience that came with repeating. "Where's Lily?"

Quinn looked at the inferno that had once held his dreams and goals.

His heart broke. He cried out, a roar of pain and denial and fury. Tears blinded him, and he shouldered Dwight out of the way. If she was still in here... A tremendous shove pushed Quinn to the ground, and when he tried to stand, Dwight was there again, holding him down, shouting at him.

Quinn watched flames devour the workshop through the open garage doors. Open. The doors were open. Quinn stood, looking at the encroaching woods. Maybe she had made it out.

Convulsive raw hope flickered to life. Dwight's fierce grip eased when Quinn headed away from the building rather than toward it. He searched through the brush. Finding Lily, that's all that mattered. She had to be here somewhere. She had to be.

And when she wasn't, despair poured out of him in great waves that brought him to his knees. It couldn't end like this. He'd finally understood what she was saying to him, practically from the first day—he didn't have to be scared of loving her.

"Come on, buddy." Dwight helped him to his feet. "We can't do much else here until the fire is out."

The research center was gone. Completely gone. The ancient pumper poured water through the open cavity of the roof.

At the front parking lot, Hilda was in command mode, but

that didn't keep her from giving him a hug when he got close enough. It was the last thing he expected from her.

"Where's Annmarie?"

"My mother took her."

Quinn nodded, tears burning at his eyes again—a thousand images of Lily and Annmarie together searing their way through his brain. The stench of fire, soot and water seeped into him until he was sure he'd never be rid of it.

"Was anyone in the building besides the three of you?"

He realized then what had struck him as odd from the moment they arrived. No one had been there. There should have been a half dozen other students working, unless they'd been doing an environmental survey. Maybe that was right. Hell if he could remember. Finally he shook his head, then said, "No, that's not right. Will Baker should have been here."

Through the raw pain the pulsed through Quinn in waves, there was another thought he couldn't quite grasp. Then it came—Cal Springfield.

"Anyone seen the U.S. Marshal?" Quinn asked. Hilda and Dwight both shook their heads, so Quinn shouted his question to the others. An awful possibility burgeoned through Quinn. The explosion was the mechanism to get Lily into the witness security program. Was this how it happened— some awful thing so they'd all believe she was dead? If it wasn't, why in hell wasn't the man right here?

"He's driving Frank Talbot's truck, right?" one of the volunteer firefighters said. When Quinn nodded, he added, "I saw him as we were coming up the hill. Looked like he was on his way to the marina."

Quinn ran to his car and climbed in. To his surprise Dwight jumped into the car with him, saying, "I figure you could use some help."

A sharp bark from the rear of the vehicle reminded Quinn about the dogs. The incongruity of it—a car full of lost dogs in this life-and-death moment—forced a laugh that morphed into a yell of frustration and fear.

He raced down the hill, the glow of the fire vivid in the rearview mirror. Black smoke billowed toward the sky, carrying with it his worst fear, greatest hope. Lily wasn't inside dead—she was with Cal.

"You figure he has a boat?" Dwight asked.

Quinn nodded. "Or a plane. Only two ways off the island."

Dwight whistled. "Lily would leave her daughter?"

"No," Quinn instantly said, the fear in his gut coalescing into a cold knot. Cal had taken Lily against her will. Quinn was as sure of that as he was of his next breath.

They stopped at the end of the road next to the marina…right beside Frank Talbot's truck. Quinn got out of his SUV. The marina had a lot of empty slips, which was usual for this time of day and this time of year. He started down the ramp, yelling for Springfield as he went.

No one answered, and he didn't see a soul. Simply boats, gently bobbing in the water, the masts and outriggers of a few boats pointed skyward. An engine rumbled to life—the distinctive rumble of a diesel engine. Quinn hit the bottom of the ramp and ran down the floating dock toward the sound, searching for the boat. There it was—Rona's fishing boat. He could see Cal and Rona inside the bridge. Where was Lily?

Movement at the stern caught his attention, and his heart stopped. Hidden from the view of anyone inside was Max…a gun in his hand.

"No!" Quinn roared. He was still yards away from the boat when it lurched away from the slip and swerved to avoid hitting another boat.

Five minutes before Quinn arrived at the marina, Lily awoke, her head pounding. She sat up, feeling the reverberation of a motor.

Rona stood at the wheel, her expression grim as she checked gauges and made various adjustments.

Confused and not at all understanding why she was on a

boat, Lily looked around and discovered that she was sitting on the long bench that lined the port-side wall.

"Rona." Her voice came out as a sandy croak. "What—"

"Don't talk." Cal seemed to appear from nowhere and eased her back down on the bench, his hands firm, his voice grim. "Save your strength."

What the heck was he doing here? He looked strange to her. She was used to him being in one of those conservative suits that shouted, "I'm a federal law enforcement agent," instead of jeans that looked brand-new and a jacket splattered with blood.

Blood…and it all flooded back. Will lying on the floor— dead. Her throat closed, and she felt the bile and fear rise, vibrating through her like the rumble of the boat engines. Explosion. There'd been an explosion.

She shook, the most awful fear drowning her. She stood again, pushing away Cal's hands. "I've got to get back. Annmarie is there and Quinn."

"There's nothing you can do."

"No!" She pushed at him. "Let me go."

"They're dead," Cal said. When she froze in complete disbelief and horror, he repeated, "They're dead."

"No!" She hit at him. "Don't say that."

At the same time Rona was asking, "You know that for sure?"

"I'm sure," he said. "You're going to a safe house, Lily."

"No!" Grief pounded through her, battering her. When she had imagined going into witness security it was to protect her daughter, to keep anyone else from being hurt or killed. If her daughter was dead, she had nothing to live for. No reason to go on. "I'm not going."

He shook her. "Yes, Lily, you are. Right now."

"If she doesn't want to go…" Rona was saying.

"I don't. I've got to see my little girl." The tears erupted. "And Quinn!" Pain doubled her over and she wailed, the cry wrenched through her broken heart.

"That's it," Rona said, shutting off the ignition. "I'm not

going anywhere. She doesn't want to go, and I'm not taking her." The cabin became abruptly quiet.

A gun—that same lethal-looking gun—appeared in Cal's hand. "We are leaving, and right now." He waved the gun toward the ignition. "Start the engine."

The hysteria that had gripped Lily washed out of her, leaving in its place a cold, odd calm.

"You're pulling a gun on Rona?" She looked into Cal's dead blue eyes. "Are you crazy?"

"She's in on the scheme with Will," he said.

"That's ridiculous. She's my friend."

"Friends can be bought out, Lily."

She stared at him, awful conclusions surfacing. "Not Rona." She swallowed. "You. You're the 'friend' who was bought."

The expression in his eyes got even flatter, and the gun was turned on her. The calm in her center froze. If Quinn and Annmarie were really dead, what did she have to live for? She'd buried her husband, and if she had to bury her daughter and Quinn, she wasn't sure she had any reason to live. *Except for the baby.* She pressed her hand against her stomach, protecting the fragile life that she wasn't even sure was really there.

She looked at Rona. She didn't deserve this. Rona caught her eye and shrugged. Lily didn't believe that gesture of surrender even for a second. Like her own family, Rona's were fishermen—resilient, determined men and women who overcame tough odds every single day.

"It was you all along?" Lily said to Cal. She didn't even care, but her thoughts raced, searching for some way to get them out of this mess.

He shook his head. "No. I'm here to clean up the shambles Will made of things."

"Not a bad ruse," Lily said. "Coming to tell me there's a contract on my life when you're the one sent to do the job. How much does it take to buy a U.S. Marshal?"

Ignoring the question, he shoved her toward the bench.

"Sit down." He waved the gun toward Rona. "Start the damn engine. No more stalling."

"You're the one who beat Patrick?" Lily asked.

"Dumb-ass kid who wanted to come clean. Come on, Rona. Let's go."

Lily pressed a hand against her head, trying to think everything through.

"Why didn't you kill me at the lab?" she asked.

The corner of his mouth kicked up. "Oh, Lily. I tried. Only you didn't stay put. You were supposed to die in the explosion, so I couldn't leave you behind to tell anyone that you knew I'd killed Will." He waved the gun toward Rona again. "Let's go."

The engine rumbled to life. Lily's gaze lit on the fire extinguisher strapped to the wall. She looked at Rona, who nodded ever so slightly. Lily moved to the corner, bracing herself and putting herself within arm's reach of the bright red canister.

Rona jammed the throttle forward. The boat shot away from the slip, then turned sharply starboard to avoid another vessel.

Cal lost his balance and crashed against the rear of the cabin. Lily ripped the fire extinguisher from the wall, yanked out the pin, and aimed the nozzle toward him.

"Drop it!" His extended arms pointed the gun toward her.

Within that instant, her daughter's face was in front of her, her daughter who he'd said was dead—the daughter he'd killed. Lily's chest tightened, the thought stabbing her. "No!" she screamed, and squeezed the handle.

Foam arced toward his contorted face, and the gun discharged.

The pain was so great in her chest, she was sure he'd shot her. But it no longer mattered, and she rushed toward him, aiming the spray at his face.

He knocked the canister from her hands.

The door crashed open and Max charged in.

"Get out of the way, Lily," Max roared, bracing a gun against the cast of his raised arm.

The boat swung port and Lily lost her balance and crashed into the bench. Max and Cal fired at each other at the same instant. Somehow, Max was on the floor, too. The two men scrambled across the floor, cursing and fighting and grunting. There was another shot and it was quiet.

No more shouts, no more struggling.

Rona eased on the throttle and brought the boat back toward the dock in a smooth curve.

Lily stared at the two men on the floor. Cal's death wasn't as tidy as Will's. She didn't even recognize him as the man to whom she had once entrusted her life. Tears blurred her vision, tears she was sure would never stop if Cal was right and her Annmarie was... Her throat closed.

The boat bounced as though someone had jumped on board. Quinn burst through the door. He looked awful, his eyes red-rimmed, soot and mud ground into his face and his clothes. He looked wonderful, solid and strong...and alive!

Lily threw herself into his arms. His closed convulsively around her and he lifted her off her feet.

"Annmarie—"

"She's okay," he said, repeating the words again and again as though he understood how much she needed to hear them. Shuddering with relief, she held on tight to him. On the heels of her relief, a certainty coursed through her as it had the very first day she met him. *He's the one.*

She became aware of him moving her out of the way, and then of others boarding the boat. Dwight and Hilda and others from the village. Friends and neighbors who were always there when the going got tough.

Quinn was carrying her out of the bridge when Hilda stopped them. "Max is still alive," she said, "and he wants to talk to you."

"I don't want to talk to him," Quinn said.

"He's dying," Hilda said.

Reluctantly, Quinn set Lily down. He knelt over Max, who

had scared a couple of decades off his life. Lily knelt on the other side of him.

Max gripped his hand with surprising strength. "Listen to the news," he said. "Lily's safe. It's over."

Quinn stared down at the man, not knowing what to believe. A few feet away someone had covered Cal's body.

To Quinn's surprise, Lily picked up Max's hand and brought it to her lips, tears once again in her eyes. "Thank you for saving my life," she said.

"Tell Dahlia…I'm sorry," he whispered, his voice trailing off. "I never wanted to kidnap her."

"That was you?" Shock laced Lily's voice. Quinn realized there was yet another part to this story that he didn't know.

"Yes," Max whispered.

Quinn looked sharply at Lily, then down at the man who smiled as the light faded from his eyes.

Gently, Lily set his hand back on his chest.

"I thought he was trying to kill you," Quinn said.

"So did I," Hilda said.

Lily shook her head, tears once again at the surface. "No, that would have been Cal. He told me that Quinn and Annmarie were dead. That my life was still in danger, that he was taking me to a safe house. When I told him I wouldn't go, he pulled a gun and threatened us."

When Quinn's inquiring gaze included Rona, she grinned. "We make a pretty good team. I made it impossible for him to keep his balance, and Lily took after him with the fire extinguisher."

"I always knew I liked you," Dwight said to Rona.

She shot him a suspicious glance. "You have a real funny way of showing it."

"And then Max came through the door. I told you," Lily said to Hilda, "he was one of the good guys."

"I wonder what he meant about the news?" she asked. "And Dahlia—I don't get that."

"Remember last spring when Ian sent Jack to be Dahlia's bodyguard?" Lily said. "After that was all over, the FBI told her the man who had kidnapped her was a suspect in a number of assassinations. If he'd ever done a kidnapping before, they didn't know about it.''

''I doubt if we'll ever know the whole story on that one.'' Hilda covered Max's face.

''I want to get Annmarie and go home,'' Lily said.

''Consider it done.'' Quinn took her hand and led her off the boat.

Chapter 17

"Mr. Quinn picked me up and ran very fast," Annmarie said a couple of hours later, concluding her story and taking a long drink of water.

Lily sipped her own water, her attention on her precious daughter. Annmarie's blond hair stood on end and her face was even dirtier than her clothes.

"And then Hilda and Mama Sara came and I went to play with Thad." Annmarie's chin trembled, and Lily pulled her close once again. "Only I didn't want to play."

"I'm sure Thad understood," Lily said, looking around the kitchen, amazed at how normal it looked after everything that had happened today. Quinn stood on the other side of the room watching them, his arms folded across his chest. He was filthy, and when she looked at herself, she saw she was just as dirty.

"There are sweatpants and shirts that will probably fit you in the bottom drawer of the chest of drawers in the master bedroom," Lily said to him, "if you want to get cleaned up."

He nodded without saying anything.

"Or maybe you'd rather go home," she said. "Since Cal is...there's no reason you have to stay."

"Trying to get rid of me, Lily?" he asked, his voice soft and steely.

"No." How could she possibly explain to the man she was simply trying to give him an out if he wanted it, needed it. "I want you to stay."

"Good, because I am. Staying." He came around the island, cupped the back of her head and pressed a kiss against her forehead. "Go take your bath. I'll be here when you get finished."

Lily took her daughter by the hand and led her to the master bath. "I think we need one of our special bubble baths."

"Me, too," Annmarie said. "With candles, too?"

"Yes." Lily turned around and found Quinn still watching them. "This is going to take a while."

"Okay."

"Probably a long while."

"Take all the time you need."

Lily lost herself in the bath ritual over the next hour. This wasn't just about getting clean, but also about cherishing her child and making sure she knew how much she was loved.

Lily's eyes filled with tears, and she could only hope that Max was right. It was really over. In her mind's eye, Lily imagined rainbows stretching into a future that she had imagined lost to her only a few hours ago.

More than an hour later, they returned to the kitchen dressed in pajamas and bathrobes. The sun had set a while ago, leaving behind a sky and water painted in shades from mauve to purple. Quinn stood in front of the window, tall and solid, everything she wanted for the rest of her life.

Annmarie skipped toward Quinn, who had showered and dressed in sweatpants and a black T-shirt that emphasized the breadth of his chest and the heavy rope of muscle in his arms.

He's the one. Thinking of the things she had to confess to him, she worried about his reaction. She hoped she had the strength to be satisfied if he was never able to share more of himself than he had already allowed. How could he possibly know he was loved since he'd never been shown that he was? She ached for the little boy who had never been loved the way she did her daughter. Showing him he was loved—that's all she knew how to do. *What about the baby?* If there was a baby…

"See?" Annmarie sat on the floor in front of Quinn and pulled off one of the fuzzy slippers. "Mommy painted my toenails and my fingernails." She held out her hands for his inspection.

"Very nice," he said, his eyes warm as he gazed down at Annmarie. "Hot-pink is my favorite."

Lily turned to the kitchen with the thought it was time to make dinner—even if tomato soup was all she was up to. The island was stacked with pots and various other containers. "My gosh, look at all the food."

"Hilda's daughter was here, along with four of her friends. Evidently they were the emissaries sent on behalf of about half the people in town—at least, that's my guess since there's enough here to feed half the village." He looked at Annmarie. "They're ready to adopt puppies."

"They can't," Annmarie said. "They're mine."

"All of them?" Quinn asked, a smile in his voice.

"Maybe they have another home somewhere," Lily said. The mother dog had clearly been someone's pet.

"I want to keep them, Mom."

Lily swallowed the sudden lump in her throat that urged her to promise her daughter anything, everything. Blinking back tears, she said, "Maybe they're lost, and maybe they have their own family that we need to find."

Quinn started to move toward her, and she shook her head. If the man held her the way she wanted right now, she'd have another bout of crying. None of them needed that.

"So," Quinn said, "want to eat dessert first?"

"Because life is short?" Lily teased. Except, as soon as

the words were out, she knew she wasn't teasing. The idea of all that she had nearly lost today made her tremble.

Quinn reached for her and pulled her close. "I listened to the news," he said, waiting until she looked into his eyes. "Franklin Lawrence was killed in a prison brawl last night."

"How could Max have known that?" she whispered, her arms tightening around him.

"I don't know, but he was right. You're safe."

She rested her head against his chest, reassured to be in his arms, even more reassured by the strong beat of his heart against her ear.

"There's something I have to tell you," she said.

"It can wait."

She shook her head. "It can't. Cal said he was here to take me into the witness security program." Her throat closed, and her vision clouded. "And I trusted him, Quinn." She swallowed and met his gaze. "And I was going to do it— leave Annmarie and you because I thought it was the only way."

"Shh." He pressed a finger against her lips. "It's over."

"You don't understand. I was going to abandon my daughter and—"

"Stop." His gaze became impossibly warm. "I know how much you love her, and I know that you'd do whatever you thought was the very best for her—including leaving her with your sister and all the others who love her."

Disarmed, she rested her head against his chest. She listened to his heartbeat, relieved and thankful that he seemed to understand.

"There's clam chowder. Want to start with that?" he asked.

"Sure." She moved out of his arms.

Through dinner she watched him and watched Annmarie, and she kept expecting to see the shadow cross his face, the one that often made him bolt when there was too much family, as now. And she wondered how to confess her suspicion she was pregnant—her hope that she was—without fearing that he'd be angry...or worse, believe she had deliberately deceived him. He didn't have much to say, and if it hadn't been for Annmarie's chatter about everything that had happened over the past two days, dinner would have been a silent one.

It wasn't until they were finished eating the chocolate cake that another neighbor had provided that Quinn met her gaze. Like her, he seemed to have a lot on his mind. She kept expecting him to say that he was leaving in the next moment...or the next.

But he stayed. Through doing dishes and through the story that Annmarie made him read to her and through another discussion about which of the puppies she should keep and through the hour that marked Annmarie's bedtime.

As soon as he kissed the child goodnight, he retreated from the room, his warm gaze offering Lily reassurance.

"I hope tomorrow isn't so scary." Annmarie snuggled deeper under the covers as Lily wound up her music box.

Lily kissed her daughter's head. "I'm sure it won't be." Lily sat on the bed and held Annmarie's hand within her own. As always, the music box did its magic, and the child fell asleep. Lily watched her for long moments, memorizing each freckle sprinkled across Annmarie's cheeks. The idea of all that she had nearly lost today—and all she had to be thankful for—filled her heart to overflowing.

She found Quinn in the living room where he stood, staring out of the big window.

Through the reflection, Lily could see that he was watching her, his expression as serious as a judge.

Finally, he turned around and pulled the ottoman toward the couch and then sat in front of her.

He clasped his hands loosely, his elbows resting on his knees, his head bent. Lily extended a hand to him, and he took it. Was now the moment that he'd tell her he needed to leave? She could only hope that it wasn't.

"Annmarie came to me with a proposal a couple of weeks ago," he said. "She was looking for a husband for you."

He swallowed. "Just for a little while…just until there was a baby." His eyes grew even darker. "I can't do that."

Lily felt her eyes fill with tears.

Quinn let go of her hand to brush the tears from her cheeks, his touch gentle. "The part I can't do, Lily, is the little while." He took her hand within his again. He cleared his throat. "Since you and Annmarie are a package deal…" He met her gaze, his beautiful eyes glistening.

Quinn's courage deserted him and, letting go of her hand, he looked away. The words, "Will you marry me?" remained stuck in his throat. No other question in his entire life had been more important, and if she said no—and if she had any sense of self-preservation at all, she should—it would just about kill him.

"Tell me about my daughter's proposal."

His gaze came back to Lily, who had never been more beautiful to him than she was right now.

"She's looking for a daddy because of that baby she wants. Somewhere along the way she decided that required a husband."

"I see." She raised her chin. "What about you?"

"Me?" Could he lay everything out there for her to see? Being that vulnerable…was the only way. He took a breath, his heart unbearably exposed. "This afternoon I figured out there was only one thing I feared more than living my life alone." He took both of her hands in his. "Living my life without you." He leaned toward her until his lips touched her loose, fragrant hair. "I can't make it without you, Lily. I want you, just you. And the little munchkin until she's off on her own in another fifteen or twenty years."

Lily's eyes shimmered and her hands trembled. "What if there was another child?"

He didn't have an answer for that, especially after she took his hand and splayed it across her tummy. His heart stopped.

"My period is late. And it's never late."

The future shifted. Annmarie and other children, too? He

took a deep breath and his heart resumed beating. "You think?"

"I honestly don't know." Her chin quivered. "I was so afraid since I'd told you I couldn't have children that you'd think I'd deceived you—"

"No." He sat next to her on the couch and pulled her into his arms, lifting her across his lap. "I want you, Lily. Whether you come with only Annmarie or children that you and I make together, I don't care."

"I love you, Quinn."

A single tear welled and rolled down his cheek. If anyone had ever said those words to him before, he didn't remember it. One thing was sure—he'd certainly never heard them before.

"I love you," he said. "Will you marry me? Will you be my forever family?"

"Yes." She kissed him, all open and giving like she always was. Only this time he knew he didn't have to guard his battered and tender heart. Not ever again.

Epilogue

"Squeeze in just a little more," Quinn directed from behind the camera set up on a tripod. In front of him everyone shuffled close together. "That's it."

The occasion was Lily's parents' fortieth wedding anniversary. This was the first time the entire family had been together since the double wedding a few months before Quinn met Lily. Her mother was determined the occasion be marked with a family photograph.

Patty and Dan Jensen, Quinn's mother-in-law and father-in-law, stood in the center of the group. Their love and respect for each other was palpable. Quinn had the feeling they were excited to be leaving for the trip to Hawaii that everyone had chipped in to buy for them.

Dahlia and Jack stood next to Dane. This was the first time Quinn had met Jack since he had been stationed overseas most of the last two years. Besides being brothers-in-laws, he and Ian were best friends, a circle they had expanded to include Quinn. According to Patty, Jack would be leaving the Army when his current hitch was up and would be pursuing a long awaited degree in architecture. Dahlia was radiant, only as a soon-to-be mom could be, her first baby due in another four months. She was also reaping the rewards for her ground-breaking research on clear-air lightning.

Rosie and Ian stood next to Patty. Rosie held six-month-old Jeremy in her arms, and Ian held eighteen-month-old Gillian. The children weren't the only thing that kept them busy. Ian ran Lucky's Third Chance, which had developed a reputation for being one of the best programs in the country for at-risk kids. Comin' Up Rosie provided thousands of seedlings for reforestation every year.

Lily stood next to Jack. Fifteen-month-old twins David and Danna squirmed in her arms. Besides the arrival of the babies, the last two years had been busy with the rebuilding of the Kantrovitch Research Center. Lily's research was showing promise much sooner than she had anticipated, and Quinn was sure that her findings would provide the foundation for a new family of antibiotics.

Seven-year-old Annmarie stood in front of her mother, her smile brilliant. "Save room for Dad," she commanded.

She had begun calling him dad the very first day she learned he and Lily were getting married, and he had adopted her a month before the twins were born. His throat tightened with emotion as it sometimes did when he thought about how close he had come to losing both Lily and Annmarie.

Jack squeezed closer to Dahlia, and a space appeared between him and Lily.

"That's it," Quinn said. "Nobody move." He set the timer on the camera, then slipped in next to Lily and took David from her.

"Smile!" Patty said. "Everyone smile."

And they did.

Of all the pictures on the mantle above the fireplace in Quinn's and Lily's house, that one became Quinn's favorite. It marked the first time he realized his dream had come true. He was part of a family. He had a wife he adored and children who were his very life. And, amazingly, he also had brothers and sisters and parents. No man could be luckier or more blessed.

*   *   *   *   *

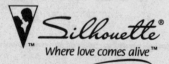

**Like a spent wave,
washing broken shells back to sea,
the clues to a long-ago death had been
caught in the undertow of time...**

Coming in
July 2003

Undertow

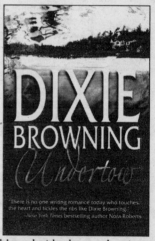

Cold cases were
Gray Hollowell's specialty,
and for a bored detective
on disability, turning over
clues from a twenty-seven-
year-old boating fatality
on exclusive Henry Island
was just the vacation he
needed. Edgar Henry had
paid him cash, given him
the keys to his cottage, told him what he knew about
his wife's death—then up and died. But it wasn't until
Edgar's vulnerable daughter, Mariah, showed up to
scatter Edgar's ashes that Gray felt the pull of her
innocent beauty—and the chill of this cold case.

Only from Silhouette Books!

Where love comes alive™

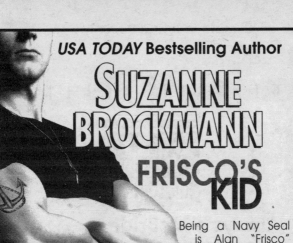

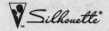

From *USA TODAY* bestselling author

EMILIE RICHARDS

comes the story of a woman who has played life by the book, and now the rules have changed.

Faith Bronson, daughter of a prominent Virginia senator and wife of a charismatic lobbyist, finds her privileged life shattered when her marriage ends abruptly. Only just beginning to face the lie she has lived, she finds sanctuary with her two children in a run-down row house in exclusive Georgetown. This historic house harbors deep secrets of its own, secrets that force Faith to confront the deceit that has long defined her.

PROSPECT STREET

"Richards adds to the territory staked out by such authors as Barbara Delinsky and Kristin Hannah.... Richards' writing is unpretentious and effective and her characters burst with vitality and authenticity."

—*Publishers Weekly*

Available the first week of June 2003 wherever paperbacks are sold!

MIRA®

COMING NEXT MONTH

SIMCNM0603